MYSTERIOUS NURSE

MYSTERIOUS NURSE

Valerie Scott

Chivers Press   •   G.K. Hall & Co.
Bath, England   Thorndike, Maine USA

This Large Print edition is published by Chivers Press, England, and by G.K. Hall & Co., USA.

Published in 1998 in the U.K. by arrangement with Robert Hale Ltd.

Published in 1998 in the U.S. by arrangement with Robert Hale Ltd.

U.K. Hardcover ISBN 0–7540–3129–2 (Chivers Large Print)
U.K. Softcover   ISBN 0–7540–3130–6 (Camden Large Print)
U.S. Softcover   ISBN 0–7838–8289–0 (Nightingale Collection Edition)

The text of this Large Print edition is unabridged.
Other aspects of the book may vary from the original edition.

Set in 16 pt. New Times Roman.

Printed in Great Britain on acid-free paper.

British Library Cataloguing in Publication Data available

Library of Congress Cataloging-in-Publication Data

Scott, Valerie, 1928–
    Mysterious nurse / by Valerie Scott.
        p.   cm.
    ISBN 0–7838–8289–0 (large print : sc : alk. paper)
    1. Large type books.   I. Title.
[PR6069.C615M97   1998]
823′.914—dc21   97–35652

CHAPTER ONE

Oliver Travers, the senior surgeon at the Royal Infirmary, Stanton, near London, was not pleased as he tugged down his face mask and turned to face Lydia Ashby, his Theatre Sister. He was a short man, hardly as tall as Lydia herself, but he seemed to grow as he let his explosive temper rise.

'Sister Ashby, you'll get rid of that nurse or I'll kick her out of Theatre myself,' he said in quivering tones. 'That's the third time today she's done something wrong, and it's just plain carelessness. I've told you before about her, and yet she's still on the team. But this time I really mean it! Get rid of her!'

'Yes, sir!' Lydia said gently, her brown eyes filled with resignation. She appreciated that Travers had every right to be angry, but she was sorry for Nurse Cole although the girl had been given too many chances to make good. 'I'll see that she's returned to ward duty immediately. She won't be with us this afternoon!'

'That's better,' Travers rasped, turning to march out of the Theatre, and Lydia signalled for staff nurse Dillon to untie her gown. She peeled off her gloves and took a good long breath as she shrugged out of her gown. It had been one thing after another for weeks now.

1

They sometimes struck a bad patch, but this present one was the longest and worst she could ever remember.

'Back at one-thirty, everybody,' Lydia called as she went to the door. She glanced around for a moment, taking in the familiar scene, and she half wished that she could return to ward duty. It had been a less demanding life, and she had known exactly where she stood in the scheme of things. But Theatre was her whole life and she didn't want to lose her position.

She stifled a sigh as she walked along the corridor to the little office, and she paused at the door before entering, knowing that Nurse Cole was inside waiting for her. She lifted a hand to dab at her damp forehead, and she knew by the temperature in the department that outside the sun was shining brightly and all London was sweltering under a heat wave.

Entering, she paused as a youthful-faced blonde looked up at her, then got slowly to her feet. There was defiance in the girl's face, and Lydia shook her head slowly. She went around to her seat behind the desk and dropped heavily into it before speaking, and she regarded her subordinate intently.

'I suppose you know your last chance has gone now, Nurse,' she said at length.

'I heard Mr. Travers shouting at you, Sister,' the girl replied. 'But I don't care. I'd rather go back on the wards than have him shouting at me all day long.'

2

'He only shouts when you do less than your duty,' Lydia pointed out slowly.

'I'm not cut out for this sort of work. There are plenty of clever nurses about. Get one of them in. Anyway, I shall be getting married in a couple of months, and then I shall be leaving nursing altogether.'

'I see. But you should do your best while you are still a nurse.' Lydia shook her head and glanced down at her hands for a moment. She could remember the time she had planned to get married. The last few weeks before the ceremony had become tense and long. But in her case the ceremony never took place, and she thought of John Seymour and wondered where he was now.

'What shall I do this afternoon then, Sister?' Nurse Cole demanded.

Lydia jerked her mind back to the present and suppressed a sigh. 'You'd better report to Matron's office at two,' she directed. 'I'll be going to see Matron now. I must have a replacement for this afternoon.'

'All right. But I'm sorry I got you into trouble.' There was still a gleam of defiance in the girl's eyes, and Lydia nodded.

'Run along then, Nurse, and try to do your duty while you're wearing the uniform.'

The girl departed quickly, her face showing relief, and Lydia sighed and let her slim shoulders slump a little. She lifted a hand to her eyes and covered them tiredly for a moment.

3

Then she got to her feet and left the office. She had to see Matron, and wanted to catch her superior before the woman went to lunch.

'Just a minute, Lydia!'

She turned at the voice and saw Jim Clare the Anaesthetist who usually worked on their team, hurrying towards her. Clare was a medium-sized man with dark eyes, and he was more than half in love with her, Lydia knew. But she never gave him any encouragement, and she valued his friendship. Her face softened as he came up with her, and then she smiled.

'Well, Jim?' she demanded. 'Anything to add to what Mr. Travers had to say?'

'He said it all, didn't he? But his bark is worse than his bite, remember.'

'He had every right to be angry. I have given Nurse Cole more chances than she really deserved. Her heart isn't in nursing any longer. She's getting married in two months, so she couldn't care less about duty.'

'I wanted to ask you to come to a party with me on Saturday evening,' he said, cutting across her thoughts.

'A party?' She was slightly surprised. 'This isn't the season for parties, Jim.'

'It never is with you,' he retorted rather grimly. His dark eyes burned with a startling intensity, and he reached out and took hold of her elbow. 'When are you going to give me a break, Lydia. You can't still be carrying a

4

torch for John Seymour!'

'No.' She shook her head. 'It isn't that at all, Jim. I don't often think about all that misery, and it hasn't left any scars on my mind, if that's what you're thinking. The real trouble is, I can't work up any enthusiasm for taking a chance on love again. I'm not afraid of getting hurt again. I just don't have any inclination to become involved. When John departed unexpectedly for places unknown I merely closed my mind to the whole sad affair, and since then I've never let anything personal get through the barriers. I'm quite happy as I am and I don't want to change my own situation.'

'Thats a pity, because I think a lot of you, Lydia, and you know it. But coming to the party with me won't hurt you! I'll make a promise to be impersonal in my approach to you. I won't try to sweep you off your feet, or anything like that. I'll just enjoy your company and let it go at that.'

'May I think about it?' she asked. 'It's only Tuesday today.'

'I'll ask you for your decision on Thursday. I daren't leave it any later than that in case I have to find someone else.'

She nodded and turned to walk along the corridor. 'I can't delay,' she said. 'I have to see Matron before she goes to lunch.'

'I'll walk towards reception with you,' he said, and fell into step at her side. 'You know, Lydia, I can't help thinking that you are making a big mistake.'

'How's that?' Her dark eyes narrowed as she looked up into his intent face. She was feeling tired and uncomfortable after the several hot hours they had spent in Theatre that morning. Tuesdays and Fridays were their heaviest days for operations, and usually they worked from early morning until late at night on both days. There were always emergencies coming in to hold up their normal lists, and the stream of patients coming to receive attention on the two operating tables that were in use seemed never ending.

'You can't cut yourself off from the most natural part of any person's life.'

'Do you mean romance?' She smiled thinly. 'Some people are not cut out for that role in life, Jim.'

'But you are! You're not a withered old maid. You're not yet thirty, and you're the most beautiful nurse in the hospital.'

'Flattery will get you nowhere,' she retorted lightly, and laughed.

'I'm not flattering you, I'm telling the truth!' He took hold of her arm. 'Listen to me, Lydia! I love you!'

His voice was trembling with emotion, and Lydia frowned as she looked into his eyes. He was deadly serious, but his words came as no shock to her. She had suspected for weeks that Jim was falling for her, and she had prayed that she was wrong. But now came his confirmation, and she felt sad because she had to disappoint him.

'Don't say anything now,' he hastened to tell her. 'I can see repudiation in your eyes. I don't want an answer. I just want you to know how I feel about you.'

'All right, I shan't say anything,' she said carefully. 'But don't build up your hopes, Jim.'

'See you this afternoon,' he retorted, and patted her arm before turning away.

She watched him striding away, and her face showed agony. She didn't want him to get hurt, but he was asking for it by maintaining his interest in her. He knew her perfectly well, realised how she felt about love and romance, and yet he was prepared to risk heartache in his bid to win her. She cringed inwardly as she went along to Administration, and she went into the Assistant Matron's office to see if Matron was still on duty.

Mrs. Lambert, the Assistant Matron, looked up from the reports she was reading at Lydia's entrance, and she nodded meaningly.

'I've been expecting you, Sister. Matron has gone, but she has left this matter in my hands. Mr. Travers was in about ten minutes ago, and I could hear his voice from in here while he was discussing the matter with Matron.'

'I've told Nurse Cole to report here at two o'clock, Mrs. Lambert,' Lydia said. 'Now who can I have to replace her?'

'There's a Nurse Wenn who started at the

hospital this morning. She went to Women's Surgical. When I saw her at the time of her application for a position here, she mentioned that she had Theatre experience and wanted a job in Theatre, but we didn't have a vacancy. Would you care to give her a trial?'

'Certainly. If she's had Theatre experience then she might be just the person I need. So long as she does her duty properly. That is all Mr. Travers requires.'

'He's a difficult man at the best of times, but when some foolish nurse can't keep the stars out of her eyes while she's on duty then it's to be expected that the fur will fly. I'll ring Women's Surgical and arrange for Nurse Wenn to join you. What time are you in Theatre this afternoon?'

'One-thirty!'

'All right, leave it with me! We'll let Nurse Wenn come to you on a month's trial, shall we?'

'That will be fine.' Lydia nodded and turned to the door. She paused in the doorway and looked back at her superior. 'Let's hope this will be the start of a calmer period,' she said. 'It's been very rough for weeks now.'

'It does go like that sometimes, doesn't it?' Mrs. Lambert looked up at Lydia for a moment, and there was thoughtfulness on her face. 'But you haven't had it very easy apart from your life here at the hospital, have you?'

'We all have a cross to bear,' Lydia retorted

8

softly.

'But you more than most.'

'I wouldn't say that. At least I've had my health. That's the most important thing in life according to my book.'

'Working here in the hospital, I must agree with you. I would put health first on my list, and without hesitation. But have you quite recovered from your broken heart?'

'Quite, and it wasn't really broken,' Lydia said, smiling thinly.

'You seem to lead quite a lonely life.'

'That's the way I like it.' Lydia opened the door, wanting to end this particular line of conversation. 'I'll look out for Nurse Wenn this afternoon.'

She departed then, feeling relieved that the conversation hadn't gone deeper, and she went to lunch, trying to thrust all personal thoughts from her mind as she did so. But she could not help letting the Assistant Matron's words roam through her mind. She had suffered a great deal in the past few years. Her mother had died suddenly from cancer, and the shock of it had affected her father so badly that he lost the will to live. It seemed that he actually died of a broken heart. Then there had been John Seymour!

Lydia shook her head thoughtfully as she ate her lunch. The heat of the day had stolen her appetite, but she forced herself to eat, knowing that more long hours in Theatre awaited her

9

that afternoon. In his present mood, Oliver Travers might work right through the list and handle a few extra cases as well. It wouldn't be the first time he had done that sort of thing.

A movement at her side made Lydia glance up, and she saw her subordinate Theatre Sister, Polly Cameron, looking down at her. There was a smile on the girl's strong face, and she sat down opposite Lydia, peering intently into her eyes.

'You look as if you've had enough for today, Lydia,' the girl said gently. She was short and blonde, rather plumpish, and she had a heart of gold. She and Lydia had been friends for a good many years, and between them they ran the Theatre, each in charge of a surgical team. Lydia was in charge of the department as a whole, but she never treated Polly as anything other than equal.

'It's been quite a morning,' Lydia admitted. 'But I've got rid of Nurse Cole. Perhaps everything will settle down again now.'

'You should have got rid of her before. You're too soft-hearted where the staff are concerned, Lydia. If I were in charge of the department I would make them jump a bit.'

Lydia smiled. 'Do you remember when we worked under Sister Agnew?' she demanded.

'Do I?' Polly Cameron grinned. 'I'll never forget that period of our lives. But enough said. Point taken. There are two ways of running a department, and your way is better than Sister

Agnew's. But you can carry that too far, Lydia, and you should know it.'

'We don't get any complaints, except from Oliver Travers!' Lydia shook her head ruefully. 'But I know I'm right in being concerned about the atmosphere that exists in Theatre. It does make all the difference. When I recall the atmosphere we used to have with Sister Agnew!' She shook her head and returned to her meal.

'Well try and humour Travers a little more, Lydia, or you'll make him hate you.'

'I treat him correctly. I'm not going to let him walk all over me,' Lydia retorted. 'And I'll always stand up for my nurses if they are in the right.'

'Good old Lydia! Champion of the underdog!' Polly's blue eyes twinkled. 'You're a strange girl, Lydia. You never think of yourself! When are you going to start planning your own life?'

'Now don't you start that again, Polly!' Lydia looked into her friend's eyes. 'We never see eye to eye on this, do we?'

'I know what I know, Lydia, and you can't fool me. You work very hard and you don't have any relaxation. How long do you think you can go on like this? When are you going to start thinking of yourself? You've got over losing your parents, and John Seymour has gone from your life. But you're missing a lot, and I wish you would unbend a little from time to time. What they say about all work and no play goes for you as well, you know.'

Lydia smiled. 'I'm doing all right, Polly. You know I don't need a lot of excitement to make my wheels go round.'

A nurse approached their table, and Lydia looked up at her. 'Excuse me, Sister, but you are Sister Ashby, aren't you?'

'Yes, Nurse, what's the trouble?'

'I'm Nurse Wenn. I've been told to report to you at Theatre at one-thirty.'

'That's right.' Lydia looked the girl over. Nurse Wenn was a tall, slim blonde with worried blue eyes, but she looked capable, and Lydia nodded. 'I understand you've had some Theatre experience, Nurse.'

'Yes, Sister. I worked in Theatre for eight months at the general hospital in Birmingham.'

'That's where you've just come from, isn't it?'

'Yes.' The girl's pale blue eyes flickered a little as she stared into Lydia's face.

'Any special reason why you left Birmingham?' Lydia asked the question out of interest. She liked to know a little about the girls who worked with her.

'Do I have to answer that?' came the surprising reply.

'Certainly not!' Lydia smiled.

'Well it was for personal reasons.' The girl was deadly serious, and Lydia felt a pang touch

12

her heart as she looked into the cold blue eyes that studied her without blinking.

'All right, Nurse. Be at the Theatre just before one-twenty. You'll be working with me on a month's trial. But if you do your work well you'll have no cause to expect to be removed at the end of a month.'

'You won't ever find fault with my work, Sister,' came the terse reply.

'Good. You sound as if you're the kind of girl I've been looking for. What's your first name?'

'Rita, Sister.'

'Very well, Nurse. Have you had your lunch yet?'

'I was just about to have it.'

'Then you'd better get away now and have it. Time waits for no one, least of all nurses.'

A glimmer of a smile touched the girl's lips and she turned away. Lydia watched her for a moment with speculation in her dark eyes.

'She seems rather sure of herself,' Polly Cameron said.

'I think she'll be all right! I like the look of her,' Lydia retorted.

'You like everyone who comes to work under you. That's why you got into hot water over Nurse Cole.'

Lydia went on with her meal, and afterwards she and Polly went back to the office they shared in the department. The time was just past one, and Lydia wanted to check through the afternoon list. They were behind schedule, as usual, and any emergencies that came in would put them further back.

'Shall I work out next week's work rota?' Polly demanded.

'You're getting eager!' Lydia looked up and smiled. 'It's only Tuesday today.'

'I want to see how we come out for next Friday. If I'm not on first call then I'll be able to get to a party that's being held.'

'You know I'll stand in for you whenever you want to go out,' Lydia retorted. 'There's no problem.'

Polly nodded. 'I'd better go and check my Theatre. Mr. Sloan won't say much, but I know he wasn't pleased this morning with the way I had arranged everything.'

'I wish I could work with Peter Sloan instead of with Oliver Travers,' Lydia said fleetingly.

'You're not interested in Peter, are you?' Polly looked at Lydia in some surprise. 'Although I will say that the two of you seem to be of similar natures and tastes. But he won't look at a woman. I fancied him myself some time ago, but he doesn't know I am a woman under this uniform. Love needs nurturing, Lydia, or it dies. I'm quite happy with Leo now. But you'll be asking for trouble if you let yourself become interested in Peter Sloan. He's strictly a no-woman man.'

'I'm not interested in him personally,' Lydia retorted. 'I just wish I could work with him

14

because he's so quiet and understanding. I don't like all the shouting that Oliver Travers does. That's not the way a surgeon should work.'

'I think he does it to relieve the tension. He's full of nerves, or haven't you noticed?'

'I've noticed, but he should have some thought for the rest of his team.' Lydia let her brown eyes narrow as she considered. 'But I'm wasting my time thinking like that because Travers always insists on having the senior sister with him.'

'But you have worked with Peter,' Polly pointed out.

'And I've enjoyed each time. He works so swiftly and skilfully, Polly.'

'You don't have to tell me,' came the swift reply. 'What I don't like about him is that he won't say what he's thinking. You never know what's in his mind. If you do a good job you don't get any praise.'

'What do you want praise for? He thanks you, doesn't he? He will always say thanks, Polly.'

'All right!' the girl smiled. 'Stick up for him if you wish. You'll have me start thinking that you like him, Lydia, if you go on like this.'

'I do like him!' Lydia caught her breath as she tried to steady her tones. 'What's wrong in liking a man like Peter Sloan? I have nothing but the greatest respect for him. I think he's a far better surgeon than his boss, although

15

Oliver Travers seems to think he's the cat's whiskers.'

'Steady on!' Polly was grinning, and Lydia smiled as she fell silent. 'If you feel that strongly about him then why don't you have a word with Oliver about changing over? I'll work with Olly. I'm sure he won't ever upset me!'

'He wouldn't hear of it,' Lydia said softly. 'And I'm not at all sure that I want to work with Peter Sloan.'

'You're attracted to him,' Polly asserted. 'I can see it in your eyes, Lydia. Don't try to deny it.'

'I wouldn't deny it because it is so ridiculous!' Lydia was smiling, but her eyes were very bright. She would not admit it to Polly, but working with Peter Sloan had always made her acutely aware of his personality. He intrigued her, and she had always felt sorry for him because of his marriage that had failed. He always seemed such a sensitive man, and she could imagine that he had been hurt badly by what had happened to him. But she was not attracted to him. She didn't like him any more than she liked Jim Clare, and Jim was always asking her to go out with him.

'Well I'm going back into Theatre,' Polly said, smiling. 'I think I'll mention to Peter Sloan that he has an unknown admirer here in Theatre. That should buck him up a bit.'

16

'Don't you dare!' Lydia said. 'I won't stand in for you again if you don't mind your own business.'

'That proves it!' Polly retorted, moving to the door. 'If there was no truth in what I'm saying then you wouldn't get upset by my words. There's no smoke without fire, Lydia. So you are interested in Peter Sloan!' A speculative light showed in the girl's blue eyes. 'Why don't you try to cultivate a friendship with him? I'm sure you could have a good time with him. He needs someone like you, and you'd find your own life vastly different with a man like him to keep you company.'

'I've got work to do,' Lydia said flatly. 'On your way, Polly, and stop talking such utter nonsense. Whatever will you think of next?'

She looked down at her lists and Polly departed, still smiling broadly, but as soon as the door closed behind her colleague, Lydia heaved a sigh and looked up from her work. Her dark eyes narrowed as she considered what Polly had said, and the girl's words seemed to have opened up an unknown avenue of thought in her mind. Peter Sloan had been lying in the back of Lydia's mind for some time, and she realised this now. But she shrugged as she forced herself to concentrate upon her work. It was nonsense. Peter Sloan was not her type, and anyway she didn't want to become involved with anyone. She had her work and that was all that mattered to her!

17

Lydia went on with her work, intent upon keeping her mind clear. But she was aware that her pulses were racing and her heart seemed to be working erratically for some unknown reason. She was suddenly wary and reflective!

CHAPTER TWO

Punctually at one-twenty there was a tap at the office door, and Lydia suppressed a sigh as she looked up and called out an invitation for her caller to enter. Nurse Wenn came into the office, and Lydia smiled and put down her pen.

'Hello, Nurse! Glad to see you here. I'll take you into the Theatre and show you around. Just keep in the background this afternoon. You won't find it difficult. Theatre work is the same practically anywhere in the country.'

'I can do anything you want done, Sister,' Rita Wenn said, and her cold blue eyes stared into Lydia's face with almost disconcerting frankness.

'Good, but I will check you out, Nurse,' Lydia said with a smile. 'This is your first day here at the hospital, isn't it?'

'That's right!' The tones were noncommittal.

'Are you living in the Nurses' Home?'

'Yes.'

'Your parents live in Birmingham, do they?'

18

'No.' The girl shook her head. She seemed reluctant to want to talk, and Lydia deferred to her unspoken wishes.

'Let's go into the Theatre then,' she said, and led the way along the corridor to the big swing doors that gave access to the Theatre.

They entered to find Staff Nurse Dillon already there, and Nurse Farnham was waiting to help Lydia into her gown. Lydia watched the new nurse as she introduced her to the others, and she sensed that Nurse Wenn was defensively hostile for some innate reason. But outwardly the girl was just shy in a new job, and Lydia hoped that was the explanation for her abrupt manner.

But Nurse Wenn soon showed that she knew what Theatre work was all about. Lydia watched her for a few moments and knew that she could be trusted to perform the duties that would be hers in the routine they had to follow.

Oliver Travers appeared in the doorway, and he paused for a moment to look at the nurses. Lydia, now fully garbed and sterile watched the surgeon as his eyes alighted upon Nurse Wenn, and she went forward as he approached the girl.

'This is Nurse Wenn, sir,' Lydia said. 'Nurse, this is Mr. Travers, the senior surgeon.'

'Have you been in Theatre before, Nurse?' Travers demanded in his clipped way of speaking.

'Yes, sir! I've had eight months' experience.'

'Good. I'm rather sharp on the correct practice here, so be on your toes at all times.' He glanced at Lydia, smiling thinly. 'Are you all ready to begin, Sister?'

'Perfectly ready, sir,' she replied. 'I'll ring for the first patient, shall I?'

'At once,' he retorted. 'Nurse,' he said to Nurse Wenn, 'come and help me into my gown.'

Lydia smiled to herself as she went to the telephone, and she called the ward to inform them the next patient was wanted. Then she went into her sequence of routine checks to ensure that everything was ready for the operation. She went to her instrument trolleys and quickly looked them over. Then she counted the mops with Staff Nurse Dillon and they chalked the numbers on a blackboard. By the time Oliver Travers appeared fully garbed for the operation his assistant had arrived and was preparing.

Lydia glanced at the clock. They were seven minutes late already. Then she heard a noise in the anaesthetics room and glanced around in time to see one of the porters latching back the swing doors. The next instant the patient was being wheeled in, and Jim Clare was there with his machine and a ward nurse was walking beside the trolley holding a drip that had been inserted into the patient's arm.

Lydia paused to run her eyes over the house surgeon who was to assist Travers, ensuring

20

that he was properly dressed. That was another small chore that came under her routine, and she recalled the time when one houseman had failed to put on the white wellingtons and Lydia herself had failed to note the omission. But Travers had not overlooked it, and she could still remember his scalding sarcasm.

The patient was transferred to the table and the ward nurse and the porter departed with the trolley. Travers approached the table and Lydia took up the sterile towels. They wasted no time, and Lydia saw Travers glance at the clock as he held out his hand for the preparation mop.

Lydia was ready, and she glanced around at the nurses to ensure they were in position and ready. She found Staff Nurse Dillon watching her, and Nurse Farnham was busy at the steriliser. Nurse Wenn was nearby, waiting for instructions, and Lydia nodded to herself. When she returned her attention to Travers she found him watching her, and his blue eyes were cold and alert.

'All ready, Sister?' he demanded sharply.

'All ready, Mr. Travers,' she replied calmly.

He took the preparation mop from her hand and went to work, and when he returned it to Lydia she handed him his scalpel. This was a simple appendectomy to be performed, and Travers went to work in his usual speedy and seemingly impatient manner.

Lydia took great care that she gave him no

cause for complaint, and as the operation progressed she found herself wondering if she could manage to switch positions with Polly Cameron. If she went to work with Peter Sloan while Polly came to Travers then life might seem totally different.

'Sister!' Travers spoke sharply, his edgy voice cutting across Lydia's thoughts, and she started a little, chagrined to discover that she had let her mind wander. All her actions had been instinctive, and Travers could not know that she was not one hundred per cent alert and with him, but she coloured a little behind her mask as she lifted her eyes to his, and she found him studying her intently.

'Yes, sir?' she demanded without a tremor in her tones.

'We shall be done here in fifteen minutes. Send Nurse Wenn to make some coffee and have it in your office as soon as we get through. I'm suffering a terrible thirst, and I want to talk to you before we get the next patient down.'

'Yes, sir!' Lydia glanced around for Nurse Wenn, and the girl came forward. 'You heard what Mr. Travers said, Nurse?' she enquired and the girl nodded. 'The kitchen is next to my office. You'll find everything there that you will need to make a pot of coffee.'

'Yes, Sister!' The girl turned and departed, and Lydia returned her attention to the operation. She sensed that Travers was watching her closely, and wondered if he had noticed that her mind was wandering when he spoke to her. She stiffened slightly as she considered, and her breath seemed to stick in her throat. The mask across her face seemed to become a gag, and she almost choked as she fought her nerves.

When the operation came to an end she sighed with relief, and walked to the door with the ward nurse, giving details of the operation. She took off her mask and stripped off the rubber gloves. She felt unaccountably tired, and her mind seemed uneasy about something which was difficult to place. She paused in the doorway and looked back to see Travers peeling off his gloves, and she knew he would soon be shouting for his coffee. She hurried along to her office and entered to find Nurse Wenn setting down a tray upon her desk.

'Thank you, Nurse,' she said. 'We mustn't keep Mr. Travers waiting or we'll never hear the last of it.' She spoke in friendly fashion, smiling, but there was no response from the girl.

'Shall I go back into Theatre now, Sister?' came the steady demand.

'Yes. We'll have another patient in fifteen minutes.' Nurse Wenn nodded and departed, and Lydia sat down behind her desk and began to pour coffee. As she put the sugar into Travers' cup there was a tap at the door and he entered.

'Thank you, Sister,' he said, sitting down

23

beside the desk. 'I've invited my assistant along, and Jim Clare. But they're giving me a moment alone with you. There's something I wish to say to you.'

'Certainly!' Lydia kept surprise out of her face, and she watched him steadily.

'Look, I know I'm not the perfect surgeon in respect of my manner. I can't help getting impatient and frustrated. I'm too sensitive in my work. I bawl you out and I find fault with everything.'

'Yes, sir!' Lydia said as he paused, and he grinned.

'But you're the perfect Sister, you know, and I do appreciate the way you put up with me without making a big thing of it. I have ridden you unmercifully in the past, haven't I?'

Lydia said nothing, wondering what was coming next.

'Well I want to know why you would rather work with Peter Sloan than with me,' he said finally.

'I beg your pardon, sir?' she demanded.

'I made myself perfectly clear, didn't I?'

'But I don't understand. I have never told anyone that I would rather work with Mr. Sloan.'

'Am I to understand that Sloan is lying about this?'

'Lying?' Lydia repeated.

'He had a few words with me at lunch. He thinks it would be in the best interests of the hospital and everyone concerned if you worked with him and Sister Cameron came with me.'

Lydia frowned as she watched his face. Had Polly said something to Peter Sloan? She recalled what had been said at her own lunch table, and she caught her breath as she imagined Polly talking to Sloan, thinking she might be helping along a situation which might have appealed to her.

'I don't know anything at all about this, Sir' she said mechanically.

'I see! Well do you want to work with Sloan? Would you prefer him to me?' he paused, and when Lydia made no reply he nodded slowly. 'Am I to take it then that you're sweet on Sloan? Well I think you're flying a bit high where he's concerned. Since he burned his fingers with marriage he's been very wary of getting caught again. But I think you might do him a power of good, so if you want to work with him then make the necessary arrangements with Sister Cameron. We all get along quite well together. I shan't mind losing you to Sloan, if you can make him any happier.'

'But I don't know anything about this, sir,' Lydia said firmly. 'I have no wish to make any changes.'

'I see. Wouldn't you rather work with Sloan?'

'I've never given it any thought.'

'Well he has!'

Lydia said nothing. She could sense the hand of Polly Cameron in this, and she didn't want to drag the girl's name into it. But she didn't want Travers thinking that she wanted to get away from him. It didn't matter to her about his abrupt manner or anything else. Duty was duty and she would not shirk it at any cost.

'I see.' It was obvious that Travers did not see, but he said so willingly enough. 'Well I hope you don't hold any hard feelings towards me, Sister, for my manner. I will tell you that I think you are the best Theatre Sister I've ever had the pleasure to work with. I can't fault you in anything, despite the way I've been treating you.'

'Thank you, Mr. Travers!' She broke off when there was a tap at the door, and when the door opened she saw Jim Clare and the assistant surgeon. They came in, Clare smiling enigmatically, and Lydia poured coffee for them.

'Coffee?' Clare demanded. 'We usually have tea in the afternoon!'

'I asked for coffee,' Travers said. 'I feel so damned sleepy. It must be the heat. Coffee should perk me up a bit.'

Lydia didn't know what to say, and she didn't want to continue the talk she was having with Travers, especially in front of Jim Clare. She narrowed her eyes reflectively as the three men talked among themselves. What had Polly

Cameron said to Peter Sloan? Why had Sloan spoken to Travers? She thought of Sloan again, her eyes showing reflective light. Her mind began to drift once more, and she started almost nervously when Clare spoke to her.

'Lydia, what is the name of that new nurse?' he demanded.

'Rita Wenn,' she replied.

'She seems to know her job very well,' Travers put in.

'Where does she come from?' Clare went on.

'Birmingham.' Lydia said.

'What else can you tell me about her?'

'Are you interested in her?' Travers asked.

'I'm always interested in a lovely girl, especially when I have to find a partner for a party I'm going to very shortly.'

'Are you taking it for granted that I won't go with you?' Lydia demanded.

'Well you haven't agreed to go with me yet, and I've asked you to a dozen different parties in the past year,' Clare retorted.

'I shan't be going with you.' Lydia spoke softly. 'But ask Nurse Wenn by all means! She's just arrived in London from Birmingham, and she doesn't know anyone here.'

'I'll ask her right away.' Jim Clare drained his cup and set it back on the tray, getting instantly to his feet and turning to the door. 'Strike while the iron is hot! That's my motto,' he said smartly.

When he had gone, Travers got to his feet. 'Thank God I'm forty-five and a confirmed bachelor,' he remarked. 'I don't have to complicate my life with the opposite sex.' He stared down at Lydia with keen blue eyes and remained motionless for a moment. 'I don't know what you're going to do about what we were talking about before we were undeservedly interrupted,' he went on, 'but you please yourself, Sister.'

'Thank you, Mr. Travers,' she replied, and there was a suddenly aching void in her heart.

'I want to start operating again in ten minutes.' Travers turned quickly and departed, and Lydia followed him out into the corridor, staring after him as he went towards the other Theatre. She went back to her own Theatre, and began to prepare for the next operation. Her brown eyes filled with speculation as she worked, and she could not keep her mind from concentrating upon an image of Peter Sloan...

They operated until six, and the time seemed to drag on and on to Lydia. She had never known a worse day for concentrating. She just couldn't keep her mind on her work.

Time and again she heard Travers talking sharply to her and she had to pull herself up instantly and continue with her duties. But each passing hour seemed to add to the confusion attacking her, until at six she was utterly weary of making the effort to

28

concentrate upon the job in hand. But eventually they were through for the day, and Lydia heaved a long sigh of relief as the surgeons departed.

She saw Jim Clare take Nurse Wenn aside, and a smile came to her lips as she imagined what he was saying to the girl. But her eyes narrowed when she saw the nurse shake her head emphatically and turn away. Jim looked towards Lydia and shrugged his shoulders despairingly, and Lydia shook her head. That was the quickest rejection she had ever witnessed, and she caught up with Clare as he left the Theatre.

'No luck, Jim?' she demanded.

'She almost bit my head off,' he replied. 'She hardly let me finish asking her.'

'Well give her a few days in which to settle down,' Lydia advised.

'I can't wait. I need someone quickly. You'll have to come to that party with me, Lydia.'

'I don't think so, Jim.' She paused when they reached the door of her office. 'See you tomorrow?'

'Yes.' He nodded as he continued along the corridor. 'You're on first call tonight, aren't you?'

'Yes.' She nodded as she opened the door of the office. 'But that's nothing new!'

Entering the office, she pulled up short on the threshold when she saw Peter Sloan seated on the chair beside the desk. Her face must

29

have shown her surprise, for he rarely made any effort to talk to anyone on the female side of the staff. She had known him two years and in that time he hadn't said a dozen words to her that did not have some connection with their work. But now he looked at her with bright blue eyes, and his face wore a sheepish expression.

'Sister Ashby,' he said. 'I wanted to talk to you before Oliver Travers had the chance to speak to you, but I guess he's said something to you since coming on duty this afternoon, hasn't he?'

'He certainly has, and I'm greatly mystified by the whole thing. Perhaps you can explain what it's all about! Your name was mentioned at the time.'

'I'm sorry about that. It really came about because Polly is worried about you.'

'Polly has been worried about me for years, but *I* always seem to make out all right,' she countered.

'It was her suggestion that you come work with me and she take your place on Travers' team.'

'She put that to me at lunch,' Lydia said.

'And I put it to Oliver Travers!' He paused and looked into her face, and Lydia felt her emotions stir slightly. He was the most handsome man she had ever met, and he didn't have the arrogance that usually accompanied a man's knowledge of his good appearance.

'And he put it to me,' she said in low tones. 'I didn't know what to say! Mr. Travers took it the wrong way, of course. He thinks I hate the sight of him because of his abrupt manner.'

'And you don't.' He smiled. 'I can imagine your surprise when he spoke to you. I'm sorry I put you into such a spot. I didn't think at the time, and I wanted to help the situation by having you with me.'

'I don't know what to say to that,' Lydia told him. 'I fear that making a change might give everyone the impression that I've taken a dislike to Mr. Travers.'

'Perhaps I put it in rather unfortunate terms,' he said. 'But really, you know, Oliver Travers has a heart of gold.'

'I know!' she nodded. 'He's told me to do what I want. I can make the change if I think fit, and he won't hold it against me.'

'I'd like you to come and work with me,' he said slowly. His blue eyes narrowed a little as he studied her face. 'They tell me that we are two of a kind, Sister.'

'By that I presume you mean Polly!' Lydia said, smiling.

'That's right. She tells me quite a lot about you.'

'So I can imagine!'

'So much so that I've begun to take an interest in you.' He sighed a little. 'Perhaps I shouldn't say that. But I have noticed that you lead a very solitary life. You don't seem to go

31

out to enjoy yourself like everyone else around here.'

'I do all right in my own way.'

'I'm sure you do!' he hastened to say. 'But I can't help feeling that perhaps you might be good for me in the same way that I might be good for you!'

She smiled, watching him closely, and she could not help feeling that this was just some pleasant dream. But she was interested in him suddenly, and knew she had been ever since Polly spoke about him at lunch. After all the time she had known him, he suddenly seemed closer to her, more important in the scheme of things. She breathed sharply, feeling a tension filtering into her which was stifling and overpowering, and she felt awkward for a moment, held under close scrutiny by his keen blue eyes.

'What I'm trying to get around to is asking you out for an evening,' he said stiffly. 'I'm sorry if my meddling has caused you any embarrassment. Perhaps I ought to see Oliver again and explain more fully what I had in mind.'

'It doesn't matter about Mr. Travers,' she said. 'Although I would like to work with you, Mr. Sloan, I think I had better stay with Mr. Travers for a bit longer.'

'Just as you wish.' He nodded slowly in deference to her wishes. 'But what about a date?'

He watched her closely, his eyes narrowed and showing that he feared the worst. But she nodded slowly.

'I'd like to go out with you for an evening,' she said.

'You would!' His face lost its tension and he came closer to her. 'I didn't think you'd say yes!'

'Is that why you asked me?' She was smiling, but there was a stiffness inside that hurt. 'I'll change my mind if you would rather not go through with it.'

'No don't do that. It's taken me long enough to ask you out. I would have done so before but I've been afraid you would decline, and I found the anticipation of taking you out far outweighed the chances of being turned down.'

'I see!' she smiled.

'When are you free?' he hurried on.

'I'm on call tonight, but I'm off duty tomorrow from two in the afternoon.'

'Good. I shall be off duty tomorrow evening. You have a flat in that block at the back of the Nurses' Home, don't you?'

'That's right. I share with Polly.'

'Of course. Then may I call for you at about seven?'

'Seven will be fine.'

'Then it's settled.' He smiled his relief and his face seemed to light up with pleasure. 'May I call you Lydia now?'

'Please do!' She nodded shyly, and felt

33

awkward again while he studied her with his keen blue eyes.

'I'm Peter, as you no doubt know. It's about time we came on first-name terms. You've been calling Jim Clare by his first name for as long as I can remember. Is there any particular reason why you've remained so aloof with me?'

'No reason at all except that you have always seemed rather more detached than is normal between Sisters and surgeons.'

'Then it's really my fault, is it?' He was smiling.

'And partly mine, I've no doubt,' she agreed.

'Well we can put matters right in future.' He was at ease now, and she could hardly take her eyes from his face. 'I shall be looking forward to tomorrow evening. You won't change your mind later, will you?'

'Not at all. I'm afraid you're stuck with me now for tomorrow evening, for better or for worse.'

'Well I'll take a chance on that,' he retorted, and his face took on a boyish expression of merriment. 'Thanks for making my day, Lydia. I've been wanting to ask you out for a long time, and I wouldn't have found the nerve to do so if Polly hadn't pushed me.'

'I'll have a word with Polly when I see her,' Lydia said in low tones.

'Don't say anything too harsh to her. She has your best interests at heart, and always has done so.'

'I know!' Lydia smiled gently. 'She and I have been the closest of friends for many years.'

'Well I'll take my leave now, bearing your acceptance with me. I'll see you tomorrow evening, Lydia, at seven.'

'I shall be looking forward to it,' she replied, and meant it.

When he had gone and she tried to settle down to her reports she found her mind strangely seething with emotion, and her hands were trembling. She retained a picture of his face before her while she worked, and found a restless sensation assailing her in a most unexpected way. She had the feeling that momentous times were about to burst upon her!

CHAPTER THREE

Lydia was called out during the evening, but nothing could break the strange spell which seemed to have settled upon her. She found herself in a mental heaven that occupied the forefront of her mind in a way she could remember she had acted when in love with John Seymour. Thoughts of John usually put a pang in her breast, but this evening when she thought of him she found no reaction, and there was a picture of Peter Sloan before her eyes, no matter where she looked.

She was tired as she went back to her flat which she shared with Polly Cameron after attending the emergency, and she stifled a yawn as she passed the Nurses' Home. The evening was still quite sunny and there were some nurses playing tennis on the hard courts set between the grass spaces around the Home and the block of flats. Lydia saw Polly seated on the grass with a number of other girls, and they called to her as she passed. Lydia paused and looked at them, then went across, dropping upon the lawn beside Polly.

'You look hot and tired,' Polly said cheerfully. 'I heard you'd been called in on an emergency. It was Mrs. Ryan wasn't it?'

'Yes.' Lydia stifled a sigh. 'Matters finally came to a head.'

'Do we have a Nurse Collister at the hospital?' one of the nurses asked.

'Nurse Collister?' Lydia shook her head slowly. 'I've never heard that name. Who wants to know?'

'There was a man enquiring earlier this evening,' Polly said. 'I told him I'd never heard of her, but he seemed to think she has started working here within the past week.'

'The only new nurse we have is Nurse Wenn,' Lydia said.

'That's what I told him! But he didn't want to take no for an answer, and I saw him asking several other nurses.'

Lydia got to her feet. 'I'm going to take a shower,' she said. 'Do you think it can get any hotter than it's been today?'

'Next month will see the peak of the weather, no doubt,' Polly retorted. 'I'll walk over with you, Lydia. There's something I want to ask you.'

Lydia smiled to herself as she waited for her friend to join her, and she guessed what Polly had on her mind. They walked on to the block of flats, and Polly was smiling as she glanced at Lydia.

'Did Peter Sloan come and have a talk with you?' she demanded.

'I expect you know that he did!'

'He told me he had spoken to Oliver Travers about us swapping teams.'

'They both spoke to me about it,' Lydia admitted.

'And what have you decided?'

'To remain as I am at the moment.' Lydia glanced sideways as she spoke.

'I'm sorry!' Polly shook her head. 'I thought I was doing right. For weeks now I've been listening to you talking about Oliver Travers, and I know you can't have been happy working with him. You're far more sensitive than I, Lydia, and I think you and Peter Sloan would get along very well together.'

'I know you meant well, Polly, but Travers seemed to think that I was tired of working with him. I am in charge of the department,

37

you know, and I do have a certain amount of responsibility. What do you think the nurses with me would think if I changed over with you? They'd think I couldn't take it, but they would have to stick it.' Lydia shook her head. 'I don't mind him, really. He doesn't worry me too much. I never let what he says get home to me.'

'But Peter Sloan is interested in you, and that's mainly the reason why I did make the effort to get you two together. You do need someone like him, Lydia.' Polly stared at her with deep concern in her eyes. 'You're so very lonely, and a man in your life would make all the difference to your outlook.'

'I had a man in my life once, remember,' Lydia said rather sharply. 'You shouldn't try matchmaking, Polly, you know. It could be rather dangerous.'

'But it couldn't hurt to be friends with a man like Peter Sloan!' Polly protested.

'Why haven't you become friendly with him?' Lydia demanded.

'I would have done long ago if he'd shown any kind of interest in me, don't you worry.'

'What makes you think he might have some interest in me?'

'He's always talking about you!' Polly looked eagerly at Lydia. 'Didn't he ask you for a date when he saw you?'

'He did, actually.' Lydia smiled.

'And you turned him down?'

'No. I agreed to go out with him tomorrow night.'

'You did!' Polly laughed lightly. They had reached the door of the flat, and she felt for the key. 'I'm so glad. I'm sure you'll never regret it.'

'You're really concerned about me, aren't you, Polly?' Lydia demanded as they entered the flat.

'Of course! We're more like sisters than friends. I do worry about you. I want to see you happy, Lydia. You can't tell me that you are. I've watched you a lot, and I have seen you looking miserable. There are times when even I can't get near you mentally.'

'Well I had quite a shock, remember.' Lydia smiled slowly. 'But I've got over it, and after such an experience one can usually build up a resistance to similar occurrences. You've been worrying more than I have about my personal life, Polly.'

'Well you're going out with Peter Sloan, and I've been trying to arrange that for a long time,' the girl retorted with great satisfaction.

Lydia took her shower, and afterwards sat upon her bed in her dressing gown, feeling ready to sleep but realising that it was too early yet to retire. She could hardly hear Polly moving around in her own room, and she smiled slowly as she considered all that had happened during the day. She pictured Peter Sloan's face and felt a little tremor of hope inside. It was strange how her mental attitude could change so suddenly. She didn't begin to understand what was happening in her mind, but she knew that her long months of loneliness were at an end. She didn't have to be told that Peter Sloan was going to become most important. She sensed that already...

The next morning she was in the Theatre office very early, and her mind was not completely upon her work. She was beginning to feel the first pangs of anticipation, and her mind was swift to realise that this was going to be a most difficult day to get through. There was a picture of Peter Sloan permanently in the forefront of her mind.

Polly Cameron was off duty this morning, and Lydia was on duty to handle any emergency that might come up. But she would be off duty at two, and then she would be free for the rest of the day. She could hardly bear to think of the barrier of time that lay between her and the moment of going off duty, but she had work to do, although much of it was merely routine. She went to check upon her nurses, and ensured that all Theatres were clean and ready for instant use.

'Where's Nurse Wenn?' she demanded when she had been around the entire department and failed to see the girl.

'She went to see the Assistant Matron, Sister,' Nurse Farnham said.

'Oh?' Lydia frowned as she looked at her

40

subordinate. 'Is anything wrong?'

'I don't know, Sister, but she seemed nervous about something.'

Lydia nodded and went on. She returned to her office and tried to do some more work, but she was feeling much too restless to settle, and as there was nothing urgent to be handled she decided to check through her desk and the cupboards.

Jim Clare came into the office a few minutes later, and Lydia greeted him warmly, although she felt guilty about having accepted Peter Sloan's invitation out when she had refused Clare many times. He obviously hadn't heard about her forthcoming date with Peter Sloan, and she felt that she ought to make some reference to it.

'Where's Nurse Wenn?' he demanded. 'I've looked through the department but I don't see her anywhere.'

'She's gone to see the Assistant Matron.'

'Oh! Anything wrong?'

'I don't know. She didn't see me before going. Are you interested in her, Jim?'

'Why not? She's a very lovely girl, and I've got to find someone to escort around. I know I'm not going to get anywhere with you. I sometimes wish I knew what really makes you tick, Lydia.' His dark eyes were narrowed and keen. 'I could have fallen in love with you if you had shown me any promise.'

'Can you turn love on at will then?' she asked

gently.

'No.' He shook his dark head. 'But I prevented myself falling in love with you. It would only have added a lot of useless complication to both our lives.'

'I'm glad you've been so realistic,' she retorted. 'But it makes it much easier for me to tell you something.'

'Oh?' He frowned as he studied her face.

'Peter Sloan asked me yesterday to go out with him, and I agreed. He's taking me out this evening.'

Clare was silent at her words, and he stared at her with a strange light in his dark eyes. Then he nodded slowly. He shrugged carelessly as he spoke.

'That proves my point then, doesn't it? You turned me down repeatedly because you didn't feel anything for me. It's a good job I didn't let myself go with you or I'd be in the lowest depths of despair now.' He studied her intent face for a moment. 'How long have you been attracted to him, Lydia?'

'I'm not attracted to him,' she replied.

'What's he got that I haven't got then?' he persisted.

'I don't think he'll ever get serious about me, but I always thought that you might.'

'I see. That's reasonable enough!' He smiled. 'Well don't worry. I'm going to concentrate upon Nurse Wenn. What's her first name, by the way?'

'Rita! But I think you'll come up against a blank wall where she is concerned.'

'Possibly. I seem to be a consistent loser, don't I?' He smiled sadly and turned to the door.

'Before you go, Jim,' Lydia said quickly. 'I'm about to check the drugs cupboard, and if you have ten minutes we can get the book signed up to date and settled. I'm off duty for the rest of the day from two this afternoon.'

'Right!' he nodded and came back to the desk. 'Then perhaps you'll make me a cup of coffee.'

'Of course!' She looked into his eyes for a moment. 'We have been good friends, Jim,' she said softly. 'I'm glad that we are going to remain so.'

'Of course we are!' He reached out impulsively and took hold of her hand. 'You're one of the best, Lydia, and I'm very happy to count you as a friend. I hope you'll get along all right with Peter Sloan. He's a good chap and I think you two could do well together.'

'Thank you, Jim. Shall I make the coffee first or will you examine the drugs cupboard?'

'Business before pleasure, eh?' He reached for the book on the desk. 'This won't take long. But you'd better be on your toes this morning because there are a couple of borderline cases of appendicitis in the wards. Either of them could well have to come down for surgery.'

'We're all ready this end,' Lydia retorted.

She unlocked the large wall cupboard and he opened the drugs book. Between them they checked the contents of the cupboard and examined the entries in the book, working out totals to see if all doses were accounted for. When they discovered that their figures were correct, Clare closed the book with a bang.

'Well that's all right,' he said. 'Since you've taken over this department, Lydia, there hasn't been a wrong entry in this book. We've never had it so good. You're very efficient.'

'Thank you, kind sir!' she retorted with a smile, and went through to the little kitchen to make a pot of coffee. She left Clare seated in the office, and when she returned with the coffee tray she found to her surprise that Peter Sloan had come in. 'Would you like some coffee?' she invited.

'Yes, please.' Sloan smiled, and his blue eyes twinkled.

'I'll get another cup.' Lydia felt her face turning scarlet for no apparent reason, and she hurried from the office and spent longer than she needed in the kitchen. When she went back into the office she found the men chatting easily.

'I really dropped in to tell you I shall need the emergency Theatre at eleven,' Peter Sloan said, looking into Lydia's face.

'We are all ready,' she said instantly. 'I'll pour your coffee, then go and tell Staff Nurse Dillon to check out the emergency Theatre.'

Her hands trembled as she took up the coffee pot, and both men seemed to be watching her actions with unusual interest. She placed their cups before them then excused herself quickly and went along to the Theatres in search of her staff.

Having warned them to be ready for the emergency operation, Lydia took a deep breath as she returned to the office, and when she entered she was surprised to find that Jim Clare had departed.

'Jim's gone to get his equipment ready for the operation,' Peter Sloan said pleasantly. His blue eyes watched Lydia's face as she moved around the desk to her seat. 'Tell me, was I dreaming that I asked you for a date? Are we going out together this evening?'

'That was the arrangement we made yesterday,' she said with a smile, his soft tones setting her completely at ease. 'You're going to call for me at seven.'

'I remember the details quite well, but ever since I awoke this morning I've had the feeling that I only dreamt it.' He smiled at her and lifted his cup to his lips. His blue eyes watched her above the rim of the cup, and Lydia was aware of tension filling her.

'I will admit that I've been filled with anticipation ever since I awoke this morning, which is unusual for me,' she said.

'Really?' he nodded. 'Well that's a hopeful sign!' He glanced at his watch. 'I'd better be

45

running along. There's no rest for the wicked, is there?' He drained his cup and got to his feet. 'Thanks for the coffee, Lydia. You make a very good cup. See you in Theatre at eleven.'

She smiled and nodded, and when he had left the office she heaved a very long sigh. His presence had affected her a great deal more than she was prepared to admit at the moment, she thought. After all the time she had known him without feeling anything at all, she was now beginning to feel only too aware of his existence.

A knock at the door jerked her from her thoughts and she went around the desk to open it, finding Nurse Wenn standing there. The girl was looking worried about something, and Lydia stepped back and invited her to enter.

'Sister, I've been to see the Assistant Matron about leaving the hospital,' Nurse Wenn said as she entered the office. 'I hope you won't think that I've gone over your head by going straight to the top, but it was rather urgent.'

'Don't worry about that!' Lydia moved back to her seat and indicated the chair beside the desk. She watched the girl's face intently as they both sat down. 'What's the trouble, Nurse? Don't you like it here?'

'It isn't that. I told the Assistant Matron the same thing. It was the first question she asked me. But it isn't that at all. I'd be only too happy to stay here, but it's impossible.'

'I don't want to pry into your affairs, of

course, but if there is anything I can do to help then you have only to say.' Lydia watched the girl's expressive face, and saw real worry in the pale blue eyes. There was something more than worry in Nurse Wenn's general demeanour, too, and Lydia firmed her lips as she recognised what she took to be fear in the girl's expression.

'Thank you, Sister. I took you for a good Sister as soon as I saw you. But there's nothing can be done to help the situation. I have to leave, and this time I expect to leave nursing altogether.'

'I'm sorry to hear that!' Lydia frowned as she watched the girl's face. 'Don't act hastily, Nurse. From what I saw of your work yesterday I'd say you have a very good future in nursing.'

'I have no choice, Sister.' The girl sighed heavily. 'I tried to get the Assistant Matron to let me leave instantly, but I have to work out a month's notice. If I could have given her the reason for my leaving then she might have let me go at once, but rules are rules, and I've got to work out my time.'

'That's a pity, if you are so determined to get away. Where would you go; back to Birmingham?'

'No!' Nurse Wenn shook her blonde head. 'I don't know where I'll go yet.'

'Then you don't have to go back home because of some family emergency?' Lydia questioned. She saw a tight smile touch the girl's lips.

'No. It's nothing like that. If it had been then I would have been able to leave immediately. But this is something personal.'

'Very well, Nurse!' Lydia suppressed a sigh. 'If there's nothing I can do for you then I hope you'll be able to work this out for yourself. But don't hesitate to talk to me if there is anything I can do for you.'

'Perhaps you would have a word with the Assistant Matron to see if I can get away any sooner than the month I have to work out,' Nurse Wenn said. 'I'd be very grateful if you could arrange it.'

'All right, I'll have a talk with her,' Lydia promised.

'Now would you report to Staff Nurse Dillon? We've got an emergency coming in at eleven.'

'Yes, Sister!' The girl sighed heavily and got to her feet. She hurried from the office, leaving Lydia staring after her with speculation showing on her face and flaring in her mind.

Lydia glanced at her watch and got to her feet. She left the department and went along to Administration, tapping at the Assistant Matron's door. Mrs. Lambert called to her to enter, and Lydia opened the door and went in. 'Sister, I was about to telephone you,' Mrs. Lambert said.

'I suspect I've come to see you on the selfsame matter,' Lydia said.

48

'Nurse Wenn?' The Assistant Matron raised her delicately pencilled eyebrows. 'Yes. Is she the reason for your visit?'

'She's just been talking to me, although she didn't say a great deal about her problems, but it seems that she's really afraid of something. She's under great pressure, and she really wants to get away from here as soon as possible.'

'I know.' Mrs. Lambert shook her head. 'Ordinarily I would have let her go, but I have been in touch with her previous hospital, and I discovered that she had remained there only three weeks. They told me she had been at her previous position only a month. It seems she has made a habit of travelling around from hospital to hospital, staying very short periods and flitting on.'

'I wonder why!'

'She's never given a reason! She told her previous employers the same thing she's told me.' The Assistant Matron shook her head. 'Frankly, I don't understand it, Sister. What sort of a nurse is she?'

'Very efficient and capable,' Lydia said instantly. 'I would like to keep her.' She glanced at her watch. 'I'll have another chat with her, but it seems as if she's determined to go.'

'I've never known a nurse travel around like that. There must be a reason why she doesn't stay long in any place.'

'Well I'll see what I can learn from her.' Lydia sighed. 'It will be a pity if I lose her because she is an improvement on the last nurse or two I've been landed with.'

'She's definitely not going to stay!' The Assistant Matron shook her head. 'Why on earth did she bother to come here in the first place if she had no intention of staying?'

'Perhaps I can find out,' Lydia said, moving to the door.

Lydia returned to the department and went into the Theatre they used for emergency operations, finding the staff nurse there and Nurse Wenn. Staff Nurse Dillon was quite capable of laying up the trolleys Lydia used, and it only remained for her to check the girl's work, finding it satisfactory. A glance at the clock on the wall warned Lydia that time was getting away, and she sent Staff Nurse Dillon to fetch Nurse Farnham. It was time they were standing by.

While the staff nurse was absent, Lydia approached Nurse Wenn. The girl's tense expression deepened when she looked at Lydia, obviously guessing at the subject which would be broached. But Lydia did not hesitate.

'Nurse, I had a word with the Assistant Matron about you, and she informs me that you've left your last two hospitals within a month of starting with them. This is strange behaviour, and there must be a very good reason for it. Are you sure there's nothing I can

50

do to help you? I'll be sorry to lose you. You're about the best theatre nurse I've come across in all my experience. Won't you take me into your confidence?'

'I can't, Sister!' The girl's voice was strained and taut with emotion. Her blue eyes showed such concern and worry that Lydia felt perturbed.

'You know your own business best, Nurse, of course, but it does seem a pity that you have to keep leaving your job so soon after starting it.'

'I told you earlier that I was planning on giving up nursing altogether. That would change the situation completely, and put an end to my problems.'

'I fail to see how changing your type of work would do that.' Lydia narrowed her eyes as a thought came to her. 'Unless you're running away from someone,' she said quickly. 'Is that it, Nurse? Is it someone who knows you're a nurse and can check up on you through the hospitals?'

The girl did not answer immediately, but her facial expression told Lydia a great deal.

'So that is it!' Lydia said. 'You're afraid of someone finding you here at the hospital.' She paused as a thought struck her. 'There was a man asking around the Nurses' Home last night for a Nurse Collister. That was the name, I'm certain. Would that have anything to do with you, Nurse?'

'Collister is my mother's maiden name,' the girl said in low tones. 'So he's here already! How did he get on to me so quickly? I'll have to leave right away, Sister. I daren't stay for the full month.'

'Look, there must be something I can do to help,' Lydia said quickly. 'Don't panic, Nurse. There must be a way of getting round your problem.'

'No!' The girl was adamant. 'I must go. I made a mistake taking another job as a nurse. I must get off duty and make a run for it.'

'You can't leave with an emergency operation on top of us,' Lydia said quickly. 'You're in no danger while you're here in the department. Don't panic, whatever you do. I'm sure there's a way out. Let's have a chat in my office after the operation, shall we?'

'If you think it can be any help,' the girl said wearily. 'But like all the other times, I shall have to be out of here as soon as possible.'

Lydia hoped not, but there was no time to give her full attention to the girl and her apparently insurmountable problems. It was almost eleven, and the operation was due to begin in a very few minutes.

CHAPTER FOUR

Lydia had worked with Peter Sloan before, but since the previous day when he had asked her to go out with him she had been thinking a great deal about him, revising many of her impressions of him and taking a keener interest in his personality and manner. Now, with the appendectomy about to commence, she found herself trembling with anticipation, and her mind was filled with rioting thought. She felt as if she were in a dream as the patient was wheeled in and transferred to the table. Routine played a great part in all operations, and Lydia had mastered every routine which applied to her. Yet this morning she was unable to do anything without having to concentrate hard upon her actions. She almost forgot to check off the mops, and Nurse Wenn brought her attention to the fact before anyone else was aware of her aberration.

'All ready, Sister?' Peter demanded at length, and Lydia nodded, unable to bring herself to speak. Her throat seemed dry and the heat in the Theatre was overwhelming.

She handed him a preparation mop and watched him paint the patient's skin. Sterile towels were to hand and she picked up a handful of towel clips, her fingers trembling uncontrollably. She could feel herself getting flustered, and try as she might she could not get rid of the feeling.

She hoped her nervousness was not showing, and glanced around at each masked face, unable to see any expression, and slowly she began to relax and feel normal. She took up a scalpel and held it out in a suddenly steady gloved hand, and when Peter took it she lifted her eyes to his and saw that he was attempting to look at her. But personal identities were forgotten now and the operation commenced without more ado.

There were no complications, and Peter proved that he was a thoroughly competent and skilled surgeon. He worked faster than Oliver Travers, and used a fine economy of movement that made him appear to hurry over his work, but Lydia knew his mind was always one step ahead of his hands, and she admired and respected him for the perfect surgeon that he was.

The operation progressed through its various stages, with no complications appearing, and when Peter finally ended his work his forehead was beaded with sweat. He sighed heavily as the patient was taken out, and Lydia came back to his side from making a report to the patient's ward nurse. They pulled down their masks at the same time, and Lydia saw a smile on his face as he regarded her.

'We did a nice job together, Lydia,' he said, glancing around to discover if they could be overheard by any of the nurses. 'I wish you would consider coming to work with me.'

'I'll think about it,' she promised.

'Good.' He took a deep breath and released it slowly. 'I'd better go and write up my report. You'll be going off duty at two, won't you?'

'Yes. I'm free for the rest of the day.'

'Lucky,' he said with a smile. 'But I'll see you this evening. Have a nice time this afternoon if you're going out.'

'Thanks. I do have some shopping to do, but it won't take long. I shall be ready at seven.'

He smiled and departed, and Lydia felt her heart lighten as she considered him. Then she dragged her mind from her thoughts and looked around. The nurses were already cleaning the Theatre, and she let her eyes rest upon the slim figure of Nurse Wenn for a moment. Thoughts of the girl's problem returned to her and she frowned.

'Nurse Wenn, come along to my office for a moment will you?'

'Yes, Sister!'

Lydia nodded and turned away, leaving the Theatre and going to the office. She had hardly sat at the desk when there was a tap at the door and Nurse Wenn entered.

'Sit down, Nurse,' Lydia said, indicating the chair. 'Now where were we before the operation? You told me you are trying to keep from being discovered by someone. Is there anything more you'd like to say about that?'

'I don't think I can, Sister.' The girl shook her head slowly. 'I've been giving it some thought and I think the only thing I can do is get out as soon as I can.'

'But who is this man and what makes you so afraid of him?'

'I'm not really afraid of him,' the girl said sharply.

'I can hardly believe that when I've learned that you didn't stay at either of your last hospitals longer than a month in each case.' Lydia spoke severely. 'You need to live a settled life, Nurse. Look, have you ever thought that if you could lie low here for a spell this man, whoever he is, might take it into his head that you're not here and go someplace else?'

'He wouldn't do that. If he thought I might have come here then he'll stay until he's certain. You told me someone was asking for a Nurse Collister yesterday. Well I told you that's me. I expect that whoever he asked told him there was no one with that name at the hospital. I can well imagine what his next question was.'

'What?' Lydia demanded.

'Have any new nurses started at the hospital in the past week!' Nurse Wenn shook her head slowly. 'That's how he always gets to me. He finds out who the new nurses are and looks them over.'

'We should be able to fool him,' Lydia said.

56

'He's learned that a Nurse Wenn has just started. Supposing we arrange for him to meet a nurse named Wenn?'

'You would help me to fool him?' the girl demanded.

'If it would help you settle down here, yes,' Lydia retorted. 'I'll do it without asking any more questions. But there are some questions which should be put to you, and one very important one at that.'

'What's that?' There was resignation in the girl's eyes.

'Are you wanted by the police?'

'No.' Nurse Wenn actually smiled as she replied. 'I've done nothing to be ashamed of. The man isn't my husband, and I haven't run away from home. It's got nothing to do with anything like that, I promise you.'

'That's a relief.' Lydia smiled. 'But I can't even guess at what the reasons might be. All this is rather mysterious, Nurse.'

'Not really. I just don't want to talk about it. But how can we get him to think I'm not here?'

'You're the only nurse who has started here at the hospital during the past week or so. It should be easy for us to get someone looking like you to pretend she's Nurse Wenn.'

'Really?' Hope shone in the girl's pale eyes. 'If I could fool him as you suggest then it would be wonderful. I'd know he wouldn't be lurking around in the shadows of my past. I'd be able to settle down and forget all about him.' Her tones softened as she spoke, and then her expression faded. 'But who would lie for me?' she demanded.

'Perhaps not for you, but I know someone who might do it for me,' Lydia said.

'Who would get mixed up in this without understanding about it?'

'Sister Cameron; my friend Polly,' Lydia retorted. 'I'll have a word with her when she comes on duty at two.'

'Would you really, Sister?'

'Yes. Anything to help. She told me about this man asking for you yesterday, so she might have seen him. If he saw her then we'll have to think of something else, but we'll play it as it comes, Nurse, and it might help you.'

'Thank you, Sister.' Nurse Wenn spoke passionately. 'I can only hope it works. If it doesn't then I'll have to change my job. I could disappear completely then!'

'Don't worry, we'll think of something,' Lydia said confidently. 'Now I'd better get my reports up to date or I shan't be ready to go off duty when the time comes.'

'I'll never be able to thank you, Sister, if this works,' Nurse Wenn said, getting to her feet and walking to the door. 'I'll keep my fingers crossed!'

Lydia smiled, and a thoughtful expression crossed her face as the girl departed. There was a first class mystery here all right, she mused. She had offered to help because she felt the girl deserved helping. But she would dearly have loved to learn more about the girl's troubles.

She returned her mind to her work and soon lost herself in the routine. She felt a disturbing sensation in the back of her mind whenever she thought of Nurse Wenn, but she kept it under control and managed to get her work done.

At two Polly Cameron walked into the office, smiling cheerfully as she paused in the doorway.

'If I know you, Lydia, you've done all the paperwork, haven't you?' the girl demanded.

'That's right. Everything is right up to date. I even got the drugs cupboard checked by Jim Clare, and the book is signed. You've got nothing to worry about except emergencies, and we had one of those this morning.'

'I don't mind taking over from you, Lydia,' Polly said, her blue eyes glinting. 'Have a nice time this evening, won't you? I'll be thinking of you.'

'There's something I want to ask you before I go,' Lydia said, leaning forward and putting her elbows upon the desk. 'Nurse Wenn! I'm worried about her. It seems there's some kind of complication in her life that won't let her settle down with us.'

'I'm sorry to hear that!' Polly spoke thinly. 'She's quite a good nurse, by all accounts.'

'I like her, and that goes a long way in her favour,' Lydia observed. 'But last evening you told me some man had been asking after a

Nurse Collister, didn't you?'

'That's right.' Polly nodded, closing the door of the office and coming to sit down beside the desk.

'Did you speak to the man himself?'

'No. One of the girls spoke to him, and I heard about it when I joined them.'

'So you don't know anything about him?'

'Nothing. Look here, Lydia, what's this all about?'

Lydia told the girl all she knew, and admitted that it wasn't much. Polly frowned as she listened, and narrowed her blue eyes. Lydia could tell that her friend didn't like the sound of the situation.

'What do you think, Polly?' she demanded at length. 'Do you think it could work?'

'I don't think we should get mixed up in it, Lydia, but knowing you, I suppose we'll have to do something to help this girl. I wouldn't hesitate if we knew more about Nurse Wenn. Why is she running away from this man? It must be something pretty serious for her to want to leave almost before she started with us, and the fact that she's left two other hospitals, both within a month of starting, makes me wonder what it's all about.'

'I'm prepared to take her on trust,' Lydia said. 'I'd pretend to be her myself, but that man has very likely asked for a description of the new nurse and someone will have described her as a beautiful blonde. You could play the part

60

without trouble.'

'Thank you for the vote of confidence,' Polly said with a smile.

'Then you'll do it?' Lydia paused and studied her friend's face. 'I wouldn't ask you if I thought there would be anything wrong in it. But I really don't think any girl should be hounded as Nurse Wenn is. Can you imagine her state of mind, having to leave three hospitals that we know of within a month of starting?'

'That's what makes me think it must be something very wrong, Lydia,' Polly said slowly. 'But I'll help out if I can. The trouble is, this man might ask one of the nurses to pick out Nurse Wenn for him, and if he sees me then he'll certainly know someone is trying to conceal something.'

'Well whatever happens, we can't make the situation any worse for Nurse Wenn, no matter what we do. That much is obvious.'

'All right, so you've convinced me!' Polly Cameron smiled. 'Now you'd better get away or you'll never be ready for this evening.'

'Don't you worry about that!' Lydia chuckled as she got to her feet. 'I'll be ready long before seven.'

'Have a nice time, won't you?' Polly moved into Lydia's seat. 'This should be the most eventful day in your life, Lydia.'

'Now don't go trying to put ideas into my head. This is just a normal date, and there's nothing in it.'

'Says you!' Polly grinned.

'Goodbye,' Lydia said in mock severe tones. 'See you later on tonight.'

'I shall want a full report of what happens this evening,' Polly warned her as she departed.

Lydia chuckled, but her face sobered as she walked along the corridor. She was worrying about Nurse Wenn, and she knew it. When the girl stepped out of a doorway at her approach, Lydia could see the worried expression on her face, and she halted when she reached the doorway.

'You can stop worrying!' Lydia told her softly. 'Sister Cameron will do it. If we can throw that man off your scent then you'll be able to settle down here.'

'Thank you, Sister. If it works I'll never be able to thank you enough.'

'You'll have to remain out of sight for a few days, no doubt, but that should be no hardship.'

'I don't go out after duty, anyway. I even make a detour to the Nurses' Home.'

'I suppose you know you've aroused my curiosity,' Lydia said with a rueful smile. 'But I'm not going to ask any questions. I don't wish to pry. All I want to do is help you settle down here. You're a good nurse and we need you. If we can accomplish that then I'll be satisfied.'

'And so shall I, Sister!'

Lydia nodded and went on, leaving the

62

hospital and walking along the sunny street towards the block of flats. As she drew near to the Nurses' Home she saw one or two men standing around, and ordinarily she wouldn't have given any of them a second look, but knowing that the mysterious man might be lurking in wait for a glimpse of Nurse Wenn made her suspicious of everyone, and she peered into their faces as she passed. None of them gave her a second glance, and she went on with her mind filled with strong imaginative thoughts.

There was a car parked at the corner of the street, and she didn't even look at it in passing, but a strong voice called to her as she went by and she frowned as she turned to see who was addressing her.

'Excuse me, Sister!' The man seated behind the wheel of the car was thickset and very dark. His teeth glinted whitely when he smiled. 'I wonder if you can help me!'

Lydia tensed as she went to the side of the car, and she studied the man's face intently as she waited for him to continue.

'I'm trying to find a nurse,' he said. There was an edge to his voice that sent a shudder along Lydia's spine, although she knew her imagination was working overtime. 'She didn't tell me which hospital she works in, unfortunately, and I've tried several of the others in this area.'

'What's her name?' Lydia demanded,

although she fancied she knew which name was on the tip of his tongue.

'It's Nurse Wenn. Do you know her?'

'Yes, I do!' A cold shiver went through Lydia despite her efforts to remain at ease. 'She's on duty right now. As a matter of fact she's working in my department. What does your Nurse Wenn look like?'

'I know she's a blonde, but that's all I can tell you.'

'You haven't seen her?' Lydia let surprise sound in her voice.

'Well it must sound strange to you, but actually I'm looking for a nurse Collister. At least, that's the name she was using when she left Birmingham. But I think she's changed her name. I believe she came into this area to work, and the only way I can find her is by checking up on any new arrivals at the hospitals around here. She's my wife, Sister, and we had a nasty row before she up and left me. I want to make it up with her, and I would if I could find her.'

'I see!' Lydia was wondering in the back of her mind if his story sounded plausible or not. 'Well I'd like to help you clear up this business as far as our hospital is concerned, Mr.—!'

'I'm Danny Elton!' He grinned disarmingly. 'Look, if I could only get a glimpse of this Nurse Wenn I'd know if she is my wife. If she isn't then I can go look somewhere else, but I can't leave here until I'm certain one way or the other.'

'Where did you say your wife came from?' Lydia watched his smooth face, and couldn't make up her mind if she trusted him or not. He looked hard and tough, but he could be speaking the truth.

'She came to London a week ago. We live in Birmingham.'

'Then I'm sorry to tell you that our Nurse Wenn is a London girl who came originally from Scotland.'

'Oh!' His dismay seemed genuine enough. 'That seems to be that then. But I would still like to see her. She might have lied about her origins.'

'That's true. But she's on duty and it is impossible to see her now. If she were on a ward I could have taken you up to see her, but she's in the Theatre department and unauthorised people are not permitted to enter there.'

'When will she be off duty?'

'She'll be on duty, with breaks, until late tonight. Look if you spoke to her over the telephone, would that help? You would be able to recognise her voice, wouldn't you?'

'Very well indeed! But nurses can't receive personal calls while they're on duty, can they?'

'No. But I'll go back to the hospital now and get Nurse Wenn into the office. I'm the Sister in charge of the department, you see. Find yourself a telephone box, give me five minutes, the ring the hospital and ask for Sister Ashby in

65

Theatre. They'll put you through to my office and I'll answer the call. But if I get Nurse Wenn into my office and tell her someone is calling, what happens if it is your wife and she won't talk to you?'

'All I'm concerned about is locating her. I can always get to see her. Just have her answer the phone and I'll know if it is her.' He paused and smiled disarmingly. 'She is the only new nurse to start with you in the past week or so, isn't she?'

'Yes.' Lydia nodded. 'I'll go and get her into the office, Mr. Elton.'

'Thank you, Sister. I'm deeply obliged. It will save me a lot of wasted time if I can tell whether it is my wife or not.'

Lydia smiled and turned away, walking back to the hospital, and she was seething with anticipation inside. She heard the car start up and pull away, and when she looked back she found it had turned the corner and disappeared. He had gone to find a telephone box. Lydia wanted to run, but she controlled her impulses and carried on in her same deliberate way.

When she went into the department again she found Nurse Wenn and led her towards the office, telling her of her encounter with Danny Elton. At the mention of Elton's name, Nurse Wenn paused and looked shocked.

'It's him!' she said sharply. 'It hasn't taken him long to get on to me. I thought I would

66

have got away from him this time, Sister.'

'Is he your husband?' Lydia demanded.

'He isn't! I wouldn't marry him if he were the last man on earth. He's lying, Sister.'

'Well he's going to ring the hospital in a few minutes. I thought it would be better to have Sister Cameron talk to him than meet him, and this might do the trick.'

They went into the office, and Polly Cameron looked up in some surprise at Lydia's reappearance. Then she saw Nurse Wenn at Lydia's back and took a deep breath.

'Ha! Something's cooking!' she exclaimed.

Lydia quickly explained the situation, and Polly shook her head slowly.

'I still say I don't like it.' She looked at the nervous Nurse Wenn. 'Are you sure he's not your husband?'

'Do you think I would leave two other hospitals in quick succession just to get away from my husband?' the girl demanded.

'I don't know.' Polly was sceptical. 'Look, I'll do what you want, but I hope there'll be no trouble from this.'

'There won't be if we can put him off.'

'When he rings he's going to ask for me,' Lydia said. 'I told him that Nurse Wenn was a London girl who came originally from Scotland.'

'And so I did,' Polly said. 'All right. I'll go through with it. I'll convince him that our Nurse Wenn isn't the girl he's looking for.'

'I told him you are on duty until late tonight,' Lydia said urgently.

Polly nodded, and a silence descended upon the office. Nurse Wenn stood by the door, a worried frown upon her face, and Lydia could feel shivers running along her spine. Polly didn't seem beset by nerves, but she started nervously when the telephone rang sharply. Lydia reached forward and lifted the receiver.

'Sister Ashby,' she said.

'Sister, I thought you'd gone off duty,' the operator said.

'I came back especially for this call,' Lydia replied.

'I'll put you through.'

There was a click, and then Danny Elton spoke. Lydia took a deep breath.

'Mr. Elton,' she said. 'I've spoken to Nurse Wenn, and she says she doesn't know you. But she's here and quite willing to speak to you if it will help. I'll pass you over to her now.'

Polly reached out for the phone and grinned at Nurse Wenn.

'Hello,' she said sweetly. 'This is Nurse Wenn. I'm sorry I can't help you, Mr. Elton.' She paused and listened for a moment, and although Lydia could hear the man's voice at the other end of the line it was unintelligible. Polly nodded from time to time, and her eyes were smiling when she looked at Lydia. 'Yes,' she said. 'I am speaking naturally. You're quite certain that I'm not the girl you hoped? Right.

Yes, I'll give your thanks to Sister Ashby. Goodbye. And I hope you find your wife. Goodbye!'

Polly replaced the receiver and smiled broadly. Lydia caught her breath, for tension seemed to have entered the office. She looked at Nurse Wenn's face and saw the girl was suffering an agony of doubt, and she realised that Danny Elton had lied about looking for his wife. If that story were true then Rita Wenn wouldn't be so worried.

'He's convinced that I'm not his wife,' Polly said. She looked at Nurse Wenn. 'He sounded quite a nice man, Nurse.'

'That's how I fell into his clutches in the first place,' the girl retorted sharply. 'Of course he's got a pleasant manner, and is attractive. But he's a cheap crook and a nasty character. I hope I've seen the last of him.'

'Well we've done all we can for you, Nurse,' Lydia said. 'Let's hope it works out now. But remember to keep out of sight as much as possible for a few days, just in case.'

'Don't worry about that,' the girl said firmly. 'I'll stay out of sight.'

Lydia nodded and turned to depart once more, and although she was satisfied with the way their deception had gone, she couldn't help wondering if she had done the right thing. But as far as that was concerned, only time would tell!

CHAPTER FIVE

The afternoon passed quickly after that incident, and Lydia felt nervous as the time to prepare for the evening came. She spent a great deal of care on her preparations, and felt unaccountably jittery when seven arrived. She was wearing a pale blue dress with three-quarter sleeves, and its simplicity enhanced her quiet beauty. Minutes went by after the appointed hour had come, and she began to think that some obstacle had reared itself in their path. But finally the doorbell rang and she went to answer it with fast beating heart filling her imagination with wonder.

Peter Sloan stood at the door, and he smiled and let his pale eyes take in her appearance as she faced him.

'Really enchanting!' he said. 'You look very lovely in your uniform, Lydia, but that dress certainly does something for you.'

'Thank you,' she replied lightly. 'I can see that we're going to get along very well together.'

'I'm not flattering you, I'm telling the truth,' he insisted, and his manner was friendly and very relaxed. She felt her tension evaporate and her pleasure increased when she realised that his professional manner had been left behind with his white coat. He was just another man now, and a very handsome and friendly one!

'And I'm ready,' she said. 'Isn't punctuality something which every woman is supposed to lack?'

'You've got your training behind you,' he retorted. 'That's whittled down any faults you might have had on account of your gender.'

She smiled. 'Will you come in while I collect my bag?' she invited.

'Thank you! I must apologise for being a bit late myself, although it was unavoidable. I got held up at the hospital. Another emergency.' He suppressed a sigh as he crossed the threshold. 'In our business one shouldn't make plans, or should be prepared to have them go awry without warning. However, the great moment has arrived, and I'm actually going to take you out.'

'You make it sound as if you've made a great achievement, getting me to go out with you,' she said lightly.

'I thought about it a great deal before I got around to asking you. On the surface it's nothing, but to me it is the end of the world. If you look into my eyes you'll see the proof of it.'

She looked into his pale blue eyes and caught her senses sway under surging emotion. Her breath caught in her throat and she released it in a long sigh.

'I've always been around for the asking,' she said.

'I didn't get that impression from my long

71

study of you. But I must admit that I made my study from a distance.' He seemed quite at home in the small lounge, and Lydia watched him for a moment in familiar surroundings, and she liked the impressions she received. 'You haven't been out with any man since John Seymour departed.'

She almost winced at the mention of the name, but she managed to contain herself, and her eyes were on his face as he spoke, making her aware that he was testing her emotions with deliberate intention. But she smiled. The name had really lost its sting now.

'John Seymour! Who was he?' She held his gaze a moment longer before looking away, and she saw his smile.

'I'm glad you've got over it,' he said softly. 'A few weeks ago you wouldn't have passed it off like that.'

'You have been studying me!' She crossed the room and picked up her handbag, removing her key and checking the contents of the bag.

'It's been a pleasant diversion.' There was an easiness in his tones which struck through to her innermost heart, and she caught her breath as she felt unaccustomed interest raising its sleepy head in her mind. She smiled at him, and he moved back to the door, opening it and stepping outside as she approached with her key.

'Where are you taking me?' she asked.

'Where would you like to go?' He watched her as she closed the door and locked it. 'We've worked in the same department for a long time, and yet I hardly know anything at all of your personal life. I know you're a quiet person, not given to gallivanting or social climbing. Poor Jim Clare has been asking you out for a very long time, without success, and I must admit that I can't really understand why you should accept me after Jim's long torture.'

'I suppose the only reason is that I know Jim would have got serious about me very quickly if I had given him any encouragement.' She looked at him sideways as she put her key into her handbag.

He was smiling, and she noticed again how handsome he was, and yet he was unassuming and very genuine. She felt her heartbeats quicken as a pang of some strange emotion fled through her. Why hadn't she noticed before that he was so attractive? Had she really been so concerned with her own misery that she failed to note life going on around her?

'And you suppose that I am made of stone and will have no personal interest in you, is that it?'

'No!' They walked down the stairs to the street, and Lydia was very aware of his nearness. It was as if his personality was vibrant with electrical impulses which attracted her because of their proximity. She was conscious that her mind was in a very receptive state, and impressions coming to her were sharper and more in focus than normal.

She was silent while he helped her into the car, and she watched him keenly. She knew his face quite well, but she was beginning to realise that there was a great deal about him that she hadn't really seen during the months they had worked together. He was forever surprising her with his cheerful disposition, which made him seem more human than she imagined. While on duty he hardly ever smiled, and she had formed the opinion that he was a dour character. But now she understood that the man she really knew was just a professional figure. The real Peter Sloan was here with her now, and he was a very different person to the surgeon she knew.

'Well this is a great moment for me, I don't mind admitting,' Peter said as they were driving in the stream of traffic. 'I've been hoping to take you out for months. Ever since John Seymour went away.' He paused and glanced sideways at her. 'You don't mind me mentioning his name, do you?'

'Not at all! It doesn't hurt any more!'

'Good. I've watched you closely during the past months, and I know you have been suffering. But it wouldn't have helped you had anyone tried to take your mind off it. It was something you had to sort out for yourself.'

'How right you are!' She suppressed a sigh and her dark eyes narrowed for a moment. She

74

searched her mind for pain, and found nothing. It didn't hurt any more, and she smiled slowly as she admitted the fact to herself.

'I lost a girl once,' Peter admitted.

'Is that why you haven't bothered with girls while you've been here?' she demanded quickly.

'Partly.' He smiled. 'There is another reason, but we won't go into that right now. But I do know how you've been feeling, and you've had my full sympathy, believe me.'

'Well it's all in the past and mostly forgotten now.'

'I shan't mention it again,' he promised. 'But I just had to find out exactly how you feel about it.'

They were silent for a bit, and Lydia looked around with interest. She was feeling very light hearted, and the void that had existed in her heart ever since John Seymour went away seemed to have filled itself in without her knowledge. She sighed silently, and her pulses raced and she found it difficult to restrain her high spirits. At long last she was free of the past!

'I've booked a table at the Brunswick,' Peter said. 'I thought you would appreciate that. Let's start off as I intend to go on!' He smiled, and she liked the way his face seemed to become animated. His blue eyes shone and his well shaven face was smooth and very clean looking.

'I haven't been out in months,' she said.

'Not socially. I know. Many's the time when I wanted to ask you out, but I was afraid of being rebuffed, like Jim Clare.'

'I might not have turned you down,' she retorted.

He glanced at her and their eyes met for a brief moment. It was like connecting two live wires together! Lydia took a deep breath as a pang stabbed through her. She moistened her lips, and her hands trembled so much that she clasped them together.

'I wish now I had asked you sooner, but it all comes to he who waits! They say patience is a virtue.'

The Brunswick was a large hotel and restaurant that was attended by the upper circles of society life in Stanton. It was usually too far for anyone to go into London proper just for an evening, but the Brunswick gave good service and was more than suitable for what was required by any young couple intent upon enjoying themselves.

They parked the car and walked into the hotel, and Lydia felt a little strange for some moments because she hadn't been out like this for so long. But when they had been shown to their table and Peter was consulting her about the menu she found her poise and felt very comfortable. She left the meal to Peter, and he selected the wine with the air of a man who knew what he was about. She watched him intently, enjoying the atmosphere of sophistication that surrounded them, and Peter seemed so very much at home that his composure seemed to infiltrate her mind.

Lydia enjoyed the meal, and the wine was delicious. It put a sparkle into her brown eyes and colour into her cheeks. Peter entertained her with an enlightening talk about the future of surgery, and she listened intently although she didn't understand the half of what he said. But later she wanted to know more about his personal life, and she asked him pertinent questions which he answered without hesitation.

'My father is the senior surgeon at St. Mary's Hospital in Mansbridge,' he said. 'I've always had surgery drilled into me. I didn't use to read fiction like other boys. I used to read medical journals and books.'

'You must have found it heavy reading,' she retorted, and he grinned.

'Surgery is my whole life,' he said. 'As long as I can remember I've always wanted to be a surgeon. But what about you? What made you want to become a nurse?'

'I don't know. It's always been the same with me. I'm never really happy except when I'm on duty.'

'That's not saying much for my company,' he retorted, his eyes studying her face.

'I didn't mean that! I'm thoroughly enjoying

myself this evening.'

'I'm only teasing!' His smile broadened. 'But I've watched you working and I know you're inspired. You get some nurses like that, and it isn't difficult to understand why they became nurses. But then again there are the others who do it because it is a job, and one has to wonder exactly why they chose it.'

'I've been getting some like that as nurses in the Theatre for quite some time now,' Lydia admitted.

'I know, and I've heard all about your stand against Oliver Travers. But it's the right way to handle Travers. He would make your life a complete misery without meaning to. He's like that. But I wish I were half as good a surgeon as he is.'

'You're every bit as good,' Lydia said staunchly. 'I've compared the two of you a great many times. I suppose it is wrong to do such a thing, but I'm always impressed by the way you don't hesitate. Your decisions are made in a split second. It's easy to see that your brain is always one jump ahead of your hands.'

He smiled. 'I hadn't looked at it that way before. But it's nice to know that I do compare favourably with the boss. I've always admired Travers. It's unfortunate that he's a bit of a bully with it. He can't help it, and I don't think he means anything by it. I don't think he even notices his brusqueness.'

'I like him a great deal, and the only time I

stand up to him is when he bullies the nurses. But as you say, I think he doesn't realise that he bullies. I don't think he means it.'

'You've got a good friend in Polly Cameron, you know.'

'I do know!' Lydia nodded. 'We've been together for years, and she looks after me like a mother hen.'

'She's been pushing you at me for a long time!'

'Really?' Lydia smiled.

'Yes! She's been telling me how lonely you are and what kind of a girl you really are. She's convinced me that I ought to get to know you better.'

'Good for Polly!'

He nodded. 'I'm beginning to agree with you. She is trying to pair us off, I know, and I don't think that's a bad idea.'

Lydia watched him, telling herself that she liked him a lot. He fitted in well with her idea of a presentable man. If they allowed it, their friendship could develop along pleasant lines. She was extremely pleased with the way the evening was going, and her happiness showed in her eyes. She could see that Peter was enjoying himself, and she was beginning to hope that he would invite her out again.

'There are one or two of our colleagues present,' Peter remarked.

Lydia looked around, spotting one or two known faces. She saw Oliver Travers with another man, and Sister Arkwright was with Dr. Sayers. Her dark eyes narrowed thoughtfully as she studied the faces of their fellow diners, and then she saw a face which caused her to catch her breath. It was Danny Elton! She fumbled for his name for a moment, but there was no mistaking his smooth features, and her heart seemed to miss a beat as she wondered why he hadn't departed after their little deception had been played out. Was he still suspicious? Did he think Nurse Wenn was the girl he said was his wife? Lydia caught her breath again, and some of her happiness faded.

Peter was watching her face, and he frowned when he saw her changing expression. He leaned towards her, taking her hand across the table.

'Is anything wrong, Lydia?' he demanded.

'No! It's all right!'

'For a moment you looked as if you had seen a ghost. Who is it at that corner table? I don't know the man, but the girl is a nurse!'

Lydia saw that he indicated Elton's table, and she looked at the man's companion for the first time, seeing that it was a nurse. That told her a great deal, and she realised that Danny Elton wasn't the kind of man to fall for any deception. He wouldn't leave the district until he was absolutely certain that the girl he was looking for was not at the hospital. The fact that he had a nurse with him proved that he was still asking questions about the mysterious Nurse Collister.

'Who is he?' Peter asked again.

'I'd better tell you the whole story,' Lydia said. 'Perhaps you can give me some advice. I did get rather a shock when I saw him over there, and with one of our nurses. I thought perhaps he had left the district this afternoon.'

She saw surprise in Peter's face, and nodded to herself. It was a surprising business, she thought, and wondered where it would end. The fact that Elton was still around bespoke of complications, and she was wishing now that she hadn't helped in the deception. But she told Peter all that had taken place, and he listened in silence, merely nodding his head from time to time. When she had told him everything she lapsed into silence and awaited his verdict. She watched his face intently as he considered.

'I suppose I would have done the same as you,' he said finally. 'But it is never wise to interfere in anything like that.'

'She's such a good nurse and I wanted to keep her.' Lydia was trying to justify her actions to herself as much as to Peter. 'She said something about Elton being a cheap crook. It's certainly true that she has left her last two hospitals within a month of commencing, and she was ready to leave us instantly. I would give a lot to know what is behind all this.'

'That's a woman's curiosity for you,' Peter retorted with a smile. 'But I must admit to feeling an urge to know the true answers myself.'

'I'm more concerned about Nurse Wenn!' Lydia shook her head slowly. 'I can see what Elton is up to. He's got Nurse Shannon with him and he's asking her questions about the nurses. Now I wonder if he can learn anything? She won't know exactly who he's talking about, and if she has seen Nurse Wenn then all she can do to describe the girl is say she's a blonde, which is what I told him. So he may think I'm telling the truth and let it go at that. The only danger is if someone points Nurse Wenn out to him, but she said she'd remain under cover for a few days.'

'I don't think you have anything to worry about,' Peter said. 'Perhaps he's leaving tomorrow. There's no reason why he should depart immediately, is there?'

'No!' Lydia shook her head, her feelings of panic receding. 'It's just my guilty conscience, I suppose.'

Peter smiled and nodded. 'Well forget about him now.' He glanced at his watch. 'It's getting late. What would you like to do now? Shall we go on to the Grotto? Do you care to dance?'

'It sounds like a good idea, but what sort of dancing have you in mind? I'm a bit old fashioned when it comes to music. Some of this pop stuff is all right, but I'd rather have the old music.'

'I must confess that I'm a bit square myself!'

Peter laughed. 'But the Grotto caters for all tastes. I'm sure you'll like it, and I can see that you're just itching to get away from here.'

She nodded, her eyes still bright. 'All right, you've talked me into it,' she said with a smile.

She was relieved when they left the hotel, for although she had seen that Elton saw her, she gave no indication of recognising him. Her thoughts were mixed as they went on to the night club.

Although she thoroughly enjoyed herself with Peter that evening, the chance sighting of Danny Elton took the edge off her pleasure and she was filled with concern for Nurse Wenn. She danced with Peter at the Grotto, and being held in his arms seemed to reawaken all her sleeping emotions. He danced well, and she followed him easily. When it was time for them to leave she did not wish to go, but time had run out on them and with reluctance they brought the evening to a close.

Lydia was silent on the drive back to the flat, and she felt very tired. Peter kept glancing at her from time to time, and she was aware of his eyes. She smiled at him, certain now that there would never be any formal barrier between them in future, even when they were on duty. When he eventually drew into the kerb before the block of flats, Peter sighed heavily and switched off the engine. He turned to her with a smile on his face.

'I'm sorry this evening has come to an end,'

he commented. 'I do hope you've enjoyed yourself.'

'I have,' she replied. 'Thank you so much, Peter.'

'Are you telling the truth?' he demanded. 'Once or twice I saw you frowning. You wouldn't lie to me, would you?'

'Never!' She shook her head emphatically. 'I'm sorry you thought I was frowning because I wasn't enjoying myself. You couldn't have been more wrong! I'm afraid I let Nurse Wenn's problems come into the forefront of my mind. It had nothing whatever to do with you.'

'Well that's a relief!' He was smiling. 'But prove that you enjoyed yourself this evening by telling me you'll come out with me again.'

'I'll go out with you whenever you ask me,' she said simply.

'When are you off duty again?'

'All day Saturday!'

'So am I! What about a trip to Southend?'

She looked into his face and plainly saw his eagerness. She nodded slowly, governed by a deep emotion which took control from within.

'That sounds exciting. I'm sure it will be quite a treat.'

'Then we'll go to Southend! We'll leave very early in the morning and return very late at night.'

She laughed lightly. A strange kind of mood was beginning to envelop her, and she liked it.

He leaned towards her, suddenly very serious, and placed a hand upon her shoulder. She stilled, thinking he was going to kiss her. But he smiled again, and patted her shoulder.

'Don't make a noise when you go in or you'll disturb Polly. Then she may not let you go out with me again.'

'Polly's all right!' Lydia insisted. 'I'd never find such a good friend anywhere else.'

'She's my friend too, for pushing me on to you,' he retorted. 'But you'd better be getting in. Tomorrow will be busy, or it will be a miracle!'

'Then let tonight fade away,' she said. 'Bring back reality. It has been really wonderful this evening, Peter, and I have enjoyed myself. Thank you for bothering over me. I shall look forward to Saturday. You'll let me know more details later, won't you?'

'Between now and Saturday,' he replied. His eyes were very watchful, and she wondered if he would kiss her. But he patted her shoulder again and then leaned across her to open the door of the car. His face came very near to hers, and she caught her breath and tried to still the fast beating of her heart. As he leaned back again he glanced at her, paused, and then kissed her lightly on the lips, without passion. He paused and kissed her again, a little harder, then smiled and drew back. 'That's enough for one night,' he said. 'Good-night, Lydia, and thanks for your company.'

She smiled and got out of the car, and although her expression had not changed she could scarcely control herself. Her pulses were racing and she felt as if her feet were not upon the hard ground. She closed the door and lifted a hand in farewell, and she dimly saw his smiling face as he started the car and drove away.

Lydia stood on the pavement and watched his progress until he was out of sight, and she breathed deeply as she tried to contain her emotions. She felt as if she had suddenly awakened from a long, blank sleep. The period following John Seymour's departure from her life had been blank and pointless, personally, but now a grey cloud seemed to have lifted from her mind and she was normal again.

She sighed deeply, filled with a rosy sensation that was warm and stimulating. She turned to enter the block of flats, and was aware that a car was coming slowly along the street towards her, moving so slowly that it seemed immediately suspicious. Frowning, Lydia turned and hurried across the pavement, but she heard a door bang and half turned to see a man coming after her, moving very fast in pursuit.

For a moment her blood seemed to turn to ice in her veins, and then she recognised the man as Danny Elton, and a shudder passed through her as she halted and turned to face him.

'Hello, Sister!' he said sharply. 'I've been waiting around a long time to see you. It seems that you have been lying to me about Nurse Wenn! Now what on earth did you want to do that for?'

Lydia was frozen in shock, and could only moisten her lips. Her mind was blank and unhelpful, and she felt as if she had been betrayed. But any complications following that deception they had tried would have been earned by her actions, she realised, and she stiffened herself to face whatever might come.

CHAPTER SIX

'Well, Sister?' Elton demanded when Lydia made no immediate reply. 'What game are you playing at, getting mixed up with other people's affairs?'

'I'm sure I don't know what you're talking about, Mr. Elton,' she said at length.

'I'm sure you do. I suppose that you saw me earlier this evening with one of your nurses. Well she told me more about Nurse Wenn than you seem to know.'

'Perhaps she's had more to do with the girl than I,' Lydia said sharply. 'And this isn't the time of night to discuss such matters. If you think I've deceived you in some way then go to the Nurses' Home and ask to see Nurse Wenn.

I went to considerable trouble this afternoon to help you, and I must say that you're not showing any appreciation at all.'

'This is a deadly serious matter, Sister, and it is only natural that I'm upset because of this.'

'You spoke with Nurse Wenn this afternoon,' Lydia reiterated. 'I'm sorry I can't help you further, Mr. Elton. Now if you'll excuse me I'll be on my way. I have a heavy day ahead of me tomorrow, and I must get some sleep.'

She moved away from him, and for a moment he restrained her with a strong hand upon her elbow. But she looked sharply at him, and heard him sigh and mutter something under his breath. Then his hand fell away and she went on, breathing deeply and conscious that he had spoken the truth. She ought not to have meddled in his affairs. But a picture of Nurse Wenn's worried, almost frightened, face came to mind and she could not be sure that she had done wrong.

Lydia went up to the flat and hurriedly prepared for bed. She was tired, and her mood of elation at the way the evening had gone was dissipating before the onset of more worry about Nurse Wenn. She tumbled into bed and closed her eyes, wanting to welcome sleep, but her mind was too embroiled in the speculation that filled her. What was the real trouble with Nurse Wenn? What sort of man was Danny Elton?

Eventually she fell asleep, but it seemed as if only a few moments had passed before an insistent hand was tugging at her shoulder, and she slowly came back to her senses and opened her eyes, to find Polly Cameron bending over her, a smile on her good natured face.

'You can't lie there all day, Lydia,' the girl observed. 'Do you want to be late?'

Lydia suppressed a groan and sat up in bed as she reached for her watch. When she saw the time she threw aside her bedclothes and hurriedly got up.

'I'll get the breakfast going,' Polly said, 'and when we're ready for it you can tell me how your evening went! Did you have a nice time, Lydia?'

'Wonderful!' Lydia smiled at her recollections. Then a frown chased away her smile. 'But there's something more important to talk over, Polly!' She pulled on her dressing gown as she told the girl about Danny Elton, and she saw a frown take hold on the girl's face.

'That doesn't sound so good. Why the devil didn't he leave after that telephone call? He's got a suspicious nature, Lydia, else this business is far more important than any of us knows. What are you going to do now?'

'I don't know!' Lydia shook her head. 'I'd better start getting ready, hadn't I?' She turned and hurried to the bathroom, and her mind was busy while she prepared for duty. After putting on her uniform, she went into the little kitchen to find that Polly had prepared breakfast, and when she sat down to the meal, Polly began to ask a stream of questions.

But Lydia could find no answers, and she shook her head as she began to eat.

'I'll tell Nurse Wenn what happened, and then it's up to her,' she said. 'We can't do anything more for her, Polly.'

'You've done too much already, if you ask me,' Polly retorted. 'I'm all right. This Elton doesn't know who was talking to him over the phone, but he does know you have a hand in this, and if he wasn't suspicious at the time then he certainly is now, and he won't leave until he's absolutely certain about Nurse Wenn.'

'If only he hadn't asked around of the other nurses!' Lydia felt a pang of desperation touch her mind. 'I expect Nurse Wenn will disappear as soon as she learns the news.'

'I can't blame her. She said something about Elton being a crook, didn't she? Do you think there's any truth in that?'

'I wouldn't know. She's a real mystery.'

Polly got up from the table and began to collect the dirty dishes. Lydia watched the girl thoughtfully, her own breakfast half forgotten, until Polly spoke sharply to her. But Lydia could not help worrying, and when they finally left to walk across to the hospital she looked around the street very carefully, half expecting to see Elton sitting around in his car.

'How will Nurse Wenn get into the

hospital?' Polly demanded as they reached the big main entrance.

'By the back ways, I suppose.' Lydia shook her head. 'For all I know she might have disappeared last night. I suppose she will have done so if she has any sense.'

'I'd give a lot to know what the trouble is!' Polly said.

'That's the least of my considerations, but I must admit that I'm intrigued,' Lydia replied.

They were silent until they reached the department, and Lydia sighed heavily as they entered her office. She handed Polly the list of operations the girl had on that day, and checked through her own, noting the serious cases and mentally alloting time to each case in order to judge the time they might finish at the end of the day.

There was a knock at the door and Lydia looked up expectantly as Polly turned to open it. Nurse Wenn stood there, her face showing such misery that Lydia automatically felt a wave of compassion for her.

'Can I speak to you a moment, Sister?' the girl asked.

'Certainly. Come in.' Lydia glanced at Polly as Nurse Wenn entered. 'I want to talk to you, Nurse. That little deception we arranged yesterday doesn't seem to have worked.' She explained what had happened last night, and Nurse Wenn nodded slowly.

'That's what I'm afraid of,' she said. 'I didn't

think he would be fooled. He's much too suspicious for that. But I don't want you getting involved, Sister. There's no telling what Danny might do if he loses his temper. I want to thank you for what you have done, but there you must let the matter rest. I'll make out on my own.'

'What will you do?' Lydia demanded. 'Are you going to leave us?'

'I'll work out my notice, and if he finds me before then it will be just too bad. If he doesn't get to me then I'll leave nursing altogether and get myself a job in a shop or a factory. Then he'll never be able to find me. While I'm a nurse it is quite simple for him to check up on hospitals.'

'Are you sure you can't tell me more about this?' Lydia asked. 'If there is anything at all I can do then just name it.'

'You've done far too much already, Sister, and I thank you for your concern.' The girl turned away, and Polly opened the door for her.

'Just a minute, Nurse!' Lydia shook her head, not wanting to leave the situation so unsettled. 'You said this man Elton is a crook who won't stop at anything. If that is the case then why not go to the police? I'm sure they'll help you.'

'That's the last thing I can do!' Nurse Wenn turned to face Lydia, and there was despair in her expression. 'If I did that I would soon be found with a hole in my head in some back street.'

'You're joking!' Polly gasped.

'I wish I were!' Nurse Wenn shook her head and turned away. 'But don't get any more involved than you are already. If Danny is suspicious of you now then you might hear more from him as it is.'

'What will he do to you if he discovers that you're here?' Polly demanded. 'Are you married to him, Nurse?'

'I'm not married,' the girl said, shaking her head. 'That was just his story. What he'll do to me when he catches me I just don't know.'

She departed then, and Polly closed the door. Lydia looked into her friend's face for a moment, and there was disbelief in her blue eyes.

'What do you make of that, Lydia?' she demanded.

'I'm sure I don't know! I find it incredible, and yet she is really worried and she wouldn't make all this up. She left two other hospitals within a month of starting at them, remember.'

'That's what gets me,' Polly said. 'I think the police should be informed, Lydia. This is all beyond a joke.'

'I have been toying with the idea of getting in touch with the police,' Lydia admitted. 'But I'm afraid of causing trouble for Nurse Wenn herself.'

'That's true. You don't know what she may

be mixed up in.'

'Well whatever it is, we're not going to learn the secret.' Lydia sighed and got to her feet. 'We'd better get into the Theatres before we're too late, Polly. I'll think about this during the morning and let you know what I decide to do. But something clearly ought to be done.'

'This is what comes of interfering in other people's business,' Polly said.

'Nurse Wenn is working with us,' Lydia pointed out, 'and if we can't take a little trouble to help our subordinates then no one else will.'

'You're right, of course!' Polly nodded and departed, and Lydia stood for a moment by the desk, lost in thought.

But nothing could be gained by thinking over the situation. Lydia realised that she didn't have enough facts to work on, and there was nothing she could do until she learned more because any attempt to help Nurse Wenn out of ignorance might make trouble for the girl.

She went along to the Theatre and paused in the doorway to look around. The nurses were busy with their preparations and Nurse Wenn was helping Staff Nurse Dillon, her face still showing worry. Lydia watched the girl for a moment, wondering what she could do to help, but no immediate solution presented itself to her searching mind. She went forward with a sigh and plunged herself in the preparations, and from then on until the end of the morning she had no time left for personal thoughts or worries.

The morning's list of cases was long and difficult. Oliver Travers seemed even more belligerent than usual, and Lydia wondered if he resented the fact that someone was trying to get her to work with Peter. But they got through the morning without too much trouble, and Lydia felt exhausted when she went to lunch.

The afternoon didn't promise to be any better, and Lydia was not looking forward to it as she went back to the department. Her thoughts were touching many things as she walked along the corridor, and when she almost walked into a man who emerged from a doorway she stopped in surprise, for it was Danny Elton, and there was a pugnacious, determined expression on his face.

'What on earth are you doing here?' she demanded sharply.

'Looking for my wife!' he retorted. 'Where is she, Sister?'

'Certainly not here!' Lydia looked around for a porter, but for the moment they were alone in the corridor. 'You'd better leave here, Mr. Elton before you get into trouble.'

'I'm not going until I've satisfied myself that my wife is not here.'

'Very well! But I shall have to report your presence in the hospital. You have no right to be here, and can only make trouble for yourself by staying.'

'I was brought up on trouble, so that won't worry me! Just take me along to your department and let me meet this Nurse Wenn. That's all I ask.'

'I'm sorry but you're out of luck. Nurse Wenn is off duty this afternoon and won't be back until tomorrow morning.'

'Where is she then?'

'At the Nurses' Home, I've no doubt.'

'I've been watching the Nurses' Home. Why haven't I seen her? That's what makes me suspicious. She lives in at the Home, but she never comes out of it to work, or returns to it afterwards. What is she, some sort of invisible woman?'

'I'm sure I don't know anything at all about Nurse Wenn. If you'll excuse me I'll get along to my department. I have quite a lot to do. I don't have to tell you that you're making a complete nuisance of yourself now, do I?'

'I can't help that. I want to find my wife.'

'I'd advise you to leave the hospital before a porter calls the police.'

Elton sneered at the word police, and Lydia shook her head and turned away. She didn't look back as she went to the department, but when she reached the door of the office she glanced around and was shocked to see Elton still behind her, the determined expression more firmly fixed upon his face.

'You can't come in here,' she gasped.

'I'm not leaving until I've made certain my wife is or is not working here.'

'I can't help you.' Lydia opened the door of the office and entered, and Elton followed her, looking around quickly as if expecting to find Nurse Wenn hiding there.

Lydia went behind the desk and sat down, reaching for the telephone, but Elton leaned forward and put a strong hand upon hers before she could lift the receiver. 'Don't do that. I easily lose my temper. I wouldn't want that to happen because you would get the worst of it.'

'I've helped you all I can,' Lydia retorted. 'This has gone too far. If you don't leave I shall certainly inform the police.'

There was a tap at the door at that moment, and Elton swung round. Lydia saw the door opening, and the next instant Jim Clare entered. He paused and stared in some surprise at Danny Elton.

'Sorry, Lydia, I didn't know you were busy,' Clare said.

'Don't go, Jim, please,' Lydia said quickly. 'I'm having trouble with this man. He's looking for his wife and won't accept that she is not employed here.'

Jim Clare frowned, but he came forward, and Lydia saw determination show in his strong face.

'You'd better leave,' he said.

'Don't try to make me,' Elton retorted,

clenching his fists. 'I want to see a Nurse Wenn to satisfy myself that she isn't my wife. There'll be no trouble if I'm permitted to see her. That's a reasonable request for a man to make who thinks his wife is working here under an assumed name, isn't it? The obstructions I've met since coming here make me think I'm on the right track and that there's a conspiracy going on to prevent me meeting her.'

'You think Nurse Wenn is your wife?' Clare demanded, and Lydia could see disappointment showing in his dark eyes. 'But she's never been married.'

'I think she's my wife!' Elton said doggedly.

'Where is Nurse Wenn?' Clare demanded of Lydia. 'It will be easy enough to settle this.'

'She's off duty for the rest of the day,' Lydia said.

'Well then, go across to the Nurses' Home and ask for her.' Jim Clare opened the door wider. 'You can't stay here. We are about to recommence operating. Leave now, and do so quietly.'

Elton glanced at Lydia with anger burning in his brown eyes. He took a deep breath and let it escape him in a long, bitter sigh.

'You'll be sorry you ever made a stand against me, Sister.' he said sharply.

'That's quite enough of that. You'd better leave before I'm compelled to throw you out.' Jim Clare stiffened a little, and Lydia caught her breath as she feared there might be

98

violence.

'Do you think you could do that?' Elton demanded.

'I can do no less than try.' Clare said, coming forward a pace and clenching his hands.

'Perhaps some other time!' Elton was quiet and deadly. 'It's obvious that I'm not going to get anywhere with you so I'll leave. But I'm not satisfied by a long chalk, and I'll be back.'

Lydia sighed with relief when he departed, and Jim Clare went to stand in the doorway to watch Elton's progress along the corridor. Then he came back into the office and closed the door firmly. His face was still showing surprise as he looked at Lydia.

'What was that all about, Lydia?' he demanded. 'Is Nurse Wenn married to him?'

'I don't think so. That's only his excuse for getting in to see her.'

'But does she know him?' Clare went on.

'She knows him all right, and wants to keep away from him.'

'Why?'

'I don't know, but you are interested in her, aren't you?'

'I am. Tell me what you know about this business, Lydia.'

'Perhaps it wouldn't be in your best interests to become involved,' she warned.

'It doesn't matter about that. If Nurse Wenn is in some kind of trouble then I'll try and help her out. I didn't like the look of that chap.

What's his name?'

'He calls himself Danny Elton, and Nurse Wenn said he was something of a crook. He's followed her here from Birmingham, and she is afraid to show herself away from the hospital for fear of meeting him.'

'That sounds bad. I wonder what the trouble is!' He shook his head slowly. 'I will find out. I've taken quite a fancy to that girl, and if I can do anything for her then I will.'

'She's off duty now, and no doubt she's over at the Home. If Elton goes there now he'll find her there.'

'We're due in surgery now,' he said, glancing at his watch. 'Damn! I wish I could speak to her.'

'Be careful, Jim. You're too nice a fellow to get involved in any trouble. That Elton certainly looks as if he could cause a lot of trouble for anybody.'

'I'm not afraid of him, but I'll be careful,' Clare said. 'You're the one who wants to be careful, Lydia. What would Peter have thought had he walked in here instead of me?'

'I don't know, but I have told him something of Nurse Wenn's trouble. What do you think it could be, Jim?'

'Almost anything! I wonder if she is his wife!'

'Somehow I don't think so!' Lydia shook her head. She got to her feet and moved around the desk. 'I'll have to hurry now or I shan't be ready for Mr. Travers.'

'Don't do anything else to upset him, Lydia,' Clare pleaded in mock serious tones. 'He was biting at everyone this morning, just like a caged tiger. I often wonder what makes him like that!'

'Perhaps he gets out of bed on the wrong side,' she suggested.

They left the office together and walked along to the Theatre, and Lydia found a certain amount of relief in throwing herself into her work. Despite her fears they were ready when the first patient of the afternoon arrived, and Oliver Travers appeared to take charge, seeming more mellow after lunch, and Lydia was thankful that her immediate world seemed to be settling down once more. She hadn't found much time to think of Peter Sloan, and her subconscious mind wanted to dwell upon him. When she called him to mind she felt strangely affected by the knowledge that he liked her and wanted to see her again, and she wondered just what it was about him that seemed to strike her favourably. She was impressed by him. That much was obvious. But there seemed to be something more, and she could not express it clearly yet.

The first operation of the afternoon proved to be complicated, and took longer than Travers anticipated. It was exploratory in origin, and such cases were always more difficult if only because the surgeon didn't know what he would find. In this case the cause of the patient's trouble proved to be exactly what Travers had diagnosed, and he removed it triumphantly; a small pear shaped growth that had interfered with the working of the spleen. Travers removed the spleen also, and then began the intricate job of closing the incision he had made.

Lydia was like a robot as she worked opposite Travers, her mind wanting to slip down from the high and demanding pinnacle of alertness on which she usually worked. Thoughts of Nurse Wenn were trying to intrude, and once or twice she felt flashes of emotion for Peter infiltrating her defences. But she held them all at bay, and when the operation was finally concluded she relaxed with a sigh and found that she was trembling inside. What followed during the rest of the afternoon was an anti-climax, and at six-thirty they were finished for the day.

With the Theatre restored to order and clean and sterile once more, Lydia retired to her office to handle the rest of the paperwork. She was on call through the evening and the night, and would remain at the hospital until ten, when she would return to the flat and be prepared to turn out for any emergency call. But she was not tied to the hospital, so long as she left information as to her whereabouts with the switchboard operator. She idly wondered what Peter was doing, and had hardly considered the thought when she heard footsteps in the corridor.

There was a sharp rap at the door a moment later, and her heart seemed to miss a beat as she imagined it was Peter. She called out an invitation to enter and watched the door opening slowly. Then a man appeared, and she saw it was Danny Elton.

He stood in the doorway with a tight grin of defiance on his face. Lydia stared at him for a moment, unable to speak. But a dull pang of fear was niggling at her heart, and she could feel her pulses racing as tension mounted inside her.

'What do you want?' she enquired.

'As if you wouldn't know!' He came forward and closed the door at his back with a bang. 'I've made enquiries at the Home but no one seems to have seen Nurse Wenn since she went off duty here this morning. Now I want to get this business cleared up so I can go back to Birmingham, and you're going to help me. I warn you that I am a hard man to cross, and that's exactly what you've done. You have crossed me for some unknown reason. I can't believe that my wife has told you anything of her past. She wouldn't do that. So I want to know what it is that's made this situation possible, and you're going to tell me.'

Lydia stared into his determined dark eyes and felt a pang of fear flutter through her breast. He evidently meant what he said, and she knew that threatening him with the police would not deter him. But she had no intention of giving in to him, and she clenched her hands as she set her teeth and dug in her mind for defiance.

She didn't like his manner one bit, and could understand why Rita Wenn seemed so afraid of him. But the girl was no longer standing alone against him. He had brought Lydia into line against himself by his arrogant bullying, and she wouldn't divulge the slightest bit of information to him for any reason. She was not afraid of him, even though she felt scared. But she wouldn't let him see that either.

He watched her for a moment, then came slowly towards the desk, and Lydia watched him with narrowed eyes, her heartbeats quickening and her face stiffening. It looked as if she was caught up in this despite her hopes, and now she would have to make the best of it.

CHAPTER SEVEN

'Well, Sister? I'm waiting!' Elton leaned his hands upon the desk and bent forward until his face was only a foot away from Lydia, and there was a sharpness about his features which reminded her of a rat, and gave her the same revulsion that she would have felt at the sight of such an animal.

'I've already told you that I cannot help you

any further, Mr. Elton, and if you persist in coming into these off-limit areas I shall be forced to tell the porters about you. They will stand no nonsense, and will probably call the police.'

'The police don't frighten me. But go on. I understand that you have to take this attitude to start with. But I'm warning you that my patience is nearly exhausted. If I start getting tough with you then you'll have only yourself to blame.'

Lydia smiled. 'You're not talking to your wife now!' she said through her teeth.

'You think I wouldn't dare get violent towards you?' He lifted a big hand as if intending to strike her, and Lydia set her teeth and continued to watch him without flinching. He was smiling, and Lydia had the feeling that this was not really happening. But it couldn't be a dream, and she pushed back her chair and got to her feet.

'If you fail to leave here immediately I shall make a report to the police. I understand that you wouldn't care to be brought to the notice of the police, so you'd better heed my warning and go while you can escape notice.'

'Who told you I might not care to come to the notice of the police?' he demanded instantly. His eyes glittered as he straightened from the desk. 'You've given yourself away there. I thought you might if I put on the pressure. You don't know a damn thing about me, Sister. So how would you know that I don't get along with the police, unless my wife told you?'

Lydia said nothing. Her mind seemed to go numb for a moment, and she realised that she had made a bad mistake. But she kept her face expressionless, and her eyes were steady as they watched his angry face.

'I mean to get to the bottom of this,' he said harshly. 'I am convinced now that my wife is here at the hospital, and I shall find her. I don't know what she's told you, but most of it will be lies. I've got to see her and talk to her. You won't be doing her any harm by arranging a meeting. In fact you can only help her.'

'I've told you I have no idea what any of this is about, and I am losing my patience by slow degrees.' Lydia kept a tremor out of her tones. 'I really will call the police if you don't leave.'

He stared at her for a moment, and tension and silence seemed inextricably mixed in the close atmosphere. Lydia would not show fear, and would not countenance browbeating. She stared him out, and when footsteps sounded in the corridor she saw a shadow cross his face. He took a deep breath and turned to the door.

'You haven't heard the last of this,' he threatened, and jerked open the door. He strode out, leaving the door open, and Lydia held her breath as she heard the newcomer's footsteps pause. But Elton hurried away, and the next moment Peter stuck his head around the door and peered at her.

'Peter!' There was a world of relief in her tone. 'Am I glad to see you.'

'What's the trouble?' He was frowning. 'Wasn't that the man we saw last night? The one who was concerned with Nurse Wenn, wasn't it?'

'That's right. It's the second time today he's been in here. He won't take no for an answer.'

'You look frightened. Has he been bullying you?' Peter moved back into the corridor and looked after Elton. But the man had gone, and when Peter came back into the office his face was showing anger. 'What's been happening, Lydia?' he demanded sharply.

She told him as best she could, and Peter listened in silence. When she finished he shook his head.

'Of all the cheek!' he said. 'Well let me catch him around here again, that's all!'

'We don't want any trouble, Peter,' she said. 'I wish now I hadn't started all this. But I thought I was helping one of my nurses.'

'Which is the right thing to do if the girl is in any trouble. But I don't like the sound of all this. I think perhaps I'd better have a word with Nurse Wenn. Where will she be at this time?'

'You won't find her anywhere, Peter. Jim Clare is interested in her, and he's going to try and do something about this.'

'Good for Jim.' Peter shook his head slowly.

107

Lydia had never seen such an expression of foreboding on his face before. 'I shall certainly do something about this man Danny Elton, however. He's not coming in here just as he pleases to upset you. I'll have a word with the porters in the first instance, but they can't be watching all the time. If he does come here again then I'll call the police. I'll put a stop to him.'

'When I suggested that he merely laughed at me,' Lydia said.

'Well he won't laugh at me,' Peter assured her.

Lydia felt easier in Peter's company, and she tried to push the incident into the background of her mind. But she could not easily forget Danny Elton's intent face, and she knew he would try again to get what he wanted. She knew another talk with Nurse Wenn was imperative, and she couldn't help speculating on the trouble that seemed to beset the girl.

'Now what did I come here for in the first place?' Peter said slowly.

'Not just to see me, surely,' Lydia retorted with a smile. 'Is there an emergency?'

'Not right now. We have a couple of patients who might need to be brought down in a hurry if their conditions change at all, but this time I did come because I wanted to see you.'

'That's nice to know.' Lydia was beginning to feel exalted in his company. A sense of unreality was collecting inside her to smooth over the ugliness which had come into the office with Danny Elton. She felt happy that Peter was going to stand up for her, but she didn't want any unpleasantness. That sort of thing had no place at all in their lives.

'What are you doing now?' he asked, sitting down beside the desk and leaning back, his bright blue eyes fixed upon her face.

'Nothing in particular. I am on call, and I usually remain here bringing my work up to date until around ten, if there are no emergency calls.'

'I see. Have you had tea?'

'I haven't bothered,' she admitted.

'Are you trying to slim?' His keen eyes studied her for a moment. 'I wouldn't say that you needed to.'

'No.' She smiled at his words and shook her head. 'I haven't found the need to diet. I lead a very vigorous life in the Theatre. I get more than my share of exercise.'

'Can you leave here to go to the café opposite? I haven't had the chance to eat yet, and I'd like to do that in your company.'

'All right!' She nodded instantly. 'You've talked me into it. I'll let Switchboard know where I'll be. How long shall we be?'

'An hour?' He was smiling faintly, his head inclined to one side, and she knew he was liking her eagerness.

She nodded and took up the telephone receiver, calling Switchboard and informing

109

the operator of her intentions. Quite a number of the staff used the café when they were on duty, and it was most convenient when they didn't have much time, or wanted somewhere to sit away from the hospital, knowing they could return to duty almost immediately.

'I'm ready,' she said, getting to her feet, and Peter arose and stood before her as she came around the desk to go to the door.

'I must tell you before we leave this sanctuary that I thoroughly enjoyed myself last evening,' he said.

She looked into his face and felt a pang starting somewhere deep within her consciousness. She nodded slowly. Her eyes were very bright, and a flush tinged her cheeks. She could see herself in his pale eyes, so close were they, and she caught her breath as she discovered a thread of excitement wending its sinuous way through her breast.

'I've never enjoyed myself more,' she admitted readily.

'And we're going to Southend for the day on Saturday?' he demanded.

'Certainly, if you wish!'

'It will be a wonderful day out!' He was eager, and he reached out and grasped her shoulders. 'Lydia, we've worked together for quite some time now, and I have always felt a special attitude towards you. I always held it in check until last evening, and I must confess that I've spent a pretty ragged day, just thinking about you. You've been in my thoughts all the time, and I've hardly been able to concentrate on my surgery because of you.'

'That won't do,' she said lightly. 'We can't have you upset by thoughts of me.'

'That's what I'm thinking at this moment, but I'm not going to turn my back upon you. That wouldn't help, and could quite conceivably make matters worse. But I think that if I kissed you it might help to allay these feelings that are running riot inside me.'

She felt her throat constrict at his words, and her eyes shone even brighter. He was looking intently into her face, and saw her imperceptibly changing expression. He sighed heavily and took her slowly into his arms. Lydia felt the tension building up inside her to an intolerable degree. Excitement fought with eagerness, and she stiffened and he bent his head towards her. Then their lips touched and she closed her eyes, quivering a little as she relaxed in his strong arms.

Peter kissed her soundly, tenderly, and held her as if he would never let her go again. She tried to hold down her emotions, but they were in revolt, and slowly she succumbed to their power and felt a rising tide of warmth and happiness sweep up within to engulf her. Before she realised it she was responding to him with all the fervour of her being, and her mind lost cohesion and sanity.

When Peter released her she opened her eyes

and stood unsteadily before him, her lips parted, her eyes bright with emotion. He stared down into her face, his eyes shining.

'Lydia, you're the most beautiful girl in the world,' he said softly. 'I've longed for this moment, I can tell you. All the weeks that went by when you were miserable about that other business, I just wanted to try and comfort you, but I had to wait it out, all the time afraid that Jim Clare might get to you before I could.'

'Poor Jim,' she said softly. 'He has been in love with me for a long time, but I think he's getting over the worst of it now.'

'Thank heavens for that!' Peter took her once more into his arms, and Lydia deliberately let herself go, clinging to him with an abandon she had never experienced before. They were both trembling when he released her again.

'Peter!' Her breath caught in her throat and she could hardly speak. 'You do things to me deep inside. I didn't think it was possible!'

'The world is full of surprise, Lydia,' he said gently. 'But come on. Let's go and get something to eat.'

She nodded and they left the hospital to cross the road to the café. Lydia felt as if she were walking on air. She wanted to hold Peter's arm, but she withheld her inclinations, walking sedately at his side instead. There were rapid changes taking place inside her which she could not begin to understand. Her pulses were racing and she felt almost overcome by the power of the usual emotions filling her.

In the café were several of their colleagues, and Lydia knew she was being eyed curiously by some of her sister nurses. But she didn't care. Peter Sloan was climbing into her life and settling down as if he intended remaining for the rest of his life. Until now she had not felt the slightest inclination for more romance, but her attitudes were changing so quickly that she hardly felt able to keep up with them.

She was almost too excited to eat, and the heat of the evening affected what little appetite remained to her, but she was hungry, having had nothing since lunch, and the afternoon had been a long, tense grind. There was the tension which had come from her brushes with Danny Elton, and this affected her worse than anything else. She remotely considered that situation as she sat and ate and talked with Peter.

'You know, Lydia,' Peter said when they had finished their meal. 'I wish we could work together. I asked the other day out of consideration for you, but now I want you to come with me because it will give me more opportunity to see you.'

'I'll see Polly about changing over then,' she said instantly. 'I'll let Mr. Travers know in time for next week, shall I?'

'Please do!' He nodded, satisfied with her unhesitating agreement. 'Life will be more bearable then.'

'You like your work, don't you?' she asked.

'Of course! There's nothing I would rather do. But even the most dedicated man will forget his vocation when a woman enters into his life. Love is the most powerful thing in the world, Lydia.'

'I believe so.' She nodded slowly, and wondered if she were falling in love with him. There were strange sensations in her breast that gave her unbelievable joy. She found her mind beginning to stretch with speculation. But she didn't think love could come so quickly. She had imagined herself to be in love with John Seymour, and had suffered a great deal when he went away under a cloud. But she had never felt these particular emotions for John. He had not got so deeply into her mind. She tried to give herself a warning. If she let Peter into her life then she would become vulnerable again, and she knew she could not take another beating in love. But she had to gamble if she wanted to find true love. Perhaps this time it would be true, but she had no way of knowing until she had triedit.

'What's on your mind?' Peter asked quietly, and she jerked herself from her thoughts and found he was watching her closely. 'I can see worry in the depths of your eyes,' he went on softly. 'You're not still worrying about Nurse Wenn, are you?'

'No!' She smiled slowly. 'I do sometimes

worry about myself.'

'What's on your mind? Is it me?'

'I was thinking about you,' she admitted.

'And that was worrying you?' He frowned. 'I don't see how I could cause you any worry. I'd do anything for you.'

She regarded him for a moment, her dark eyes wide with speculation. Then she nodded.

'It's nothing more than the worry any girl would feel when she is preparing to let a man come more fully into her life.'

He nodded his understanding immediately, and his eyes narrowed. For a moment they looked into each other's eyes, and then he reached out and took her hand.

'Lydia, I wouldn't give you a moment's worry or disquiet,' he insisted.

'I don't think you would,' she replied.

'Then are you prepared to take a chance on me?'

'Yes!' She nodded slowly, and felt a pang stab through her as she spoke.

'Good!' He glanced around, then looked into her eyes once more. 'Come on, let's get out of here. Let's go back to your office where it's quiet.'

She nodded and they got to their feet. Peter paid the bill and they departed, and this time he held her arm as they went back to the hospital.

Lydia was almost breathless with excitement, and a series of thrills were darting through her. She had never felt so elated, and her mind was quivering with speculation. What on earth was happening to her? She was almost beside herself with excitement, and she knew this was only the start. When time passed and they drew even more close together she would find deeper emotions to control, and she wondered if she would be equal to the task.

When she opened the door of her office she paused, for Nurse Wenn was inside, sitting by the desk, and the girl leaped up as the door opened, her face showing great fear. Lydia glanced around, half expecting to see Danny Elton as well, but the girl was alone.

'Sister, I must talk to you,' Nurse Wenn said quickly. She paused when Peter showed himself behind Lydia, and for a moment she was tense with fear. Then she recognised him, and her tension fell away.

'I'd like to talk to you, Nurse,' Lydia said quickly. She held the door for Peter, and when he entered the office she closed the door. 'I think you'd better tell us a little more about this business you're involved in. Danny Elton has been here twice to see me in his desire to get to you, and he threatened me into the bargain. I can't help feeling there's more to this than I imagine, and if you want me to continue trying to help then you'll have to let me know exactly what is going on.'

'I'll see to it that Elton doesn't start any violence,' Peter said sharply.

Nurse Wenn looked at him, and Lydia could

116

see reluctance in the girl's face. She guessed what was in the girl's mind, and hastened to reassure her.

'I have no secrets from Mr. Sloan, Nurse. I've already told him all I know about you.'

'You can rely on me to help in any way I can, if you explain exactly what the trouble is,' Peter said.

'Thank you,' the girl gasped. She was under considerable mental pressure. 'But I'm dreadfully sorry that you've become involved as it is. I wish I hadn't agreed to your helping me, Sister. You don't know what you've let yourself in for. I've been out of the way most of the time this afternoon, because I saw Danny outside the Home when I left off at lunch time. I've just come back, and Danny isn't there, but Eddie Garrett is!'

'Who's Eddie Garrett?' Peter demanded.

'He's one of Danny's particular friends, and he's a violent man. They work together around Birmingham. I've got to leave, Sister! I daren't stay here now Garrett has arrived. They'll get to me in no time, and I'll suffer for all the trouble I've given Danny.'

'What's this all about, Nurse?' Peter demanded.

'I'd rather not say.' The girl shook her head emphatically. 'They can't hurt you if you don't know.'

'You make it all sound most mysterious.' Lydia shook her head slowly. 'It's gone too far

117

now for you to keep quiet about it. If it is as bad as you make it seem then you should get in touch with the police.'

'I can't do that, and Danny knows it.'

'Why not?' Peter came to the desk and stood looking down into the girl's worried face. 'Have you done something you're ashamed of? Is it something that's against the law? Is that the hold this man Elton has over you?'

'It's something like that!' The girl hung her head for a moment, and her stiff shoulders slumped a little.

Lydia shook her head slowly, at a loss to know what to do. She knew now that Danny Elton was a nasty type, and she didn't wonder that Nurse Wenn was afraid of him, but she couldn't understand why the girl had to give way to her fears. The police would soon deal with Elton, and anyone connected with him.

But Peter was more determined. He hadn't been subjected to the fear that Elton had evoked in Lydia. He continued to question Nurse Wenn, although the girl would not divulge anything.

'I'm not going to say anything at all about it,' she said in tones of great finality. 'You've proved that you've tried to help, and you've gone too far in that for your own good. I thought it might have worked. If Danny had swallowed that story and gone away then all well and good. I might have been able to settle down here. But he's still around and he won't

118

go now. What's happened has made him suspicious, and I know the kind of man he is. Rather than bring his anger and violence upon you, I'll go. That's what I've come to tell you, Sister. I'm leaving now, tonight, and I am not coming back.'

'But you can't do that, Nurse!' Lydia protested. 'There must be a way to get round this. I don't like admitting defeat, and you shouldn't give up so easily.'

'I know what I'm doing, but you don't,' the girl rejoined firmly. 'I can't let anything happen to you because of this. This is the only thing I can do. I'll go, and I'll take my trouble with me.'

'If only you'd tell us something of this trouble,' Peter said. 'Nothing on earth should be able to force you to do something against your will. If you're happy here then stay. As far as I can see there's nothing to prevent it. One man can't make all that much difference. As I've said, the police will do something about him if he's making himself a nuisance.'

'It isn't as simple as all that,' Nurse Wenn said sadly.

'If only you'd trust us enough to give us a chance of helping you,' Lydia said. 'Are you certain there's nothing we can do? Is that man Elton your husband, Nurse?'

'He's not, although there was a time when I thought he would ask me to marry him!' There was bitterness in the girl's tones. 'But that was

before it was too late, before I found him out.'
Her voice quivered and Lydia thought she
would break down and cry, but she stiffened
her features and held on to her self control.

'Well if he has that kind of a hold upon you
then I fail to see why you can't get rid of him,'
Peter said. 'You're a nurse, and you ought to
be able to follow your vocation without
hindrance or fear.'

'I thought like that, but I'm sure Danny
would kill me if I did not do what he wanted.
That's why I ran out on him twice before. But
each time he's found me, traced me because
I've come back to a hospital, and now there's
nothing left for me but to flee again, and get
myself a job in industry, or a shop or office.
Then he won't be able to find me.'

Lydia nodded slowly, seeing that the girl's
mind was made up.

'You know your own mind best,' Lydia said.
'I do hope you'll be doing the right thing, that's
all. If you must leave tonight then you'd better
get packed and be off. I'll try and straighten it
out with the Assistant Matron in the morning.'

'You'll be walking straight into Elton's
hands,' Peter said slowly. 'He'll be watching
for certain, and you'll be making it easy for him
to get you. Look, why don't you try another
bluff, only this time I'll help, and if it works it
will certainly put him off your trail.'

'I don't want you to become any more
involved,' Nurse Wenn said slowly.

120

'I don't mind, if it will help you!' Peter said eagerly. 'Look you pack your bags and Lydia and I will drive you to the bus station. Take a bus out of town, and get off before any destination. I'll pick you up along the road and bring you back to the Nurses' Home. If Elton sees you leaving he may follow, and if you can get off the bus unseen then you have a very good chance of covering your tracks.'

'It sounds as if it might work,' Lydia commented. 'What about it, Nurse? You've got to stop running somewhere or you'll be running for the rest of your life. Why not make your stand here, among friends?'

The girl considered for a moment, then nodded slowly.

'All right,' she said in despairing tones. 'I'll try it.'

At that moment there was the sound of footsteps in the corridor, and they all froze. Lydia especially thought it was Danny Elton returning, and her heart seemed to miss a beat as the footsteps came quickly nearer to the office. But Peter acted quickly, going to the door and departing, closing the door at his back.

CHAPTER EIGHT

Lydia raised a finger to her lips as Nurse Wenn opened her mouth to speak, and they heard Peter's voice outside. Lydia could see that the girl suspected the newcomer was Danny Elton, and they stared at one another in silent fear. Then the door opened again and Peter entered, holding the door wide for the newcomer, and Lydia let her pent up breath go rapidly when Jim Clare walked in. He paused on the threshold and looked around, his face lighting up when he saw Nurse Wenn.

'What's going on here?' he demanded. 'I've been trying to find you all evening, Nurse Wenn.'

'I think perhaps I'd better explain,' Peter said. 'I was about to try something that might help Nurse Wenn, Jim. If you're willing to help out it might work even better.'

'Fire away,' Clare said instantly. 'Anything to help a pretty nurse. She certainly needs help from those of us she knows.'

'But I hardly know any of you,' Nurse Wenn said tensely.

'You work with us, and that's good enough,' Clare retorted. His dark eyes were glinting, and he smiled as he looked at Lydia. 'You look as if you expect the hospital to fall in on you,' he commented.

'It is getting a bit tense,' Lydia retorted. 'But listen to what Peter has to say. Perhaps you can give your opinion, Jim.'

Peter quickly explained his plan for throwing Elton off Nurse Wenn's tracks, and Clare agreed that it was worth a try.

'Elton is seated in his car outside the Nurses' Home now,' Clare said. 'The best thing to do, I imagine, is get Nurse Wenn into the Home unobserved and let her pack, then let Elton see her coming out to get into your car. You can drive her away, and I'll fall in behind you. I'll keep an eye on friend Elton, and if he tries to follow you then I'll block his way. Once you get out of sight you're as good as clear, and whether you put Nurse Wenn on a bus or sneak her back into the Home again is up to you.'

'You might get into trouble by interfering so openly,' Nurse Wenn objected.

'It doesn't matter about that.' Clare shook his head firmly. 'If we can get Elton off your back by this trick then all well and good. I'm willing to risk the trouble for you.'

'Then you go with Nurse Elton into the Home,' Peter instructed Lydia. 'I'll give you fifteen minutes, then pull up in front of the Home. Make no secret of coming out when you're ready. We want Elton to see us.' He glanced at Jim Clare. 'Which way is Elton's car facing, Jim? If I come up from the opposite direction it will mean he'll have to turn around before he can follow us. That should give us a

123

better start.'

'Now you're thinking like a fox,' Clare said, grinning. 'His car was facing this way, so if you enter the road from the Stradbroke Road end you'll be right. I'll pull in front of Elton and wait for his move. I'll block him, don't you worry. You'll get away all right.'

Lydia looked at Nurse Wenn, and saw hope showing once more in the girl's face.

'Are you willing to try this, Nurse?' she demanded.

'Yes, if you're so set upon helping me. I'll never be able to thank you for this.'

'Don't even consider trying,' Jim Clare told her. 'But you had better get moving if you want to make this look good. Make sure Elton sees your cases. We'll take care of the rest.'

Lydia suppressed a sigh as they left the hospital, and she led Nurse Wenn along the corridors to the back door that let them out into a small courtyard giving access to a street behind the hospital. It was a little-used exit, and a porter appeared as Lydia wrestled with the stiff lock.

'This isn't allowed, Sister,' the porter said firmly.

'It's something of an emergency, Frank,' Lydia retorted. 'I never bend the rules, you know. But this is necessary.'

'All right!' The porter came forward and turned the key for her. 'But don't make a habit of this, will you?'

'I promise not to.' Lydia smiled as she led the way outside, and she glanced both ways along the street to ensure the way was clear. There was no sign of Elton, and she sighed a little as Nurse Wenn joined her and they hurried on a round-about way to the rear of the Nurses' Home.

When they reached a corner of the street that ran behind the Nurses' Home, Nurse Wenn peered around the corner, then drew back in alarm, and Lydia felt her pulses race as she saw the expression of fear which came to the girl's face.

'Eddie Garrett's car is near the back entrance,' the girl said.

'And Elton will be watching the front entrance!' Lydia nodded.

'I knew it wouldn't be so easy,' Nurse Wenn said.

'We're not beaten yet.' Lydia took hold of the girl's arm. 'There's a side door that gives access to the boiler house. If we can get in through there, no one will see us entering the building.'

'I don't like this at all,' Nurse Wenn said in nervous tones.

'There's nothing to worry about. If the worst comes to the worst, Peter and Jim will keep Elton away from you.'

'There'll be trouble, I know there will,' the girl said sharply. 'If anyone gets hurt I'll have it on my conscience for the rest of my life.'

'Hurt!' Lydia frowned, and the girl's seriously spoken words sent a pang through her. 'Is this business as bad as all that, Nurse?'

'That's what I keep trying to impress upon you,' the girl said.

'Well we've gone too far now to let anything stop us.' Lydia shook her head. 'Come on, let's try that boiler house entrance.'

They crossed the road, and Lydia kept between Nurse Wenn and the car that was parked near the back door of the Nurses' Home. She felt a little bit ridiculous because it all seemed so unreal, but a glance at Nurse Wenn's taut expression warned her that this was anything but a game to the girl. They reached the door in the wall that led into the boiler house, and Lydia held her breath as she tried it. She clenched her teeth when it refused to budge, and at that moment Nurse Wenn grasped her shoulder.

'Sister, look!'

Lydia half turned, saw the direction the girl was looking, and turned her eyes the same way. Her heart missed a beat when she saw the powerful figure of Danny Elton on the front corner of the Nurses' Home. He was pacing up and down in front of the building, and was casually peering around as he turned at the extreme limit of his self imposed beat to retrace his steps. In a moment he was going to glance their way, Lydia realised, and she thrust her weight against the door again, hoping against hope that it would open. It didn't move an inch, and Lydia pushed Nurse Wenn to her left, inserting herself between the girl and Danny Elton. She looked again at Elton, and saw that he was glancing their way. The fact that Lydia was in uniform attracted his immediate attention, and she gasped when he began to walk towards them.

'What can we do?' Nurse Wenn demanded.

Lydia thrust against the door again, but it wouldn't budge, and she knew no one used the boiler house during the summer.

'Let's make a run for it,' she said urgently. 'Round to the back entrance. We can get inside before that other man realises what is happening.'

They took to their heels and ran back the way they had come, and as they turned the corner into the back street Lydia looked round and saw Elton chasing them, and gaining quickly. But it wasn't far along the street to the back door, and they were breathless as they reached it. Lydia glanced at the man in the car at the kerb, and she saw him staring until he recognised Nurse Wenn. But by the time he started getting out of the car they were at the back door and scrambling into the building.

Lydia slammed the door after they passed through, and pushed home the heavy bolt. She sagged against the door and tried to catch her breath, and a hand tried the door, causing her to stiffen. She looked into Nurse Wenn's eyes and saw extreme fear on the girl's face. Outside two men were talking angrily, and Lydia recognised Danny Elton's voice.

'We'd better get up to your room and pack those cases,' Lydia said. 'The sooner we get you away from here the better.'

'I couldn't agree more,' the girl said. 'But I'm afraid Danny will come into the Home looking for me.'

'If he does I shall call the police,' Lydia said firmly, and the girl was too scared to protest. A heavy hand tried the door again, and Lydia firmed her lips. 'We'll leave it locked, and get upstairs before they can reach the front door again,' she declared. 'We can check their whereabouts before leaving, and if they are watching front and back still, we'll leave by that boiler house door.'

'Danny will know for certain that I'm here now,' Nurse Wenn said. 'He'll never go away until he gets me. I think the best thing I can do is go with him. It will save a lot of trouble, and he'll only get me in the end.'

'Don't be such a defeatist,' Lydia retorted. 'Come on.'

They hurried into the front of the building and ascended the stairs to Nurse Wenn's room. Lydia went to the windows, which overlooked the road outside, and her lips tightened when she saw Danny Elton pacing up and down out front. There was no sign of the second man, but Lydia knew the two of them could not cover the three exits from the building. There had to be a good chance of getting away.

Nurse Wenn hurriedly threw her clothes into two cases, and in a matter of minutes she had packed everything. Then they went to the windows again, and Lydia saw Elton still pacing up and down outside the main door.

'At least he hasn't come in here after you,' she said, looking into Nurse Wenn's worried face.

'That doesn't mean anything. He doesn't really want to attract the attention of the police. He may threaten that he doesn't care, but he does.'

'Then why don't we call the police and tell them about this?'

'Because if they start asking questions I might get into serious trouble as well as Danny.'

'Does that mean you've broken the law because of Elton?'

'Yes.'

'And you don't want to talk about it?'

'No.'

'All right. I won't ask any more. Look, there's Peter's car.' Lydia smiled when she saw the vehicle pulling in at the front entrance.

'But I'm not going down there while Danny is standing right in the entrance,' Nurse Wenn said in shocked tones. 'He'll grab me! Then there would be trouble.'

'Perhaps you're right. Look, stay here and

wait until I come back.'

'What are you going to do?'

'I'll go down and get Peter to drive around the side and park near the boiler house door. You can get out of the building that way.'

'But I thought the whole object was to let Danny see me with my cases!'

'So it is!' Lydia suppressed a sigh. She felt frustrated for a moment. Her dark eyes narrowed as she stared at the street below. Then she stiffened. Jim Clare's car had come into sight and was parking near Elton's on the far side of the street. 'I think I'd better go down and have a word with Peter. Perhaps he can suggest something.' Lydia looked into the girl's eyes and saw fear in their pale depths. She reached out a comforting hand and grasped the girl's shoulder. 'Don't worry. With Peter and Jim around, Elton won't be able to do anything.'

'I don't know so much about that!' Nurse Wenn shook her head. 'I still think I ought to go to Danny. It will save you all a lot of trouble.'

'Nonsense. Now you just stop thinking like that, and stay here until I get back. If you do try to go to Elton, I'll call the police and tell them all I know.'

'You wouldn't!' Stark fear showed in the girl's face.

'I would. So that's an end to it. Stay put, Nurse.'

The girl nodded slowly and sat down on the foot of her bed. Lydia studied her face for a moment, then left the room, closing the door silently. She hurried to the ground floor, and took a deep breath as she moved to the exit. She could see Elton's powerful figure pacing to and fro, and Peter's car at the kerbside. She could imagine how Nurse Wenn was feeling as she felt nervousness attack her, but she thrust her weaknesses away and walked boldly out into the evening sunlight.

Elton paused and looked at her when she appeared, and Lydia went on without faltering. She fully expected him to say something, but he had seen Peter in the nearby car, and he merely stood watching her as she crossed to the vehicle, opened the door and got in beside Peter.

Peter was tense, and his lips were firm against his teeth.

'Well?' he demanded.

'She's up in her room, packed and ready to go, but we had trouble getting into the building, and you can see it will be even more difficult to get her out.' Lydia glanced towards the still watching Elton.

'I've been wondering what to do,' Peter admitted. 'We don't want any trouble unless it is absolutely necessary.'

'There mustn't be any trouble at all,' Lydia said firmly. 'But I have an idea. Elton has a friend watching the rear of the Home, but there is the boiler house door at the side of the building. If you drive around to it I'll bring Nurse Wenn out that way.'

'But we want Elton to see her leaving with her cases, don't we?' Peter demanded.

'We do, but if there is a confrontation between them anything might happen. What do you think?'

Peter glanced at the watching Elton. Lydia could almost see what was passing through his mind by the fleeting expressions on his face. She shook her head.

'No violence, Peter,' she said firmly.

'Don't worry about that. I'm not a violent type.' He smiled. 'I can take care of myself, of course, but I've always been a defensive type of person.'

She nodded. 'What shall we do?'

'I wish I knew!' He sighed heavily. 'What does Nurse Wenn think about this situation?'

'She feels that she ought to go with Elton because it will save a lot of trouble all round, and he'll get to her in the end, anyway!'

'I'm not so sure of that. A girl doesn't have to submit to such circumstances in this day and age. If she doesn't want anything to do with him then she has the right to stay away from him. I'll go and have a word with Elton. I'll try and warn him off.'

'You'll be wasting your breath,' Lydia said, and got out of the car as Peter alighted.

Elton narrowed his eyes as they walked up to

him, and Peter motioned for Lydia to stay back. She heard a car door slam and looked around quickly, seeing Jim Clare getting out of his car at sight of them and following them. She felt a measure of relief that Jim was determined to back them up, and returned her attention to Danny Elton.

'You're playing a funny game, Sister,' Elton said sharply.

'It's not as stupid as the one you're playing,' Peter retorted. 'If you don't give up this idea of pestering Nurse Wenn then I shall call the police.'

Elton's face turned ugly at the mention of the police. His eyes brightened and he put a hand into his jacket pocket. 'You don't know what you're saying,' he retorted. 'This is none of your business. I have every right to see my wife.'

'I don't believe she is your wife,' Peter said, glancing around at Clare as he came to stand at his side. 'She denies it out of hand, and now she's going to leave this place and get on a bus. We are going to see that you don't interfere with her. What you do after she's departed here is your business, but you won't accost her in any way while she's in our company.' He looked at Lydia. 'Go and fetch her down, will you?'

'She won't come down while he's here,' Lydia said.

'And I don't blame her,' Jim Clare said

sharply.

'Listen to me, Elton, if that's what your name is! You might think you're pretty tough bullying women, but you'll find me at least a different proposition. Nurse Wenn is leaving here, and you're not going to do anything about it. If you try you'll get exactly what you're asking for.'

'There's no need to talk like that,' Peter said.

'Oh yes there is!' Clare retorted, his eyes flashing. 'It's the only language his type understands. Do I make myself clear, Elton?'

Danny Elton grinned, but his face was ugly, and Lydia felt a nervousness take hold of her. It seemed that Nurse Wenn's words were coming true. Nothing was going right, and it seemed that Elton would get his own way. She glanced around the street, and her pulses leaped when she saw a uniformed constable getting out of a Panda car just along the street.

'I've a good mind to call that constable along here,' she said desperately. 'He'll know exactly what to do about this situation.'

Elton stiffened at her words, and looked around, his eyes narrowing when he saw the policeman. Lydia, watching him closely, saw his alarm, and she smiled, suddenly feeling sure of herself. Elton was a crook, and he wouldn't willingly draw attention to himself.

'Look, she's my wife, I tell you,' he said thickly. 'All I want is to talk to her.'

'But she doesn't want to talk to you, Elton,'

134

Jim Clare said. He looked around to see where the policeman was, and saw the constable entering a shop. 'He's gone in there for a packet of cigarettes. If you haven't started to go by the time he comes out then I'm going to call him and tell him you're making a nuisance of yourself. We're all pretty well known by the police around here, but not in the way I imagine you're known to them. If you don't want more trouble than you can handle then you'd better get into your car and take off.'

Elton breathed harshly, and for a moment Lydia saw brutal anger in his features. But then he shrugged his shoulders and turned away abruptly, moving to his nearby car and getting into it. He started the engine and drove away fiercely, turning the corner at the end of the street and disappearing.

'Phew!' Jim Clare took a deep breath. 'He's a tough character and no mistake, but he's certainly afraid of the police. I'd give a lot to know what is behind this situation. But you'd better get Nurse Wenn down here and into your car. I'll leave my car here and travel with you, just in case Elton has any more ideas about this.'

'Lydia, go and fetch Nurse Wenn down here,' Peter said.

She nodded and hurried into the Home, but met Nurse Wenn on the stairs. The girl had started out of her room as Elton departed.

'Were you watching the scene?' Lydia

demanded as she took one of the girl's cases.

'Yes!' The girl's tones were thick with emotion. 'I thought there was going to be real trouble. What made Danny leave like that? I've never known him to back down that way?'

'We threatened to call a policeman,' Lydia said. She was feeling more sure of herself now. The police were a weapon which they could use against Elton, it seemed. 'We told him you were leaving here, and no doubt he'll be watching to see where we take you.'

They went out to Peter's car and hurriedly got into the vehicle. Jim Clare got into the back with Nurse Wenn, and Lydia sighed heavily in relief as she got into the front with Peter and they drove away from the kerb.

'Are we going to the bus station?' Peter demanded.

'You can drive in that direction while we look to see if we will be followed,' Jim said. The tone of his voice suggested that he was enjoying this.

'We'll have to get in touch with the hospital shortly in case there's an emergency,' Lydia said to Peter. 'I was forgetting we are on call. They won't know where to get in touch with us.'

'Elton's car is coming along behind,' Clare suddenly reported, and Lydia turned in her seat, an icy pang stabbing her through the heart when she saw the following car. 'Do you think you can lose him, Peter?'

'You've been watching too many gangster films,' Peter retorted. 'That sort of thing isn't done in England.'

'Well we can't drop Nurse Wenn off at the bus station or she'll be picked up by Elton immediately. If you can lose Elton then we could take Nurse Wenn to my flat, and she can stay there for the night. Perhaps I could share with you, Peter.'

'That sounds like a good idea!' Peter glanced at Lydia. 'I don't suppose it will matter if Nurse Wenn doesn't stay at the Home does it?'

'Under the circumstances it won't matter at all,' Lydia said. 'What do you think of the idea, Nurse?'

'Anything you suggest,' the girl retorted.

'Good, then that's settled the problem.' Clare was grinning. He turned and peered through the rear window. 'There are two men in that car behind. If you can lose them, Peter, they'll never know where to look.'

'You're right of course!' Peter nodded grimly. 'But I'm not going to start breaking the speed limit or anything like that. I'll drive to the traffic lights and try to catch them as they change. If we can get across on the change then we'll lose them easily.'

They all sat rather tensely, and Jim Clare kept an eye on the car that was following them. Lydia tried to relax in her seat, but she was too aware of the tension about her, and she felt overheated and very tired. It had been an exhausting day without all the trouble which had come to her since surgery finished. But if they could keep Nurse Wenn out of Danny Elton's hands then it would all have been worth it.

Peter drove on steadily, and Elton kept some little distance behind. Lydia tensed when they reached the traffic lights, and they caught the changes wrong, having to stop themselves, with Elton pulling in close behind, and they stayed together when the lights changed again and they went on. But Peter went on to yet another set of lights, and knowing the town better than Elton, managed to suddenly shoot ahead as he approached the lights, catching amber and passing through, and Jim Clare, looking behind, declared with great satisfaction that Elton had pulled up.

Peter drove on faster then, taking side streets and changing direction a great many times, to finally pull in at the kerb by the block of flats where Jim Clare lived, and Jim and Nurse Wenn bundled out of the car and hurried off the street.

Lydia sighed heavily in relief as she looked around for signs of Elton's car. But the street was deserted, and she smiled at Peter.

'We've succeeded, it seems,' she said.

'But the worst part is still to come, isn't it?' he queried.

'Nurse Wenn still has to come to work, and that's where the danger will lie.' Lydia nodded.

'But she's got nothing to lose, has she? Elton might have got hold of her this evening but for us. That's the only thing in her favour. She's got nothing to lose.'

'We'd better be getting back to the hospital.' Peter glanced at his watch. He smiled at Lydia, and she felt her tension fading. 'It's been a hectic time,' he commented. 'But it's always like that when I see you.'

CHAPTER NINE

Time seemed to stand still in the following three days. Lydia could not forget about Nurse Wenn and Danny Elton, and although the girl came on duty at her usual times, there was a great deal of worry in her, and Lydia felt some of that dark emotion communicated to herself. But they didn't see Danny Elton around. They had lost sight of him at the traffic lights and never saw him again in the ensuing days.

Jim Clare shared Peter's flat, and Nurse Wenn stayed in Jim's flat. Lydia could tell that Clare was becoming interested in Rita Wenn, and she felt it was a good thing because the girl needed a friend.

But on the Saturday Lydia forgot all about the problems which had beset them. She and Peter went to Southend for the day, and the weather was benign. The sun shone perfectly all day and by slow degrees Lydia lost her inner fears. She found it difficult to get accustomed to not looking around for Elton, and she realised, during the long and happy day, that her nerves had been taking a beating by the nervous incidents which had occurred.

Peter showed himself to be a cheerful and carefree man away from the hospital. He was gentle and kind, warm hearted and human, and Lydia could not remember the last time she had enjoyed herself so much. They mixed with the holiday crowds and had a great time. But eventually they had to think of returning to Stanton, and as they walked to the car, Lydia began to experience a curious sense of let-down, and her nervousness returned as they began the drive back.

'Tired now?' Peter demanded when they were speeding back towards London.

'Almost exhausted,' she replied, forcing a smile. 'It's been heavenly, Peter. Thank you so much for such a wonderful time.'

'It's been a great pleasure to me,' he replied. 'Lydia, I feel really close to you now. Each succeeding day is breaking down the distance that has existed between us.'

'Have you felt a sense of distance between us?' she demanded.

'Strangely enough I have. There's always been formality between us. But apart from that I've always felt that you were too beautiful to be approached. That may sound strange to

140

you, but it is the way you've affected me in the past. Perhaps it was on account of your unhappy affair. I don't know. But I'm glad all that is behind you now.'

'And so am I!' She smiled softly as she considered.She had at one time thought all that bitterness and heartbreak would never lose vividness, would not fade away to manageable proportions, but now it was all gone, and there wasn't even an ache left behind to remind her of it.

'I suppose you know I'm more than halfway to being in love with you!' Peter spoke softly. 'I've always had a high regard for you, but since I kissed you I've been captivated. Today, spending all these hours in your carefree company, has done much more to bring us closer together.'

'I'm beginning to feel the same way,' she confessed glancing at him. 'It isn't a bad thing, is it Peter?'

'Certainly not! I think it's the best thing that has ever happened to me!'

'I hope the unfolding of the future will prove you right,' she told him.

'I can tell that you're exactly right for me,' he went on, watching the road ahead. 'You've made great differences to my life already, you know.'

She basked in the warmth that his words evoked, and she longed for the moment when he would take her into his arms again. She knew she would have been highly elevated all these past days since they had first gone out together if they hadn't had the complications that Nurse Wenn brought into their lives.

Lydia let her eyes narrow as she considered that episode. But it seemed over and done with now. Danny Elton hadn't shown his face again after that never to be forgotten evening. Yet there was a sense of foreboding in Lydia's mind which warned her that trouble was still likely to spring from the seeds she had sown in interfering in the first place.

But Nurse Wenn seemed much happier of late, and there seemed to be something in the air between the girl and Jim Clare. Nurse Wenn was still using Jim's flat, and Clare was sharing with Peter. But the general situation would gradually sort itself out, and Lydia could only hope that nothing went wrong.

'What are you thinking about?' Peter asked shortly.

She stirred and looked at him, a smile on her lips. 'I was just thinking how all the tension seems to have slipped away over the past few days.'

'Nurse Wenn, you mean!' He smiled as he glanced at her. 'I have been hoping that we've seen the last of Elton. It was a bit hectic, eh?'

Lydia nodded, comfortable in the knowledge that there were no distractions now to keep her mind from this fascinating man. She put out a hand and touched Peter's arm, and he smiled tenderly at her. Their glances told more than a breathful of words, and she felt happiness rising inside her, killing the last of the ghosts that existed in her mind. The past was now completely dead and she didn't have to worry about it any more.

By the time they reached Stanton the evening was turning gloomy, and Peter parked on the outskirts and took her into his arms. He kissed her time and again, his fervour arousing a kindred sensation in her own breast, and when they were both breathless he leaned away from her with a smile on his lips.

'I've been waiting all day to do that,' he declared.

'What prevented you in Southend?' she demanded.

'I don't know!' He shook his head. 'I'm not old fashioned, but I can't bring myself to make a spectacle in public.'

'Lots of couples weren't so inhibited,' she said.

'So I noticed.' He chuckled, and Lydia leaned towards him, filling her mind with sweet impressions of him. She kissed him, and he took her strongly into his arms.

They stayed until it was time to think of parting, and she was reluctant as she realised that the last minutes of their long day together were running out. All good things had to come to an end! The thought was in her mind as she sighed sharply, and Peter heard the sound and smiled at her.

'Don't you want to go home?' he demanded.

'I don't want the day to end.'

'That's how it goes. But there is one consolation.'

'What's that?'

'There will be other similar days. We can go out each week if you wish. It's only a matter of making sure we get off duty together.'

'That knowledge makes me feel better.' She leaned back in the seat and nodded slowly. 'It's a sign of the times, Peter, feeling like this.'

'I'm glad to hear you admit it. I know now that you do feel something for me!'

'I do!' She put her heart and soul into her words, and he kissed her again before driving on.

When they reached her flat, Lydia sighed again. She was beginning to slip down from the high pinnacle of exhilaration that had gripped her all day, and her thoughts turned towards the morrow.

'I'm on first call all day tomorrow,' she said.

'So am I! We'll get together!'

'That sounds exciting.' She felt better. 'I usually spend quite a time at the hospital when I'm on call. That's one of the penalties of being in charge of the department.'

'I'll look in on you about ten, and we'll see what the situation is then. There's no need for us to stay in even though we are on call. If we were in Casualty it would be different, but usually our weekends are relatively free of emergencies.'

'If there ever are any, they usually occur when I'm on duty,' Lydia said.

'Well we'll be working together, if that's the case.' He smiled as he took her hands in his. 'Are you going to see about working with me all the time?'

'I'll have a talk with Mr. Travers next week,' she promised.

He kissed her again and then they parted, and Lydia watched him drive away before going into the block of flats. She was tired but very happy, and there was a song in her heart that filled her with lilting pleasure. This was the start of true love. She knew it as plainly as if she had been told by some divine intelligence. Love was the greatest gift of life, and it was hers now for the taking.

Polly Cameron was still up when Lydia went into the flat, and the girl poured her a cup of coffee before they sat down to discuss Lydia's day. Despite her tiredness, Lydia gave her friend a good account of her day, and Polly nodded knowingly when she looked into Lydia's flushed face. 'I can smell romance in the air,' she said at length. 'It's not just the simple boy and girl affair, is it, Lydia? This is for keeps, isn't it?'

'I rather fancy that it is,' Lydia admitted with a tired smile.

'I knew it would come about. That's why I

145

did my best to get you two together, Lydia. It stood out a mile, in my estimation, that you two were meant for each other.'

'Talking about getting us together, are you still bent upon working with Oliver Travers?'

'Do you want to work with Peter now?'

'Yes, if it can be arranged.'

'Well arrange it. I'll have a word with Travers shall I?'

'I think you'd better let me have a word with him,' Lydia said with a smile.

'All right, so long as you do.' Polly stifled a yawn. She glanced at her watch. 'My word! Just look at the time. I can remember when you'd always be in bed by ten-thirty, no matter what day it was. Times have certainly changed for you, Lydia, and I'm very happy about it.'

'You've been a good friend, Polly,' Lydia said softly. 'I don't know how I've got through some of my days in the past, but you have always been there in the background, and your presence alone has done a lot to help me.'

'That's what friends are for,' Polly retorted with a smile. 'Look what you've done for me in the past!'

Lydia got to her feet and put an arm around Polly's shoulder. 'What sort of day have you had while I've been lazing away at Southend?'

'The usual run of things. We had an emergency this afternoon. Travers tried to bully me, but he can't get away with it with me as much as he can with you, and you hardly let

146

him have any rope, do you?'

'Between us we make his life a proper misery,' Lydia said with a laugh.

'He needs to be kept in check or he'd have us wearing leg irons on duty. But it hasn't been a bad sort of day. I shan't dream about it, though, like you'll probably do about your day.'

Lydia smiled and they said goodnight and went to their respective rooms. Lydia could hardly keep her eyes open now, and she hurried to get into bed, sighing heavily as she slipped between the cool sheets, and no sooner had her head touched the pillow than she was drifting into a sound sleep. She knew no more until Polly shook her gently awake next morning and placed a cup of tea on the bedside cabinet.

'I thought I'd better call you,' Polly said, sitting on the foot of the bed. 'I know you like to get across to the hospital for a bit.'

'Well there will be a nurse on duty, and someone has to keep her company.'

'Or chase her up,' Polly said, smiling. 'Who is on duty this morning?'

'Nurse Wenn!' Lydia's eyes narrowed for a moment.

'Well I'll start cooking you a breakfast. Bacon and eggs do you?'

'That's our usual Sunday morning fare.' Lydia threw aside the bedclothes, and got up. 'I'll take a quick shower while you're putting on the pan.'

They usually handled the chores between them, and in the years they had been together they had arrived at a very comfortable arrangement which worked quite well. Lydia took her shower and put on a clean uniform, and by the time she was ready for her breakfast the aroma of eggs and bacon was assailing Lydia's nostrils and making her aware of her hunger. She went into the little kitchen to find Polly flushed and busy.

'You're just in time,' Polly said cheerfully. 'One breakfast coming up. Do justice to it, my girl, and you won't put a foot wrong all morning.'

Lydia sat down at the table. 'I'll do this for you next week,' she promised.

'Our system has worked well through the years,' Polly said loftily. 'Do you remember when we were students together? What feasts we used to have after lights out in the dormitories!'

'And Sister Tutor sneaking around like a jailer, quoting all the gems of wisdom she had acquired in thirty years of nursing!' Lydia smiled. 'It doesn't seem ten years ago, Polly.'

The girl shook her head. Lydia glanced at her watch and suddenly realised that time was fleeting away, and she ate her breakfast with great relish.

'I'll do the washing up,' Polly said. 'You'd better get across to the hospital.'

Lydia took her leave and enjoyed the short

walk through the sunlight to the hospital. Her mind returned to the previous day, and she felt a wave of joy sweep through her at the recollection of the pleasures she had experienced with Peter. What a pity the day had to end! She smiled wryly and entered the hospital, going swiftly to her department and looking for the nurse on duty.

She found Nurse Wenn in one of the Theatres, and the girl greeted her cheerfully. In the days that had ensued since their confrontation with Danny Elton, Rita Wenn had settled herself to the routine of the hospital, and her despair and worry had been pushed beneath the surface of her mind.

'Good morning, Sister,' she greeted Lydia.

'Good morning, Nurse!' Lydia studied the girl's intent face, and saw brightness in her blue eyes. 'How are you this morning?'

'Very well, thank you. Are there likely to be any emergencies today?'

'There are always one or two patients on hand who might need sudden and urgent surgery, Nurse,' Lydia replied. 'But I've had no warning of an emergency yet. You have enough to keep you occupied while you're on duty though, haven't you?'

'Yes, Sister. I'm going to sew new tapes on all the gowns. Some of them are rather worn.'

'We haven't had the chance to talk about your future.' Lydia watched the girl's face for reaction to her words, but Nurse Wenn didn't even blink. 'You're still occupying Jim Clare's flat, aren't you?'

'Yes. He's been most considerate. I've been very fortunate in having such good friends here. If it hadn't been for all of you I don't know where I'd be right now.'

'Are you glad you've stayed with us?' Lydia demanded.

'Very glad. If I hadn't taken your advice I would still be running.'

'You still don't want to tell what was wrong in your life?'

'I'd rather not. You've become far too involved as it is. I can't understand why Danny let it go like this.'

'You haven't seen or heard from him since that day?'

'No.' Rita Wenn shook her blonde head.

'Do you think he believes you went away from here?'

'I don't know. But he won't give up looking for me. He may go on to try and locate me, but I feel certain that when he doesn't find any trace of me he'll come back here, because this was the last spot he saw me.'

'And that's why you can't move back into the Nurses' Home!' Lydia shook her head slowly. 'Have you thought of trying to get a flat somewhere, or a couple of rooms?'

'That's what I'm trying to do. Jim doesn't mind how long I use his flat, but I know it must be most inconvenient for him, and for Mr.

150

Sloan too. You've all been so wonderful to me. I'll never be able to thank you.'

'The fact that you're still with us and apparently more happy and less worried than before is enough for us,' Lydia said lightly. 'You're a very good nurse, and you deserve the chance to follow your vocation.'

'I am happier than I've ever been,' Nurse Wenn said with a sigh. 'I had begun to think that I was not meant to be happy in this life!'

She spoke with such emphasis that Lydia was a little surprised, but the girl's words opened Lydia's mind to the unhappiness which she had suffered. It made Lydia feel all the better for doing what she could to help. She felt good as she turned away to go to her office. She had done more than her duty, and that was always very satisfying.

There was some paperwork to be brought up to date, and work lists for the coming week to work out. Lydia sat down at the desk and threw herself into her routine with an exuberance which proved her high spirits. She hummed to herself as she worked, and time fled by unnoticed. It wasn't until footsteps sounding in the corridor attracted her attention that she gave any thought to her surroundings, and then she put down her pen and heaved a long sigh. She had been working almost an hour, and now her work was almost up to date.

She was expecting Peter to call, and when

there was a tap at the door she hoped he had arrived. Calling out an invitation, she took a deep breath as happiness welled up inside her. The very thought of seeing Peter sent thrills along her spine and filled her with butterflies. She watched the door as it opened, and then Peter stood before her, smiling cheerfully and showing in his expression that he loved her more than anything in the world.

'You look as if you've been busy,' he commented, staring at her paper strewn desk. 'I'm not interrupting anything, am I?'

'Certainly not. I've almost finished, as a matter of fact. But how are you this morning?'

'Fine!' He came into the office and closed the door. When he advanced to the desk Lydia got to her feet and went around it, to push herself into his arms. He kissed her lightly, then with growing passion, and Lydia closed her eyes and felt herself being uplifted to that wonderful plane of ecstasy which usually awaited her within the circle of Peter's arms. 'That's what I like,' he said huskily. 'You're eager to come to me. I can hardly believe my good fortune, you know. What a wonderful girl you are, and you've become interested in me.'

'I've never been happier,' she said simply. 'Being in your company fills me with the greatest joy.'

'You say the sweetest things!' His eyes were filled with a brightness that enhanced their pale blue colouring. 'Life gets more interesting day

152

by day. That's the art of living to the full, isn't it?'

'So they say,' she retorted lightly.

The telephone shrilled at that moment, startling Lydia so that she jumped a little, and Peter smiled as he released her and let her take up the instrument.

'Not an emergency, I hope,' he said.

'It probably is,' she replied, and transferred her attention to the call, giving her name. The switchboard operator answered.

'Sister, is Mr. Sloan with you?'

'Yes, he is! What's the trouble?'

'An emergency! Mr. Clare has just been brought into Casualty, but they want him to come in to you.'

'Jim Clare!' Lydia could not prevent her tones rising in surprise. 'What's wrong with him?'

'He was found a short time ago with skull injuries. He's in a very bad way, I'm afraid. Would you warn Mr. Sloan to stand by to assist in the operation? Mr. Travers has been notified and will be in shortly. I'm getting in touch with the rest of your team now.'

'Very well. We'll be ready when the patient arrives.' Lydia replaced the phone and looked up into Peter's face with bewilderment in her dark eyes. She repeated what the operator had told her, and saw shock show on Peter's face.

'Good Lord!' he declared. 'I was about to ask you about Jim. He didn't come to my flat last night to sleep. I was about to ask you if Nurse Wenn had found herself a place, and I was thinking it a bit odd that Jim didn't tell me he wouldn't be around.'

'Nurse Wenn is still using Jim's flat,' Lydia said sharply. 'I was talking to her only a short time ago. She's here on duty now. But there's no time to ask questions. He's been found with serious head injuries and they're bringing him up as soon as Mr. Travers gets here. The questions can wait. We'd better get ready for the operation.'

They hurried from the office and Lydia found herself rising to the emergency. Her mind was clamouring with urgent questions, but they did not count. No doubt a lot of people would be asking questions later, and her own were of little account. Her job was to prepare for the operation, and she went into the Theatre with only that object in mind. But shock was filling her with intense power, and she could hardly bring herself to explain to Nurse Wenn what had happened...

CHAPTER TEN

Nurse Wenn took the news with even greater shock. Lydia saw how the girl's face paled, and Nurse Wenn clutched at her arm as if her equilibrium had failed.

'Where was he found?' she demanded.

'I don't know. Was he with you last evening?'

'Yes, he was, but he left at about eleven to go to Mr. Sloan's.'

'Then he was all right at eleven!' Lydia frowned. 'I don't know if he's been involved in a car accident or what. There were no other details.'

Nurse Wenn tightened her grip upon Lydia's arm. Her blue eyes were narrowed and coldly bright. She looked like a girl in the lowest depths of despair.

'Danny has done this,' she said in trembling tones.

'Elton?' Lydia was startled by the girl's words. She thought it over, and found her mind rejecting the thought. 'Surely not, Nurse. Even he wouldn't go that far.'

'But he would! I've been telling you this all along.' There was a note of panic in the girl's tones. 'I knew Danny wouldn't let matters rest. He's always got to get even with people who cross his path.'

'We'd better wait until we know more about the circumstances surrounding Jim's injuries,' Lydia said firmly. 'For heaven's sake don't repeat to anyone what you've just said to me. Pull yourself together and start preparing for Jim's arrival. There's only one way in which we can help Jim right now and that's to make sure the surgeons can get on with their job as quickly as possible.'

The girl nodded and turned away, her shoulders stiff, her hands trembling, and Lydia stared after her for a moment, her mind leaping swiftly from suspicion to suspicion. But she couldn't accept that Danny Elton was responsible for Jim's injuries.

Staff Nurse Dillon arrived shortly after, and was bursting with news about Jim Clare. She spoke in high pitched tones as she helped Lydia prepare the instruments and lay up the trolleys.

'They've got him in X-rays at the moment,' the girl said. 'He's in a bad way, Sister. He was found in an alley by a policeman. It seems he was lying there all night. Someone attacked and robbed him.'

Lydia did not know how to answer, so she remained silent, but she could see that Nurse Wenn was taking the news badly. There were tears in the girl's eyes. Lydia wanted to say something to comfort the girl, but she remained silent. It wouldn't do to say anything about that part of the situation which they knew only too well. But Lydia could not accept that Elton might be responsible. She kept denying it to herself, afraid to let her mind believe it, because if that was what had happened to Jim for the way he had opposed Elton, then the same thing could happen to Peter, and to herself.

Her doubts nagged at her mind, but she went through her routine as if she hadn't a care in the world. Oliver Travers arrived, and Peter was with him. Lydia heard them discussing the x-rays that had been taken of Jim Clare's injuries, and the gravity in the expressions of both surgeons filled Lydia with foreboding. Peter came across to her when Travers went to scrub up, and Lydia was glad she was wearing a face mask because it hid most of her worry from Peter's shocked eyes.

'How is he?' she demanded.

'In a very bad way, I'm afraid. Someone gave him a real going over. He's got a broken jaw and a broken nose, but the real worry is the skull fracture. They'll be bringing him up in a moment. Are you all ready in here?'

'Yes.' She nodded briefly. 'Peter, I must tell you that Nurse Wenn thinks Danny Elton is behind this.'

Peter stared at her silently, and she could not see his expression plainly. She heard him sigh heavily, and then he nodded slowly.

'To tell you the truth that was the first thought that came to my mind. I didn't want to admit it, but you've brought it out into the open. There is a policeman at the hospital. He will wait until Jim regains consciousness in order to find out what happened to him.'

Lydia told him what Nurse Wenn had said about Jim leaving her at eleven.

'So he was coming to my place.' Peter nodded slowly. 'We shall have to let the police know that much, Lydia.'

157

'I think they should be told everything about Danny Elton!'

He nodded slowly, agreeing with her though reluctantly. Lydia saw Oliver Travers returning, gowned and masked, and she pulled her mind from her speculative thoughts and hurried to make her final preparations. Peter went to Oliver Travers, and Lydia knew they were discussing the case.

When Jim was brought in on the trolley, Lydia had to make an effort to forget his identity. It was just another patient! She tried to impress the thought upon her mind. But the anaesthetist at the side of the trolley was the man who usually stood in when Jim was off duty, and Lydia missed the sight of Jim's powerful figure.

They quickly transferred Jim to the table, and a porter made adjustments to the table while Oliver Travers had a final look at the x-ray plates. Lydia moved her trolleys into position and checked their contents once more, fighting against her thoughts, trying hard to keep her mind upon what she was doing. When she looked at Jim's face, so stiff and pale, she could hardly recognise it as one that she knew, and her nerves were taut and she felt at screaming pitch.

Travers came to the side of the table, his pale blue eyes narrowed under the glare of the overhead lights. He looked at Lydia, asking the usual unspoken question, and she inclined her head. 'All ready, Mr. Travers,' she said, and there was a quiver in her tone.

'This is going to be very tricky,' Travers commented as Peter came to his side. 'I don't know if we will be able to save his life. These injuries should have been attended to hours ago. If he had been found at the time of the incident there wouldn't have been any complications.'

Travers was practically talking to himself; thinking aloud, and no one answered him. He stared down at Jim Clare for a moment, then glanced sideways at the anaesthetist, hunched on his seat by his machine.

'How is he now?' he demanded curtly.

'You'd better start as soon as possible,' came the ominous reply.

Lydia took a deep breath as if she were about to plunge into deep water, and she had to collect her wits and force herself to concentrate. She turned to her trolleys and for a moment she did not know what instrument Travers would require. Then her training asserted itself and she was ready to begin.

'When you're ready, Sister,' Travers said curtly.

The operation began, and Lydia felt as if she were taking part in a living nightmare. Try as she might she could not forget the grave suspicions that flooded her thoughts. Danny Elton! She pictured the man's face, and felt a shiver of fear trickle through her. Was it merely

159

coincidence that Jim had been attacked with robbery as the motive, or had Elton been responsible, and made it appear as if robbery had been the reason for the assault?

She was in a frenzy of indecision. Her subconscious mind controlled her actions, made her hold out the right instrument at the right time for Olivers Travers, and anyone watching her would have been impressed by her quick efficiency, but she hardly knew what was going on. Time did not exist for her. When she glanced at the clock on the wall she hardly noticed the position of the hands. All she was aware of was that Jim Clare lay helpless under their hands, and they were fighting for his life.

Travers relieved the compression set up by the skull fracture, and for the moment there was nothing else he could do about that particular injury. The nose and jaw injuries were treated afterwards, and the morning was almost at an end when Travers was at length satisfied that he had done all he could.

Lydia felt reaction striking through her as Jim Clare was wheeled out to be taken to a side ward. She sagged a little, feeling faint and uneasy, and when Travers had taken his leave, Peter came to her side, his face mask dangling upon his chest, his face showing the extent of his shock and worry. Nurse Wenn came to their side, and Lydia was further shocked to see the girl's tearful manner.

'Will he be all right now?' the girl demanded

in high pitched tones.

'He has every chance now,' Peter replied softly. 'But it's out of our hands. All we can do is pray.'

'I want to tell the police what happened,' Nurse Wenn said.

'But you don't know what happened,' Lydia took hold of the girl's arm with a gentle hand. 'Don't upset yourself too much. We all feel very keenly for Jim, but you mustn't blame yourself for this.'

'It is my fault, no matter what you say.' Nurse Wenn sighed bitterly. 'I told you I should have gone when I had the chance. I warned you that something like this might happen. I know Danny Elton!'

'We don't know yet that Elton is responsible for it,' Peter said gently. 'Take hold of yourself, Nurse. It won't help if you become hysterical.'

The girl nodded miserably. 'I'm sorry, but I know I'm on the right track. I was afraid this might happen. Elton has done it before.'

'If he is responsible then I assure you he won't get away with it this time,' Peter said in determined tones. 'A policeman is going to be at Jim's bedside, but we'd all better have a talk with him.' He looked into Nurse Wenn's strained face. 'Are you prepared to talk now?' he demanded.

'Yes.' The girl nodded emphatically. 'I don't care what happens to me. I want to see Elton suffer for this.'

'Even if your past has to be revealed.'

'I don't care about that.' The girl turned away as her tears began to flow.

'Well I'll go and see that policeman, and we'd better all hold ourselves ready for questioning.' Peter patted Lydia's shoulder and turned away.

Lydia watched him as he left the Theatre, and she shook her head slowly. This was a calamity! There was no other word to describe the situation. If Jim died! She cringed at the thought and tried to thrust it away, feeling that if she didn't let it take root in her mind then it wouldn't come about. She threw herself into helping clean the Theatre, and even mopped the floor when all the other work was done. Staff Nurse Dillon watched with surprise on her face, and Lydia paused to tell the girl to get away off duty while she had the chance. But Nurse Wenn stayed with her, and they had almost finished their work when Peter returned, standing in the doorway to call their attention.

Lydia walked slowly towards him, and saw a man standing at his back. Nurse Wenn accompanied her and they went out to the corridor. They both studied the stern face of the man with Peter, and he quickly introduced them.

'This is Inspector East! Inspector, this is Sister Ashby and Nurse Wenn.'

'Thank you,' the Inspector said. He had

162

dark eyes that seemed to be able to bore right through one's exterior. 'Mr. Sloan has given me some details of the trouble you've had with one Danny Elton. Perhaps you'd care to give me the background story to this trouble, Nurse. I understand that Elton followed you to Stanton from Birmingham.'

'Yes, Inspector,' the girl said wearily. 'Perhaps I ought to have spoken to the police about this long ago. It would certainly have saved a lot of trouble. But Danny Elton is known to you, or the police in Birmingham, as Frankie Mason. He's got a record as long as your arm.'

'That's all very interesting, but if we can go somewhere private I'll take a statement from you.' The Inspector glanced at Lydia enquiringly.

'You can use my office, Inspector,' she invited. 'Perhaps you would care to talk to Nurse Wenn privately in the first instance. There are certain things she may wish to keep from our ears.'

Nurse Wenn turned grateful eyes to Lydia, who smiled encouragingly and patted the girl's arm.

'Tell the Inspector everything, Nurse,' she said.

'I will, but it won't do much good,' Nurse Wenn said. 'If Danny is responsible for this then he won't be taken for it. He wouldn't have done it himself. He'll have a perfect alibi in case

163

he's questioned. That's the way he works. The police won't be able to prove anything.'

'Well you tell me everything you know and leave the detective work to us,' the Inspector said with a tense smile.

Lydia led the way to her office, and she and Peter went along the corridor to the Theatre again when the Inspector had entered the office with Nurse Wenn. They were silent, each filled with foreboding. Then Lydia looked into Peter's face, and her expression showed him the extent of her worries.

'I blame myself for what's happened,' she said softly. 'If I hadn't insisted upon interfering with Nurse Wenn's life then none of this would have happened.'

'That's the wrong attitude to take and you know it, Lydia,' Peter said softly. 'Look, you did the right thing. You wanted Nurse Wenn to stay here and you are her superior. If you hadn't interested yourself in her welfare then you would have done less than your duty. You can see that, can't you?'

'I suppose so. But Jim would be all right now if I hadn't enlisted his aid.'

'He came into it eagerly, because he was interested in Nurse Wenn, so that lets you out,' Peter went on. 'Look, if we're all going to try and shoulder the blame then let me get into the act. I realised more than you the results that might come from our intervention. So why didn't I insist upon informing the police? No, it won't do, Lydia!' He spoke sternly. 'I'm not going to let you shoulder the blame. Why should you have the luxury of it?'

'It's no luxury, I assure you,' she said softly.

He smiled slowly as he patted her shoulder. 'Look, I think Jim will pull through this, and when he's conscious he'll be able to throw some light upon this business. In the meantime I suggest you refrain from condemning yourself. It won't help you or Jim. I think the Inspector will get to the bottom of it one way or another, and if that chap Elton is responsible for the attack on Jim then he will be brought to book, have no fears about that.'

'I can't help wondering exactly where Nurse Wenn fits into all this,' Lydia said wonderingly.

'It will all come out in the wash,' Peter said firmly.

'I hope so.' Lydia looked around for something with which to occupy her mind. But the Theatre was spotless now after the operation and she shook her head slowly as she still tried to get on terms with the shock that enveloped her mind. She glanced at the clock on the wall and saw it was almost time for lunch. 'We'd better get this business with the Inspector settled before going to lunch,' she mused. 'I wonder what Nurse Wenn is telling him.'

'I just hope she's telling him the truth and holding nothing back!' Peter's blue eyes shone fiercely for a moment. 'I'll check with him when he's finished with her. This business has got to be settled one way or the other now.'

They chatted on, and Lydia felt her tension increasing as the minutes slipped by. But finally Nurse Wenn appeared at the door and informed her that the Inspector wanted to talk to her, and Lydia took her leave of Peter. She told Nurse Wenn to go to lunch, and they walked in silence along the corridor until they came to the office. There Lydia paused, and she put a hand upon Nurse Wenn's arm.

'I hope you've told the Inspector everything, Nurse,' she said.

'Everything about what happened since I've been here,' the girl replied. 'What went on before doesn't apply, you know. But if they should need to know the rest then I won't hesitate to tell them.'

Lydia nodded and waved the girl on along the corridor. She took a deep breath as she entered the office, and the Inspector got to his feet to welcome her.

'Well I think I have a pretty complete picture of what happened here some days ago, Sister. I've learned a lot from Nurse Wenn, and what she had to say was in part borne out by what Mr. Sloan told me. I shan't ask you to go through your story of the events, but I will ask you a few questions to elaborate on certain points.'

'I'll help you all I can, Inspector!' Lydia told

him.

'I would have been pleased to have received a report of all this as it was happening,' he said severely as they both sat down. His piercing eyes held her gaze for a moment, and Lydia felt most guilty as she watched his immobile face.

'My instincts were to inform the police, but I had to have some consideration for Nurse Wenn. She feared a great deal of trouble for herself if the police were notified.'

'No doubt, but it would have obviated this present trouble, and if Elton is responsible for the attack upon Mr. Clare then a report to the police earlier would most certainly have spared him his injuries.'

'I quite agree with you,' Lydia said.

The Inspector nodded and glanced down at the notes he had taken while talking to Nurse Wenn, and for a moment there was silence in the little office. Lydia could hear the thumping of her heart, and she watched the Inspector's face until he looked up at her again.

'Sister, tell me what happened to start all this off. When did you discover there was trouble in Nurse Wenn's life?'

Lydia explained how the girl had come to her wanting to give notice almost as soon as she'd started. She went on to tell of her talk with the Assistant Matron about Nurse Wenn, learning that the girl had left two previous hospitals within a month of commencing duty. Slowly, the Inspector drew a complete picture of the events which had taken place from Lydia, gaining her impressions and point of view. Lydia answered him readily, and when he was satisfied he nodded briefly.

'We shan't know exactly what happened until we are able to talk to Mr. Clare, of course,' he said slowly. 'But you are positive that you haven't seen Danny Elton around the hospital since that evening you pretended that Nurse Wenn left the hospital.'

'I'm quite sure. I have automatically looked for him when entering or leaving the hospital. We lost him at the traffic lights, as I explained, and I haven't seen him since.'

'Then it is possible that he imagined Nurse Wenn really did leave. She had run away from two other hospitals when he discovered her whereabouts.' The Inspector closed his notebook and got to his feet. 'Thank you for your help, Sister. I may need to come back to you again, but I know where to find you should that be necessary. If you do see Elton around the hospital in the future please let us know.'

'I will, Inspector. I only wish I had done so when my instincts warned me to in the first place.'

'That's usually the case,' he retorted.

Lydia opened the door for him and they both went into the corridor. Peter came up, and Lydia remained by the office while he walked the Inspector to the end of the corridor. When Peter returned, Lydia sighed heavily.

'I'm relieved that's over,' she said.

'I shan't be happy until Jim has recovered consciousness and can tell what he knows,' Peter retorted. His eyes were filled with worry as he looked into Lydia's face.

'Is Jim going to be all right?' she demanded.

'I wish I could answer that with confidence.' He shrugged and shook his head. 'We've just got to wait and see, Lydia.'

She glanced at her watch. 'I'd better go and have lunch,' she said. 'Shall I see you this afternoon?'

'I'll come in here to see you.' He took her arm and they walked along the corridor. Lydia could not summon up her joy at their contact. Her mind was filled with the shock of the morning's incident concerning Jim Clare, and she still could not believe that it had really happened as they parted and went their separate ways.

Lunch was something to be hurried over, and afterwards Lydia could not remember clearly what she had eaten. She went to the ward where Jim was to enquire after his condition, and learned there was no change. Sister Leyton, in charge of the ward, was as shocked as everyone else, and they chatted for some moments, indulging in speculation as to what had happened to Jim Clare, but Lydia said nothing of what she thought was the real cause of the trouble.

When she returned to the Theatre she found

169

Nurse Wenn waiting to speak to her, although the girl was off duty for the rest of the day. They went into the office, and Lydia sat down at the desk, waiting for the girl to broach the reason for her appearance.

'Sister, I'm in love with Jim Clare,' the girl said. 'He's been so kind to me. But what's happened to him is because he tried to help me. I shall never be able to live this down, and now I feel the only thing I can do is leave the hospital as I was going to in the first place.'

'Don't be foolish, Nurse,' Lydia retorted. 'After all that has happened you should increase your determination to stay. If Jim is suffering now because he helped you then that's all the more reason why you should stay. But we don't know what happened to him yet, so don't start jumping to conclusions.'

'It's not so much that I'm afraid Elton will come back for me, but if he was responsible for what happened to Jim then the same thing could happen to Peter, or you.'

Lydia could not argue with that, and she knew she had been worrying subconsciously about that very likelihood. But she dashed the fears from her mind. They had all acted in good faith, and she knew they had done the right thing. That was all there was to it. Whatever came of their actions would have to be faced unflinchingly.

'You'll have to stay to learn how Jim gets over this,' Lydia said slowly. 'He thinks quite a lot of you, you know. It wouldn't be fair to run out on him at a time like this. You could find a great deal of happiness here when things improve.'

'I don't want to leave for my own sake but for yours. I know I ought to stay now because there's a good chance that Elton won't come back, especially after what's happened to Jim. But I can't take the chance, Sister. If anything happened to you or to Peter then I'd never be able to forgive myself. It's hard enough for me to take this business as it is. My brain would never be able to take any more.'

'I sympathise with you, but you must hang on. I'm blaming myself for part of this, but it doesn't help to accept guilt. One has to go on as if nothing happened, and there's always hope that order and happiness will come out of all this.'

'I don't want to go. The Lord knows I've been happy here. I have never felt happier. But if something else should happen then how would I be able to face it?'

'The police are taking a hand now, so I'd leave all the worry to them.' Lydia shook her head as she stared into the girl's face. 'You shouldn't reproach yourself, Nurse. You have every right to live your own life, and that fact alone prompted us all to help you. We took the trouble and the risk to help you, so repay us by accepting that help.'

'I wouldn't leave until I know how Jim will

be, but he'll probably hate the sight of me when he recovers.'

'Nonsense, Don't start thinking up obstacles. That isn't going to help. Just take it as it comes in future, and make sure you don't give Elton a chance to get at you.'

'Don't you worry about that!' The girl shook her head. 'I take all the precautions I can.'

Lydia nodded. She heard footsteps in the corridor, and hoped it was Peter coming to see her. She felt the need of reassurance, and Peter was the only person in the world who could help her in that respect. She could understand how Nurse Wenn was feeling, but no blame could be attached to the girl in any way, and it was imperative that she remained at her post during this crisis. Jim Clare might need the girl in the very near future, when he became conscious again and aware of the need for a fight to full recovery.

The footsteps paused outside the door, and Lydia smiled at Nurse Wenn.

'Look, forget all this nonsense about leaving, at least until Jim has recovered. Find out what he thinks of the situation before making any decision.'

'All right.' The girl spoke reluctantly, and they both looked towards the door as it was opened. 'I'd better go now. If this is Peter then he'll want to see you alone. Thanks for giving me good advice, Sister.'

'I'll see you later,' Lydia responded.

The door opened and Peter looked in, his face grave, and Lydia felt her heart lurch as she read his expression. Nurse Wenn paused on her walk to the door, and they could tell that something was wrong. Was it Jim Clare's condition? Had he taken a turn for the worse?

CHAPTER ELEVEN

It seemed an age before Peter spoke, and Lydia felt as if time paused in the interval. She took a deep breath, and there was a sudden lump in her throat as she asked the inevitable question.

'What's wrong, Peter?' She waited a moment then added: 'Is it Jim?'

'I'm afraid his condition has deteriorated and there is cause for concern,' Peter said softly. 'I've just had a consultation with Travers, and the situation is not good. But we've done all we can for him. All we can do is wait and hope, and that's always the hardest part.'

'Poor Jim!' Lydia took a deep breath. 'If only we knew what happened to him.'

'If only I could have been with him last night when he left the flat,' Nurse Wenn said passionately. 'This waiting is going to be the worst period of our lives.' She went on to the door, and paused to glance back at Lydia. 'What am I going to do?' she demanded. 'Just what am I going to do?'

She didn't wait for an answer, but went out quickly and closed the door. Peter frowned as he looked into Lydia's taut face.

'What was all that in aid of?' he demanded.

'She feels that she's caused us enough trouble and thinks she ought to leave.'

'But that would be ridiculous after all the trouble we've gone to.'

'That's what I told her.' Lydia shook her head. 'Peter, I was just thinking how happy we were yesterday! Isn't it amazing how one's feelings can change so abruptly in such a short time?'

'That's life, my love,' he said slowly, his face troubled. He looked at her, saw her distress, and went close to put an arm around her shoulder. 'Try not to think of it,' he said softly. 'I know it's dreadful about Jim. But we did what we thought was right, and no matter what happens, none of us must take any blame for the situation.'

'We didn't expect this sort of thing to happen,' Lydia said thinly. 'We don't even know if Elton is responsible, and that's the hardest thing to face. It might be a coincidence! People are attacked and robbed even in these benighted days. But it seems too much of a coincidence to me.'

'I'm inclined to agree with you, but we must keep an open mind.' He patted her arm. 'Look, Lydia, I don't know about you, but I could do

174

with a nice cup of tea.'

'I'll make one.' She turned instantly, relieved to have something to do to occupy her mind.

Peter followed her into the little kitchen and stood with her, chatting lightly, trying to raise her spirits while his own were low. They were both badly shocked by what had happened, and shortly, Lydia turned to him.

'Peter, we have to face facts. We do it all the time in our work, so we'd be foolish to forget the practice in our daily lives. We've got to assume that Elton was responsible for that attack on Jim, and we've got to take precautions.'

'Don't worry about it. I've already mentioned this to the Inspector. He's promised to have someone to keep an eye on us and this place for the next few days.'

She smiled. 'You're far wider awake than I am!' she retorted.

He took her into his arms and kissed her. For a moment there was a tender expression on his face, and Lydia caught a fragment of the happiness they had been getting to know before this situation developed. She clung to him as if the very strength of her feelings would revert everything to their previous footing.

'Don't worry,' he said softly. 'Everything will be all right. I know I can't promise anything about Jim, but it's out of our hands where he's concerned. It's going to be a trying period for all of us while this tension lasts, but it will pass, and I hope we shall all come through it safely.'

'How long will this crisis surrounding Jim last?' she asked.

'It's hard to tell. I wouldn't like to commit myself. We can only wait.'

'Has his family been notified?'

'Yes. I expect his parents will come down to see him. They will want to know what happened, but we can't tell them the truth. The Inspector will see them when they arrive.'

'We can't say anything about Elton because there's no proof yet.' Lydia narrowed her eyes as she thought. 'I hope the police will soon get to him.'

'They will, don't worry.'

Lydia made the tea and they sat down in the office. Silence enveloped them, and Lydia could not help feeling low. She was very near to tears, and her thoughts did not help. She could not force them away from the situation.

'Look,' Peter said at length. 'We've got to get out of here. Why don't we let Switchboard know that we'll be at my flat? We can go round there and forget all about this for a bit.'

'All right!' Lydia accepted the idea immediately. She knew the atmosphere of the department was affecting her. She lifted the telephone receiver and called the operator, passing on Peter's instructions, and then she got to her feet, feeling easier already with something definite to do. 'I'm ready if you are,' she said lightly.

They left the hospital and walked in the sunlight of the bright afternoon. Lydia took a deep breath and exhaled slowly. She looked around with eyes that slowly accepted the scenery, and she felt the weight upon her mind lifting imperceptibly.

At Peter's flat they sat chatting, and the rest of the afternoon fled with increased tempo. They had tea, raiding Peter's refrigerator for food, and he admitted that he had stocked up in the hope of getting her to visit him.

Later they walked back to the hospital, but there were no emergencies to occupy their time, and Lydia eventually went back to her office while Peter went to check on Jim Clare's condition. There was some paperwork for Lydia to take care of, and she started in on it with every intention of getting it finished. Her mind worked against her and she struggled with her thoughts, eventually winning through. By the time Peter returned to her with news that Jim was holding his own she had finished her work and felt easier because of it.

'I'll see you to your flat,' Peter said when they were ready to call it a day. 'If Polly isn't at home then perhaps I can stay with you for a bit.'

Lydia nodded, liking the idea, and she informed Switchboard of her future movements. When they left the hospital she could not prevent herself looking around furtively for a glimpse of Elton, and although she saw nothing suspicious she could not help realising that tension was filling her again. It was going to be like this all the time until Elton was found or the police cleared him, she knew.

Polly Cameron was not at home, and they spent a pleasant hour together in the flat. But when it was time for Peter to depart, Lydia felt more than ready to go to bed. She had been subjected to a great deal of tension during the day and this had worked heavily upon her nerves.

'Before you go, Peter,' she said as they stood together in the tiny hall of the flat, 'call the hospital and find out how Jim is.'

He nodded and took up the telephone, putting through a call to the hospital, and learned that there was no change in Jim Clare's condition. Lydia felt a pang of hopelessness touch her mind as she heard the words, but at least there was no worsening of Jim's condition, and that counted for much.

Peter kissed her tenderly, and told her to lock the door as soon as she departed. He kissed her again and Lydia reluctantly opened the door for him. She kept a picture of his face in her mind after he had gone, and she locked the door as he had instructed.

Alone in the flat, she paced the little sitting-room, her mind still in a turmoil. But no peace came to her, no matter the direction she turned her mind. Time was the only solution, and time was unable to co-operate in any way except its inexorable passing.

Lydia went to bed in the hope that she would be able to fall into slumber quickly and effortlessly, but lying in the dark did not aid her. There were too many conflicting thoughts in her mind, and fear was present, digging at her with cruel talons. She was not afraid for herself, but she knew that if Elton had attacked Jim Clare then the same horrible thing could quite easily happen to Peter.

There was guilt in her mind as she tried to sleep. She heard Polly come in, and the girl was very quiet, as usual. But a floorboard in the hall creaked whenever someone stood on it, and Lydia heard the faintest protest that it made. She felt relieved in the knowledge that Polly had come and lay listening for further sounds of the girl's presence. When she heard her doorhandle turning slowly she tensed and felt a pang of suspicion. Sitting up in bed, she switched on the bedside lamp and stared towards the door, which was opening slowly.

A man stepped into the doorway, and Lydia felt a scream of shock rising into her throat, but she could not utter it. Her throat constricted and she felt stifled. But in the same instant she recognised the man, although she couldn't place him immediately. His face was familiar, and she swallowed her fear and took a deep breath. In that instant she recalled the man's identity. It was Eddie Garrett, the man who had helped Danny Elton to watch the Nurses' Home.

'Don't scream, Sister,' Garrett commanded, 'and you won't get hurt.'

'What are you doing here?' Lydia heard her tones, but they sounded forced and unreal to her own ears.

'I've got to talk to you, that's what. I don't like this any more than you do, so don't panic. I've got to give you a warning. Nurse Wenn is still here at the hospital, isn't she?'

Lydia did not answer immediately. She was marvelling that she could sit so calmly in her bed while a stranger confronted her. But this was so unreal she could hardly believe it was happening.

'You'd better co-operate, Sister.' Garrett came to the foot of the bed and stared at her with intent eyes. 'You've been making things tough for Danny Elton, and he doesn't like it. If you're not careful you're going to find yourself in a lot of trouble.'

'If I were you I'd get out of here as fast I could and then leave town altogether,' Lydia said firmly. 'Just who do you think you are, bursting in here like this?'

'Don't make things hard for yourself, Sister!' He smiled thinly.

'You're making things hard for yourself, and so is Elton,' Lydia retorted. She was breathing heavily, but otherwise she was not alarmed by this man's presence. But when she thought of Jim Clare her breath began to come a little faster, and she could not help wondering if this man was responsible for what had happened to Jim. She wanted to ask the inevitable question, but refrained from doing so. Garrett must have a very good reason for coming here like this, and she wanted to know what it was. She had no intention of divulging any information that might help Elton.

'Look, I'm only doing a job, so stay quiet and let me ask the questions. Then I can leave. I've been watching you all day in the hope of getting close to you for a little chat. But that doctor didn't leave your side very often, did he?'

'That's none of your business. What do you want with me? I suppose you know I'll call the police after you've gone.'

'Now that wouldn't be a very wise move,' he retorted.

'I don't want to have to resort to threats, but you ought to know from Rita's manner that there is something to be afraid of. So play smart, Sister, and you'll be all right when this comes to an end.'

'What is it all about?' Lydia demanded, and saw him shrug.

'Look, I want to know if Rita is still working here at the hospital. You should think yourself lucky that I came here and not Elton. You asked for a lot of trouble by standing out against him. I'm surprised he hasn't given the

181

word for some of you to be taught a lesson.'

'Are you trying to convince me that he hasn't?' Lydia demanded.

'What do you mean?' His eyes became alert and watchful.

'Jim Clare was badly beaten last night. It's too much of a coincidence for it to have been the work of a casual thief. He was badly hurt, and his wallet was taken to make it seem as if robbery was the motive. But I know what happened, don't I?'

'Who's Jim Clare?'

'He was one of the two men with Rita and me on the night she left the Nurses' Home.'

'I remember him, but what about him?'

'Don't try to make me believe you don't know that he was attacked and robbed last night.' Lydia smiled thinly.

'No!' He shook his head. 'I didn't know. Hey, is that why the police were at the hospital this morning?'

'That's right.'

'And you think Elton had some hand in this beating?'

'Who else?'

'And you told the police all about the trouble that was going on here a few days ago?' He began to sound excited, and Lydia wondered if she had done the right thing in giving him the information. 'Hell, what is Elton trying to do to me? Have you told the police all about us?'

Lydia made no reply, but she stared at him with an expressionless face. His face began to show signs of uneasiness, and he glanced towards the door.

'If you have told the police everything then it's likely they have got someone watching out for you. Look, I'm telling you the truth when I say I know nothing about anyone getting beaten up. I won't even ask you any more questions. Just sit where you are and I'll take my leave.'

He turned abruptly and hurried to the bedroom door, and Lydia held her breath, afraid that he wouldn't leave. But he left the room and a moment later she heard the outer door bang. Her breathing resumed then and she slipped hastily out of bed and pulled on her dressing gown. She was unsteady as she went to the door of the bedroom, and she was half afraid to peer out into the hall. But she steeled herself and looked, sighing heavily when she found it was deserted. She hurried to check the lock on the outer door, then sat down on a nearby chair and began to tremble.

But she shook her head to rid herself of the fear that tried to overwhelm her mind. Reaching for the telephone, she called Peter, and was pleased when he answered almost immediately. When she explained what had happened he uttered a loud ejaculation, and demanded to know if she were all right.

'Yes,' she said. 'There's nothing to worry

about as far as I'm concerned. But what I learned has made me think a great deal.'

She began to explain what had been said, and Peter listened in silence, without interrupting. When she lapsed into silence he cleared his throat as if he were filled with excitement and said: 'Lydia, you'll have to call the Inspector and tell him about this.'

'Do you think so?' She stared across the hall for a moment. 'I'm inclined to forget it. We can only make matters worse by doing more than we have already done.'

'Leave it until the morning then and see how you feel about it then, but I would call the Inspector if I were you.'

'I'll think about it,' she promised, sighing heavily. 'Good night now!'

'Good night, and make sure that door is bolted on the inside.'

There was a noise at the door, and Lydia tensed as a key grated in the lock. But it was Polly Cameron who walked in, and Lydia acquainted Peter with the news.

'Secure yourselves then,' he said. 'See you in the morning.'

Lydia hung up and turned to face Polly, who immediately launched herself into a monologue about Jim Clare. 'I warned you in the first place that it might be dangerous to meddle in Nurse Wenn's affairs,' Polly ended. 'That girl was very worried for herself, and she told you what Danny Elton was like. Now Jim

184

Clare is in a critical condition, and he may well die from his injuries.'

'Don't, Polly, please!' Lydia shook her head. 'I've been reproaching myself for this ever since I heard about Jim.'

'I'm sorry. I suppose it's been a very bad day for you.'

'It certainly has!' Lydia debated whether or not to tell Polly about Eddie Garrett's visit, and decided against it. But she bolted the door as she returned to her bedroom. 'Good night, Polly. See you in the morning,' she said tiredly.

Polly wished her good night and Lydia went into her room, sighing heavily as she closed the door, and although she was desperately tired she had never felt less like sleeping. Her thoughts were rushing in a torrent through her mind and speculation was rife. But she got into bed and resolutely fought her brain. Eventually she did succeed, and sleep claimed her, taking her senses away and leaving her blessed relief. But it would all start up again next morning, she thought wearily as she lapsed into slumber...

The shrilling of the telephone dragged her back from sleep, and Lydia started nervously as the sound cut through her mind. She switched on the bedside lamp and sat up, unsteady and trembling, her wits scattered, but she snatched up the telephone receiver and automatically gave her name.

'Switchboard here, Sister,' came the sharp

reply. 'There's an emergency for you. It's one-twenty now. Mr. Sloan would like to be in Theatre at two.'

'Thank you!' Lydia stifled a yawn and rubbed her eyes. 'I'll be right over.'

She replaced the receiver and got up from her bed. This definitely was not her most fortunate period! The thought crossed her mind as she hurried into the bathroom to wash, and the cold water enlivened her a little. But she felt stark inside as she hurriedly dressed. Then she let herself silently out of the flat and departed swiftly for the hospital. This was just another aspect of her duty, she told herself as she walked quickly through the deserted streets. One was never really off duty in these circumstances. She looked around through narrowed eyes, feeling sombre and cold, and once again her thoughts were filled with nagging doubts of the situation that surrounded them...

CHAPTER TWELVE

There was activity in the Theatre when Lydia arrived. Nurse Farnham was there, and the girl had switched on the sterilisers and filled the sinks in the anteroom with hot water. She had brought out the jar of rubber gloves and the sterile gowns that would be needed, and Lydia congratulated the girl before going on to scrub preparatory to garbing herself in sterile clothes.

Lydia hung her uniform in a locker and pulled on white wellingtons, while trying to fight her tiredness. The short sleep she'd had seemed to have made her feel worse instead of better, and she stifled a yawn as she tied her face mask.

'Any news come through about this emergency, Nurse?' she asked when she joined her subordinate.

'It's an appendectomy, Sister,' the girl replied. 'I've got everything ready now.'

'Good. I'll just check over my trolleys. You've got the first general set in the steriliser, have you?'

'Yes, Sister,' the girl replied automatically, and Lydia smiled behind her mask.

'Set up the blackboard then, and write up the mops.'

Lydia turned to her trolleys, leaving the girl to get on with the rest of her duties. They knew exactly what had to be done, and they never wasted any time. The nurses were able to work without supervision, although Lydia always checked everything to ensure nothing was overlooked.

Peter arrived, his face showing strain and lack of sleep, and he scrubbed quickly and garbed himself. Lydia turned to check him when he came into the Theatre, and she was

187

satisfied that he was correctly dressed. He came instantly to her side, and she could tell by the way his eyes shone that he was smiling.

'We could have done without this,' he commented. 'How are you feeling? You look very tired.'

'I shall be all right. Is this a case that we've had in a ward?'

'No, it's an outside case, and the patient didn't call in his doctor until it was almost too late.'

The swing doors were thrust open and a porter appeared. A ward nurse was pushing a trolley on which the patient lay, and Lydia felt a cold pang strike through her when she looked at the anaesthetist and saw it wasn't Jim Clare. She had instinctively expected Jim to be there as always, and she shook her head slowly and sighed heavily as she went forward. Her thoughts swung towards Jim again and she could not shake them away from the subject.

The patient was placed upon the table and Peter was in a hurry to commence. Lydia went through the preliminaries with him, her hands shaking for some unknown reason, and then the operation commenced. She felt easier as she handed Peter the scalpel, and his eyes met hers for a moment before he returned his attention to the patient and poised the scalpel for the initial incision.

Once they started, the operation proceeded smoothly, with no complications, and Lydia found her tiredness receding in the face of the exigencies of the moment. She lost all knowledge of time, and was faintly surprised when the operation came to a close and Peter began finishing off. She had worked automatically, ready with whatever instrument he needed, and her needles were threaded and ready as he called for them. But time had fled by despite her ignorance of it, and when the blessed moment of returning the patient to the care of the ward nurse came, Lydia sighed with relief and turned quickly to help Nurse Farnham with the cleaning up.

Peter came to her side, his face mask dangling, his face showing great strain. His hands trembled as he took hold of Lydia's shoulder.

'I'll see you home when you get through here,' he said.

'No, Peter. You look all in, and you're on duty first thing in the morning. I shall be all right. You get away and have as much sleep as possible.'

'I shan't be able to sleep for worrying if you'll get home safe,' he retorted.

'Nonsense. What could possibly happen to me at this time of night?'

'Who would have thought that chap would enter your flat?' he countered.

She smiled thinly. 'That was quite a shock, but he didn't intend me any harm, and he was really frightened when he left. He fully expected the police to burst in on him at any moment.'

'I can't help wondering what will happen when he makes a report to Elton,' Peter said, shaking his head. 'I still don't like this, Lydia. Anything could have happened to you in that flat. I think the police should do more to protect you, especially after what happened to Jim.'

'We still don't know what happened to Jim,' she pointed out, and Peter nodded slowly.

'Well hurry up and I'll see you safely to your door,' he insisted.

Lydia nodded, knowing that he wouldn't be satisfied until he had seen her home. As she turned to get on with her work she said:

'Why don't you go into the office and make yourself a cup of tea while you're waiting for me?'

'That's a good idea. I'll make you one as well. You look as if you could do with something.'

When he had gone Lydia sighed heavily and returned to her work. It didn't take her long to get through her chores, and Nurse Farnham was practically finished when Lydia turned around to help her. Between them they put the finishing touches to the Theatre and then Lydia switched off the lights. They walked along the corridor together until they reached the office, and then Nurse Farnham went off to the Nurses' Home.

Lydia went into the office and found a cup of tea waiting for her. Peter was seated in the chair beside the desk, and he was asleep. She stood looking down at him for a moment, a gentle smile on her lips, and then she shook him gently—awake.

'Come on, Peter,' she said. 'I told you to go straight home. You'll feel like nothing on earth in the morning.'

'Had your tea?' he demanded, getting unsteadily to his feet.

'I won't bother now. All I want to do is get into bed.' She took his arm and led him towards the door, switching off the light as they departed, and she was feeling utterly weary as they walked towards the exit.

The deserted streets had a fresh breeze blowing along them, and Lydia felt herself awakening as they walked towards her flat. They had the streets to themselves, and when they reached the door of her flat, Peter put his arms around her, kissing her lightly.

'See you in the morning,' he said tiredly, and she returned his kiss and opened the door. He waited for her to enter before turning away, and Lydia sighed as she bolted the door.

Then she went to bed, and she almost fell asleep before her head touched the pillow. She was still sleeping soundly when Polly shook her arm next morning.

When Lydia opened her eyes she could hardly see, and there was a buzzing in her ears.

She felt so tired she wished it were only just bedtime instead of morning, and she stifled a yawn and pushed herself into a sitting position.

'I don't think love is any good for you, Lydia,' Polly observed. 'You look as if you've just crawled into bed instead of having spent the night there.'

Lydia smiled thinly and explained about the emergency, and Polly's face changed.

'You lie there a little longer and I'll get breakfast ready,' the girl declared.

'No. I'm awake now. I'd better get up or I may never find the energy to make it.' Lydia thrust aside the bed clothes and got to her feet. 'What a trying time this is!' she declared.

'That's love for you,' Polly said with a chuckle.

'It isn't Peter that I'm thinking about,' Lydia replied . . .

They walked across to the hospital together, and Lydia tried hard to force her mind to relax. But she had the sensation that something was very wrong somewhere and she couldn't dispel it. She mentally crossed her fingers as they entered the hospital, and the first thing she did was enquire after Jim Clare's condition. When she learned that he had made some progress during the night her fears lessened, and she felt almost normal. When she reached her office she was actually humming to herself.

But a shock awaited her when she went on a routine check of the Theatres. Nurse Wenn had not reported for duty. Lydia went back to the office and called Jim Clare's number. She tapped her fingers impatiently on the desk top while she waited for a reply, but there was nothing, and a pang of fear throbbed through her as she listened to the insistent ringing. When she was more than certain there would be no reply she hung up and sat for a moment thinking it over.

What could have happened to Nurse Wenn? Had she made good her threat to disappear? Lydia set her teeth into her bottom lip as she considered. She didn't think the girl would run out while Jim Clare lay very seriously ill. The girl was in love with him!

But Lydia knew she could not afford to waste any time. She lifted the receiver again and called the police station, asking for the Inspector, and when he came to the phone she told him of Nurse Wenn's non-appearance and also about Eddie Garrett's visit to her the night before.

'I'll check on Nurse Wenn,' the Inspector said, taking Jim's address. His tones sounded harsher as he continued. 'I wish you had called me last night about this man's behaviour.'

'He didn't harm me,' Lydia retorted. 'Have you picked up Danny Elton yet?'

'I'm afraid I'm not permitted to divulge the extent of our enquiries, or the progress we're making,' came the reply. 'I'll act upon your information this morning, and I'll probably be in touch with you during the day.'

The line went dead and Lydia replaced her receiver. There was a frown on her face as she got to her feet. Duty called, and she had never felt less like doing her duty.

When Peter arrived she hastened to tell him what had happened, and his face turned bleak when he learned of Nurse Wenn's non-appearance.

'I don't like the sound of that,' he said. 'You ought to have called me as soon as you learned of it. I would have gone around to Jim's place to find out what happened.'

'It's in the hands of the police now, anyway,' Lydia said. 'I even told them about that man Garrett letting himself into my flat last night.'

Peter nodded. His pale blue eyes showed signs of great tiredness as he looked at her. 'I shall be very relieved when all this is a thing of the past,' he commented. 'I love you very much, Lydia, and I want the opportunity of having your full attention when I tell you so. But this business is like a dark cloud hanging over our heads, and until it has been blown away there's nothing much we can do about leading our own normal lives.'

'That thought has been in my mind for days,' she admitted. 'I don't like this any more than you do, Peter, but I would do the same things again if we had this time to live again.'

'I'm sure you would. That's one of the things I like about you. I've never come across a more selfless person than you. I like to do what I can to help my colleagues and fellow travellers through life, but you pass me easily in your selflessness. But you should save something for yourself, you know. You have to live too.'

She smiled slowly. 'I'm sure we'll get in our share of living before we die,' she said.

He chuckled, and for a moment the tension and the worry faded and Lydia felt the true power of love in her mind. Then the clouds closed in again and she sighed heavily.

'We've got a large list today,' she remarked. 'We'd better get started or we'll never be finished.'

'I wish I had time to see what's happened to Nurse Wenn,' he retorted.

'Better leave that to the police,' Lydia told him wisely.

'Perhaps you're right!' He turned and opened the door of the office. 'Come along then. The sooner we get started the earlier we shall finish this evening, and I want your company when we get off duty. It seems such a long time since Saturday.'

Her eyes turned dreamy as she thought of that day at Southend. It did seem as if an age had passed by since then. All the trouble that had come in the last two days had pushed all the vivid memories into the background, and she could not help feeling sad because of it. There seemed to be an ill fate working against them now!

The day turned out to be as long as Lydia imagined it might be, and the hours seemed filled with drama and tension. Nothing seemed to go right in Theatre. Oliver Travers was not pleased with anything, and he showed it in his usual manner of snapping and shouting. They worked a nurse short because of Nurse Wenn's absence, and Lydia was more than weary by the time the morning came to an end. But there was still the afternoon waiting to be touched, and her lunch seemed unappetising and too much for her.

But the hours passed by, slowly and surely, and when they reached the end of the list it was to discover that Peter had suffered almost as badly as she during the day. His work had not been smooth and easy. He was still in Theatre with a complicated case when she was ready to go home, and she left a note for him in the office before taking her leave.

She went home and took a welcome shower before changing, finding the cool water refreshing, and after she had put on her best dress she felt a little more human. She had asked Peter to come for her when he was ready, and she tried to occupy her mind with anything that would hold her attention in order to keep her thoughts from the trouble they seemed to be in.

Her mind was filled with conjecture about Rita Wenn. She found she could take no more of the speculation that filled her brain, and she called the police station to enquire if there was any news of the missing girl. The Inspector spoke to her and said there had been no sign of Nurse Wenn at Jim Clare's flat. Even the girl's cases and clothes were missing.

'It seems to me that she's run out rather than face the music,' the Inspector said sharply. 'I shall have her picked up, of course, because we need her evidence.'

'I don't think she would run out, Inspector!' Lydia said firmly. 'She had fallen in love with Jim Clare, and she would worry too much about him to go off without any word at all.'

'Then what do you suppose has happened to her?'

'I just don't know, but I don't like this. You haven't picked up Danny Elton yet, have you?'

'I'm afraid I'm unable to comment on the state of the case.'

'Well I'm sure you haven't, and I think Elton has got to her now. Her life could be in danger, Inspector, if what happened to Jim Clare is anything to go by.'

'I quite understand the situation, Sister Ashby,' the Inspector retorted. 'I assure you we're doing all that is possible to find Nurse Wenn and to get the man or the men responsible for what happened to Mr. Clare.'

'I'm sure you are, Inspector,' Lydia said with a sigh. 'But I'm dreadfully worried about this business.'

'I'll keep you informed of the progress we

might make, Sister,' came the gentler reply, and Lydia thanked him and hung up.

Waiting for Peter to come for her was a difficult thing to do, Lydia discovered. She tried to read and she paced the room, but there was a tense restlessness inside her that would not relent, and she had to take all the pangs of worry and the fears that overloaded her mind. When the telephone rang she rushed to it like a tigress protecting its cubs, and snatched it up breathlessly. It was Peter, and she had hoped it might be news of Jim Clare or Nurse Wenn.

'Lydia, I'm sorry, but I can't get away from here yet. There is another case coming in and I've got to handle it. I should be off duty, but there's been some rearrangement here this evening. I wouldn't count on seeing me this evening if I were you. If you have anything else to do then get on with it.'

'Peter! I'm sorry to hear that. I was looking forward to being with you this evening.' Lydia sighed sharply. 'But it can't be helped. All right! Don't worry about it. Duty comes first, as we all know. But it is hard to accept at this particular time.'

'You need to get a good night's sleep tonight,' Peter said firmly. 'What with last night and all the worry of yesterday! I can imagine the state of your mind. Try and have an early night and get plenty of rest.'

'That's easier said than done, but I'll follow your instructions to the letter,' she said,

198

laughing lightly.

'That's my girl,' he said, apparently satisfied. 'Look, I have to ring off now. I'm due back in Theatre.'

'Goodbye then, Peter. See you tomorrow.'

'Time will pass,' he retorted, and hung up.

Lydia felt even worse after that. The knowledge that she would see Peter that evening had kept the worst of her depression at bay, but now there was nothing to help, and she felt a blacker mood than any she had experienced begin to settle upon her. She paced the room until she could stand the silence and the solitude no longer, and she took her handbag and left the flat, intending to take a stroll until bedtime.

Her thoughts were in a groove. They embraced Jim Clare and Nurse Wenn, with Garrett and Elton thrown in for weight, and nothing she could do would erase them from her mind. She walked past the hospital and paused on a corner to stare at the massive building. Her thoughts idled for a moment, and she felt a measure of comfort flit into her mind because she was part of the great organisation that operated from there. They did a wonderful job with the sick. The knowledge boosted her spirits. No matter what came of this business worrying her, she had done her best in the service of the sick, and she realised then that she had been blaming herself for everything that had come about since

Nurse Wenn came to them. If she hadn't taken an interest in the girl's welfare then none of this would have happened, and Jim Clare would be on duty now, as fit as she or Peter.

She shook her head and turned away, and Lydia knew she was trying to force self-pity to overtake her mind because she was so deeply weighed down with feelings of guilt.

The evening was bright and warm, although she had no thoughts to spare for the weather or even her surroundings. She walked mechanically, and it wasn't until she entered the nearby park that she became aware that she was being followed. The realisation came slowly, and it was a shock when she finally turned and saw Eddie Garret standing a few yards away, watching her intently.

As soon as he saw that she had seen him he came forward quickly, and Lydia looked into his face with no feelings of fear. She felt anger rather than anything else, for what little peace of mind she had remaining fled instantly at sight of him.

'What are you doing here?' she demanded abruptly. 'Am I to get no peace from you? Last night you broke into my flat, and now you're following me around. What do you want?'

'Look, I don't like this any more than you do,' he retorted. 'I wish I'd never left Birmingham! But when you work for Danny Elton you never quit. I've got to ask you some questions, and if you try to make things awkward then you'll suffer for it. Not at my hands, I hasten to tell you. I'm not a violent man, and Elton has enough of that type running around for him.'

'I suppose one of them attacked Jim Clare,' Lydia said, her tones filled with scathing contempt. 'Elton won't always get away with it, you know.'

'Try telling him that,' came the swift retort. 'Look, I don't want to see anything happen to you. Just answer me a few questions and it will all be over as far as you're concerned.'

'Where is Rita Wenn?' Lydia demanded.

'Rita?' He shook his head slowly. 'I don't know. I was about to ask you the same thing!'

'Well she's disappeared!' Lydia sighed heavily. All the trouble that had come about because of her efforts to keep Elton away from the girl had been for nothing. Rita Wenn was gone and Jim Clare could have been spared that beating which almost claimed his life.

'Is this on the level?' Garrett demanded.

'I have no need to lie to you. She was staying at Jim Clare's flat. She was on duty yesterday morning until lunch time, and after that she disappeared.'

'That's bad. Elton is convinced you still known where she is. This is the last place he saw her, and he knows she hasn't left.'

'Well you can tell him she's gone now. She took her cases with her. And if Elton hopes to find her by checking other hospitals then he'll be wasting his time. She told me earlier that she would change her job in order to disappear completely.' Lydia lapsed into silence and stared across the park, her thoughts speculating on Rita Wenn's whereabouts. 'There's one thing you can tell me,' she said slowly.

'What's that?' Garrett seemed more friendly now, and Lydia was not afraid of him.

'Why is Elton so determined to get her back? She isn't his wife, is she?'

'Is that what he told you?' Garrett shook his head slowly. 'No, Rita isn't his wife. Until she made her break with him she was completely under his influence. He had her stealing drugs from the hospitals where she worked.'

'What!' Lydia was shocked, and her face and eyes showed it. 'You're joking!'

'I'm not!' He shook his head. 'And I shouldn't have mentioned it, obviously. But I'm getting tired of Elton and his ways. If I could quit I'd do so, don't you worry. But there's no way out for me. Look, if I were you I wouldn't wander around town alone like this. If Elton decides to get back at you for the way you helped Rita then he'd find it easy to grab you.'

'Was he responsible for what happened to Jim Clare?'

'I don't know! I wouldn't be surprised. He cursed a lot that night you got Rita away. He threatened all of you, and if one of the doctors has been hurt then it's more than mere coincidence.'

'That's what I thought, and the police do, too.' Lydia looked into his face with intent eyes.

'Did you tell them about me entering your flat last night?' he demanded.

'Yes. What did you expect?'

'Then this is worse than I feared. I'll have to get away from here whether I want to or not. Look, I gave you some good advice. Don't go out alone until Elton has decided to leave here.'

'Is he still in Stanton then?'

'He is.'

'And is Nurse Wenn with him?'

'No! I swear that she's not. That's why I came to see you. Elton wants her badly.'

'Why? To steal more drugs?'

'I shouldn't have told you that, and you'd better forget that I did.' He shook his head. 'I wouldn't want to be in your shoes if Elton learned that you know about it.'

'I'm not likely to tell him!' Lydia shook her head and began to turn away. She glanced along the path that led to the exit, and her heart seemed to miss a beat. The Inspector and another plain-clothes man were coming towards her, and she knew by the expression on the Inspector's face that he had some idea of Garrett's identity. But Garrett was too intent upon his advice to notice the police, and his first intimation of trouble was when a heavy

203

hand was laid upon his shoulder.

Lydia would have laughed at the expression which came to Garrett's face when he turned to look into the Inspector's hard face, but this was too serious an incident for laughter. He offered no resistance, and admitted his name when the Inspector challenged him. He was led away, eyes downcast, face showing that he realised the trouble he was in, and Lydia felt a small pang of sympathy for him.

The Inspector smiled cheerfully before departing. 'I've had you followed,' he said. 'I thought perhaps Elton might try to make contact with you again, especially when Nurse Wenn disappeared. I think I have a chance now in cracking this case. I shall need a statement from you, Sister, about your conversation with Garrett. But I'm hoping he'll tell me where Elton is. I've ascertained that Elton hasn't returned to his old haunts.'

'Garrett told me Elton is still in Stanton,' Lydia said.

'Then we'll get him!' The Inspector turned away. 'You'd better stay at home until this present emergency is over. I'm a bit short-handed, and a man has to watch you all the time you're out. Will you help by not giving Elton the chance to get hold of you?'

'By all means, Inspector! I'll go home immediately. You'll find me there if you should need me at all.'

She turned and walked to the nearest exit,

and hurried home, her mind filled with more speculation. Her hands trembled as she unlocked the door to the flat, and she slipped home the bolt after entering. But when she turned she sensed that she was not alone in the flat, and a frown touched her smooth forehead as she wondered if Polly had come off duty so soon after Peter's telephone call. She turned to the little sitting-room, but the door was ajar, and as she faced it she saw it opening wider. The next instant Danny Elton stepped into view, and there was an ugly expression on his face despite the grin that clung to his lips.

'Don't scream or do anything foolish,' he said. 'It's time we had a little chat.'

But Lydia couldn't have screamed even if she'd thought of it. The shock of seeing him had robbed her temporarily of all powers, and she could only stand and stare at him.

CHAPTER THIRTEEN

'You're smart, Sister,' Elton said, advancing towards Lydia. 'But at the same time you've been very foolish. You ought to have known just how determined I am. I expect Rita told you a lot about me.'

'I'm not afraid of you,' Lydia said firmly, and she stared unflinchingly into his face. 'In fact I feel sorry for you. The police will get you before very long, and then you'll realise the error of your ways.'

'Just answer my questions and you'll not get hurt,' he said sharply. 'I don't need a sermon from you.'

'You must be getting nervous, coming here yourself. Can't you trust your man Garrett any more?'

'He hasn't met with much success,' came the taut reply.

'He's just been arrested,' Lydia said, a thin smile touching her lips.

Elton's powerful figure stiffened at her words, and Lydia saw his uneasiness quite clearly in his eyes.

'He accosted me in the park, and was talking to me when the police arrived.'

'You informed the police about him?'

'I reported that he broke into here last night, the same as you've just done. The police know quite a lot about this business and you'll have a lot of questions to answer when they finally catch up with you.'

Elton began to look apprehensive. He moistened his lips, and Lydia could see that he wished he hadn't come. She smiled slowly. This was how it should be!

'Where is Rita?' he demanded.

'What is your interest in her? Why do you have to hound her like this?'

'You'd better answer my questions, and truthfully, or it will be the worse for you.'

'I've told you I'm not afraid of you,' Lydia retorted. 'I'm not Rita. I don't have her guilty conscience. But even she has made a stand against you, hasn't she? And she's really disappeared this time. She didn't report for duty this morning, and she went from her flat with her luggage. No one knows where she is.'

'I don't believe you,' he snapped. His face took on an ugly expression.

Lydia smiled. 'That's your privilege,' she said. 'I'm telling the truth, but I can imagine that a man like you wouldn't be able to recognise the truth when confronted with it.'

He seemed about to strike her, but although she tensed inside, Lydia did not change her calm expression.

'The police are watching me,' she said. 'That's how they caught Garrett. He came up to me in the park and they pounced. I didn't even know they were there.'

'Did they follow you here?' he demanded.

'I don't know. But they seem to think I need watching after what happened to Jim Clare. There was no need to beat him up like that.'

'Leave off or you'll make me cry,' Elton retorted harshly. 'It seems as if you've spoiled everything for me around here, so why shouldn't I get my own back on you?' He grinned evilly, and Lydia felt a momentary pang of fear. But she forced it out of her mind and smiled thinly.

'Even you must have some intelligence,' she

said. 'Assaulting me can only make your trouble worse. The police know all about you, and if you go back to Birmingham you'll be picked up. There's no escape for you.'

'They have to prove everything against me,' he retorted, 'and with Rita gone they're going to have a tough time getting anywhere.'

'They'll find her. You managed to find her after she left her last two jobs, and the police have more resources than you.'

He smiled thinly, but it was obvious that he was uneasy. Lydia hoped he would leave without causing trouble, but she could not understand why he had risked coming. If Rita had disappeared then surely Elton knew where she was. Or had the girl left of her own accord because of what had happened to Jim? Did she really fear that something similar might happen to the friends who had helped her? Lydia looked into Elton's face and knew why Rita Wenn had been so afraid of him.

The telephone rang shrilly, causing Lydia to start nervously, and Elton stepped between her and the instrument.

'I'd better answer that in case it's an emergency call from the hospital,' she said.

'You don't answer it,' he retorted.

'Tell me why you have come here this evening,' Lydia went on. 'You know I'll do nothing to help you.'

'You would if you thought your boy friend might get a dose of the treatment that was 'handed out to Clare,' Elton said.

'So you did harm Jim Clare!' Lydia caught her breath, and a cold pang touched her heart. She paused and waited for him to speak, but he said nothing, and she took a deep breath to steady her fast beating heart and asked the next question. 'What is it you expect me to do for you?'

'Rita was a great help to me, working as she did in the hospital. I need something quickly in large quantities, and you're going to get it for me.'

'Drugs?' Lydia smiled and shook her head. 'I'm sorry. But I would rather die first. I wouldn't lift a finger to help you even if it meant saving my own life.'

'How do you know it would be drugs?' he demanded, his face showing a harsh expression. 'Has Rita said anything to you about her former life?'

'She told me everything,' Lydia lied without a qualm. 'But you won't make such a fool out of me.'

'Not even if I tell you that at this very minute your boy friend is in danger of getting the rough treatment? I have only to make a telephone call and his fate will be sealed.'

For a moment Lydia was worried, but she didn't let Elton see it. Then she forced a smile.

'I think you're overstepping the mark now, trying to involve me in your crookedness. But the police are watching Peter, and you couldn't get near him.'

'The police can't watch him twenty-four hours a day. I can have him picked up any time I like. I know he's still on duty at the hospital, and the minute he walks out of the door I can have him.'

'I refuse to help you, and I shall inform the police of this conversation at the first opportunity.'

'We'll see just how tough you are,' Elton said.

The telephone was still ringing, and the insistent tone cut across Lydia's nerves. She clenched her hands and set her teeth, determined not to let him see her fear. But he noticed her actions and grinned.

'I know exactly how you feel. This isn't the first time I've put the squeeze on a girl. How far do you think I would have got in life if I hadn't been able to get around females? Rita did what I wanted, and so will you, if you know what's good for you.'

Lydia shook her head, facing him quite calmly. She smiled at him, her face devoid of expression.

'You would kill me before I agreed to take any step calculated to help you,' she said firmly.

The telephone stopped ringing, and the silence was unbearable. Lydia took a deep breath, aware that menace had crept into the atmosphere. But she would not show her fear.

210

She faced Elton and kept her face free of expression. It was an effort to remain unconcerned because she knew what he was capable of, but she also knew that the first sign of fear in her make-up would finish her. He would be brutally quick to take advantage of her feelings.

'I want you to go to the hospital and bring me the contents of your drug cabinet,' he said. 'I am quite familiar with the routine of your department. Most hospitals are alike in administration and working. Rita has told me a great deal, so don't try to pull the wool over my eyes. If you value the health of your boy friend you will do what I ask with no hesitation.'

'You don't seem to understand about people like me,' Lydia countered. 'Peter is similar. We would rather suffer than break faith with our ideals. No matter what you did to me, or threatened to do to the man I love, you'll never get me to do what you want.'

His face slowly changed expression, and real fear began to fill Lydia. She made an effort to remain expressionless, knowing her manner was the only thing she had to fight him with. If she could convince him that she was above threats then there was little he could do, apart from beating her, and she was prepared to take that because of what had happened to Jim Clare. But she was afraid all the same.

Elton crossed to the telephone and lifted the

receiver. He dialled a number and waited for a few moments, then began to speak to someone, and Lydia's blood seemed to run cold as she listened.

'That's right,' Elton said. 'They've picked up Garrett, but he was never any good, so don't worry about him. Listen, I pointed out that surgeon to you yesterday, didn't I? Well he's still on duty at the hospital and I want him picked up the minute he leaves. You know where to take him. Hold him there until you hear from me again.'

Lydia scarcely heard any more, but Elton went on talking, giving instructions to combat the situation as it existed, and Lydia felt sick with fear for Peter. She knew she couldn't just stand by and let these men get to him. But there was nothing she could do cooped up here with Elton. If she went to the hospital she might be able to raise the alarm in some way. Anything constructive would certainly help, and she could always refuse at the last minute to do what Elton wanted.

'Wait a minute,' she said in cowed tones. 'Cancel that order about having Peter picked up. I'll do what you want.'

Elton glanced at her, a smile on his lips, and he watched her for a moment while he judged her.

'All right,' he said. 'I'll give you a chance to prove you're on the level.' He spoke into the telephone again, countermanding his previous instructions. Then he replaced the receiver and turned to her. 'Don't get the idea that you'll be able to fool me,' he warned. 'I wasn't born yesterday. I shall be right with you the whole time, and if I get the slightest idea that you're going to try and pull a fast one then you'll wish you had never been born.' He put a hand into a pocket and pulled out a flick knife, which he showed to Lydia. 'If I use you as a target it won't be the first time I've knifed someone,' he said sharply. 'Don't misjudge me, Sister. I'll use it if I have to, and I don't care who gets hurt so long as I get in the clear. Do you understand?'

'I understand!' Lydia took a deep breath and tried to still her unsteadiness.

'Come on then!' He moved to the door and opened it, and Lydia took a deep breath as she moved towards him. 'Stay close to me, and we'll enter the hospital by the back door that you used.'

'There will be nurses on duty in the Theatre. I don't think they've finished operating yet!' Lydia was trying to think of any excuse which might hold water.

'Then you must introduce me as your friend, or something. But don't forget that I have the knife and that I'm not afraid to use it.'

'How can you hope to get away with this? Surely you know I shall tell the police as soon as you leave.'

'What makes you think I'll leave you in one

piece?' He grinned evilly.

'You wouldn't go so far as to kill me for a few drugs.' Lydia smiled confidently although she was feeling far from happy.

'I'll fix it so you want to keep quiet about this,' he said.

Lydia didn't believe him, and wondered if he could be so desperate as to steal drugs in such an audacious fashion! The thought warned her to be very careful.

They left the flat and walked to the hospital, using the back ways, and when they reached the small back gate in the side road Lydia was hoping against hope that they would find it locked. But it opened easily to Elton's hand, and Lydia felt her nervousness increasing as they went in.

Elton stayed very close to her, and Lydia was torn between two desires. She half hoped they would meet a porter who would question Elton's presence, and yet she felt afraid that someone might get hurt if it came to that. But Elton had to be stopped somehow, and she racked her brains for a way to prevent him carrying out his plan.

When they reached the department she was petrified in case they ran into Peter or Polly Cameron, but there was a team still working in one of the Theatres, and she knew they were safe from interruption for quite some time.

'Into your office,' Elton snapped, and their feet echoed in the tiled corridor as they hurried towards the office. Lydia tried to hang back but Elton seized hold of her arm and almost dragged her along. 'Don't give me any trouble,' he snapped.

When they entered the office Lydia stumbled to her desk and leaned upon the corner. Elton stood with his back to the door, glaring at her, and his face was positively ugly.

'You'd better remember what I said,' he warned again. 'I won't be foiled, and you'd better know it.'

Lydia said nothing. Her mind was working fast, and she was trying blindly to think of some way in which she could outwit him. On the other hand she wanted him to get away from the hospital before Peter finished in Theatre. The less people there were around the less likelihood of anyone getting hurt, she thought dimly. But her mind was not functioning in top gear. She was scared and this was affecting her judgement.

'Now then,' he went on. 'You have the keys to the drug cupboards locked in that top right hand drawer, haven't you?' He indicated the desk, and Lydia moved around to it, sitting down and trying the drawer.

'The drawer is locked,' she said. 'I don't have the key for it. The Sister on duty keeps that in her possession.'

He came around the desk to her side, his face ugly again, and when he took the knife from his pocket Lydia shuddered. But he used the weapon to open the drawer, and she picked up the small bunch of keys.

'That's better. We can go into the two Theatres not being used and empty them. Then we'll hang around until they finish in the Theatre they're working in.'

'You can't stay around here,' Lydia said in shocked tones. 'There are nurses on duty, and someone is always in and out of the Theatres.'

'I don't care about that.' His tones were edged with harshness. 'Let's get on, shall we?'

Lydia did not get up from the desk quickly enough for Elton, and he cursed as he seized her arm and dragged her upright. His dark eyes blazed for a moment, and Lydia heard his sharp intake of breath.

'I'm getting impatient,' he said. 'Do as I say and do it more quickly.'

He thrust Lydia towards the door, and just before she reached it she saw the handle turn. The door opened slowly. Lydia gasped, for Nurse Wenn appeared in the doorway, her face pale, her lips compressed as she peered at them. Elton uttered a curse and came forward, reaching out to seize hold of the girl's arm.

'Where the devil have you come from?' he demanded.

'Save your breath, Danny,' the girl retorted. 'I'm here, and that should be good enough for you. I've come back to help you, but on one condition.'

'I don't work on conditions,' Elton said

arrogantly.

'I'll help you on the condition that you don't harm any more of these people. They're fine people and only did what they thought was right.'

'It's a pity my idea of what's right doesn't coincide with theirs,' Elton said. 'But you've got the right idea, Rita. I won't bother with anyone if you'll help me now and come away with me afterwards.'

'That's what I'm here for, Danny,' the girl said softly. She tried to avoid Lydia's eyes, but Lydia wouldn't let her.

'Don't be a fool, Nurse,' she said. 'You know you'll get into a lot of trouble over this.'

'I'd rather face that trouble than have you take it. It's my fault that Danny is here at all. He followed me. So it's only right that I take him away. You leave this to me, Sister. You tried to help me and the least I can do is help you and your friends.'

'But what about Jim Clare?' Lydia demanded.

'Jim will be all right. I telephoned the hospital about half an hour ago and was told that he's now coming through his crisis. He's going to be all right.'

'That's good news, but what you plan to do is not the way to celebrate it.'

'We're wasting time,' Elton said harshly. 'Come on, Rita. Lead the way to the first Theatre. I want all the useful drugs in the cupboards.'

'Leave it to me. I know where everything is,' the girl retorted. She turned to the door and Elton took hold of Lydia's arm as they departed from the office. They went along the deserted corridor to the nearest of the three Theatres, and Lydia was praying that they would meet no one. It would be bad enough to lose the supplies of drugs, but it would be much worse if someone were hurt by Danny Elton.

Rita Wenn was stiff and edgy as they entered the Theatre. She held out her hand for the keys Lydia still carried, and Lydia shook her head slowly as she handed them over under Elton's keen gaze.

'You know you'll never get out of his clutches if you do this, Nurse.' Lydia said.

'Cut the cackle and stay out of the way,' Elton said roughly. 'Come on, Rita. I haven't got all day. The police have picked up Garrett, and I want to get out of this town as fast as I can.'

The girl walked to the large cabinet on the wall and unlocked it. Lydia shook her head slowly as she watched, and Elton took hold of her arm and led her closer, keeping a close watch on her. Lydia thought of the knife in his pocket and remained silent and amenable.

'Hurry it up, Rita,' Elton said. 'Get that stuff into your bag. I see you've got the one you always use. You came prepared. I'm going to forget all about your lapse for this. I knew you

218

wouldn't let me down. But give me a shot of something now, will you? I need it badly. I haven't been able to get anything for a couple of days, and my personal supply has run out.'

Lydia gasped as Elton rolled up his sleeve, and she saw the needle marks on his forearm. She understood a great many things then, and a little knot of deeper worry came into existence in her mind because she knew Elton was an addict and likely to do anything.

'Can't you wait until we get out of here?' Rita demanded. 'I don't want any trouble here, Danny, and someone might wander in at any moment.'

'Give me a fix now, and then we'll think about getting out,' he retorted. His grip tightened on Lydia's arm. 'We shan't have any trouble getting out because I'll cut this girl's throat if anyone tries to stop us. It'll be like old times again, Rita. I wish you hadn't found those principles that began to bother you. But it's all right again, now, eh?'

'Everything's all right now,' the girl responded. She was busy at the cabinet, and when she turned to face them Lydia saw a hypodermic in her hand. Rita was smiling as she came towards Elton, who thrust out his bared forearm to her.

Lydia watched with sinking heart. Rita administered the injection and then walked back to the cabinet. She looked back over her shoulder at Lydia.

'That's why Danny picked me up in the first place,' she said. 'I've been getting drugs for him for a long time. I did the wrong thing by running out on him. He needs me, and now I'm taking care of him again.'

'But you can't hope to get away with this!' Lydia gasped.

Elton grabbed at her arm and she half turned towards him, fearing he was about to attack her, but he was crumpling helplessly, falling heavily to the ground, and Lydia caught at him, lowering him gently to prevent his head cracking against the tiled floor. She was startled out of her wits, and could only stare down at him, realising that he was unconscious and defenceless. Rita came forward swiftly and checked Elton's condition.

'Lydia, for heaven's sake snap out of your shock and fetch the Inspector in!' the girl said urgently. 'Danny won't be out more than a few minutes.'

'The Inspector!' Lydia could only stare at the girl.

'He should be in the corridor if his timing is correct,' the girl went on, and hurried across the Theatre to the door, thrusting it open to peer outside.

Lydia stood watching, unable to take her eyes off Elton's unconscious form. When she heard voices in the doorway she looked up to see a group of people coming in, and Peter was with them. There was the Inspector and two

220

policemen, and Polly Cameron was following, intent upon seeing what was happening.

Peter came immediately to Lydia's side and put an arm around her, filling her with reassurance, and the two policemen took charge of Elton, one of them snapping handcuffs on the man's thick wrists. Lydia leaned against Peter, almost overcome by the swiftly changing events. The Inspector stood speaking with Rita Wenn for a few moments, and then, as Elton was carried out, Rita came to Lydia's side.

'Your face is a sight to see,' she said cheerfully, although her features were pale and she was obviously labouring under great tension and nervousness. 'I went to the police yesterday afternoon after going off duty, and I told the Inspector everything. He advised me to disappear until Danny showed himself again, and I stayed in the police station until Eddie Garrett was picked up. Eddie told the Inspector that Elton was waiting for you in your flat, and he warned that Danny would use that knife on you if anyone tried to get at him. So it was decided that I should come in and pretend I'd forgiven Danny. I didn't think it would work, but it did, and when Danny wanted that fix I gave him something to put him out instead of the drug he's crazy for.'

'You certainly fooled me,' Lydia said slowly. 'I thought all our efforts had failed.'

'I'm in a lot of trouble,' the girl declared, 'but

221

it will sort itself out, with the Inspector's help. I'm hoping Jim will want to see me again when he's well. It was falling in love with him that finally decided me to do something drastic to break the hold Danny had over me.'

'But you were trying to break that hold before you came here,' Lydia said happily. 'I'm so glad for your sake, and I certainly hope you'll find the happiness you so richly deserve.'

The Inspector came across, having been content to let Rita Wenn do his explaining for him. He smiled at Lydia.

'I shall need statements from everyone involved in this,' he said.

'But that can wait, Inspector,' Peter interrupted. 'I have something to say to Sister Ashby before you start getting her story. Let Nurse Wenn take care of you until later.'

The Inspector nodded and departed with Nurse Wenn and Lydia sighed heavily as Peter took her arm and led her towards the office. When they entered he closed the door and placed his back against it. He held open his arms for Lydia and she hurried into their strong circle.

'You said you had something to say to me,' she remarked, looking up into his face.

'Actions speak louder than words,' he retorted with a grin, and kissed her soundly. For a few moments silence reigned in the office, and Lydia felt her mind emptying of tension and worry under the pressures that his lips forced upon her. But these were pleasant pressures, and she felt her burden lifting slowly and inexorably from her shoulders.

'Peter!' She said his name in breathless tones as he released her in order to look at her. 'Is it really all over now?'

'At last,' he said, kissing the tip of her nose. 'Now we can begin to live normally, wonderfully. I've got great plans in my mind that I'm sure you'll be dying to agree with.'

'If they're anything like the idea of spending the day at Southend last week then I do want to hear them,' she said with a smile.

'These ones are better and bigger,' he said, grinning. 'But we have plenty of time to go over them now. Plenty of time!'

*   *   *

Lydia closed her eyes as he kissed her again, but she mentally agreed with his words. She wanted to tell him so, but actions did speak louder than words, and she was quite content to stay in his arms. She had the feeling this was the way it would be for the rest of her life. Now the mystery of Nurse Wenn had been solved she would be able to give the proper attention her own life merited, and that was the only determination remaining in her mind. She returned his kisses with flaring eagerness, and a low voice in her mind insisted that the fine future she planned for them would be far better than she could imagine...

We hope you have enjoyed this Large Print book. Other Chivers Press or G.K. Hall & Co. Large Print books are available at your library or directly from the publishers.

For more information about current and forthcoming titles, please call or write, without obligation, to:

Chivers Press Limited
Windsor Bridge Road
Bath BA2 3AX
England
Tel. (01225) 335336

OR

G.K. Hall & Co.
P.O. Box 159
Thorndike, Maine 04986
USA
Tel. (800) 223–2336

All our Large Print titles are designed for easy reading, and all our books are made to last.

Serie
La Jauría Intergaláctica

ⓒ Wild Parra (compilador)
ⓒ 1ª edición, Fundación Jóvenes Artistas Urbanos, 2020
Pueblo Nuevo, calle 2, # 3-33, San Cristóbal.
Táchira – Venezuela, 5001.
Teléfonos: +58 276 3532839

Correos electrónicos
fundajau@gmail.com
lajauriaintergalactica@gmail.com

Sitios web
http://fundajau.blogspot.com
http://lajauriaintergalactica.blogspot.com

Ilustraciones y diagramación
ⓒ Omau

Prólogo y corrección de estilo
José Leonardo Guaglianone

Hecho el Depósito de Ley
Depósito legal Ta2020000044
ISBN 978-980-6979-19-2

—En el siglo XXI, como en cualquier otro - dice Fryes, ofreciéndome una taza de té-, solo existen dos destinos tolerables: el de científico y el de artista. El primero danza al borde de la extinción física del cosmos. El segundo, al filo de la muerte del alma. Luego, se han hecho imposibles.

—Y no son ya diferentes.

Luis Britto García

PRÓLOGO
DE LA CRISIS SANITARIA GLOBAL A LA
CREACIÓN LITERARIA DE FICCIÓN ESPECULATIVA

I. UN CONTINENTE PLURICULTURAL Y UN GÉNERO LITERARIO DIVERGENTE

El género literario y narrativo originalmente conocido como "ciencia ficción", mejor traducido como "ficción científica", o posteriormente precisado en su diversidad como "ficción especulativa" (Harlan Ellison *dixit*[1]), en Latinoamérica, cuenta con una reducida pero significativa trayectoria de antologías de cuentos, que han cumplido con la reconstrucción documental de un repertorio valioso pero escaso, disperso y olvidado, hasta hace pocos años, en nuestras tierras. Ocurrido, quizás, debido a cierta infravaloración o desprecio hacia el género desde la crítica literaria local más reducida, academicista y con limitada influencia en las comunidades lectoras; así como a un desinterés por parte del sector editorial comercial y/o bien con preferencia por obras angloeurocentradas; así como un desconocimiento general, de los referentes propios y su potencial, por parte del gran público.

Ciencia ficción y/o ficción especulativa latinoamericana. Menos infrecuente de lo que pareciera a primera vista, dicho género en nuestros países y sus historias de la literatura, en constante reconstrucción documental, ha implicado un origen paralelo con las obras fundacionales del género en el campo cultural anglosajón y de otras culturas del mundo. Así como una imbricación, estereotipada o compleja, con otros géneros literarios más aparentemente "propios" de las culturas latinoamericanas, como la leyenda popular o tradición oral folclórica, la fantasía, la fantaciencia, el realismo fantástico, el llamado realismo mágico del "*boom* latinoamericano",

---

1 . Harlan Ellison: "Introducción: Treinta y dos augures", en: Harlan Ellison (Comp.) [1967]: *Visiones peligrosas I*. Barcelona (España): Ediciones Martínez Roca/Ediciones Orbis (Biblioteca de Ciencia Ficción, Vol. 10), 1983. pp 31-42.

o, como lo redefiniera y rebautizara el escritor y crítico cubano Alejo Carpentier: real maravilloso. Todo esto, en el contexto de una tradicional historización anglocentrada del género, con su "prehistoria" popular-masiva *pulp*; sus Edades de oro y plata; su "Paradigma Campbell" (Jhon W. Campbell Jr.) o Primera Revolución de las décadas treinta-cincuenta, junto a su evolución *new wave* (nueva ola) o Segunda Revolución, de las décadas sesenta-setenta del siglo xx (Isaac Asimov *dixit*[2]). Junto a sus modalidades estilísticas transversales de *soft* y *hard*, en relación al nivel de realismo científico y justificación teórica de los planteamientos ambientales, escenográficos, narrativos y lógicos de los relatos. Haciendo de la caracterización del "estilo" uno de los principales problemas de definición y debate crítico en nuestros países y en los estudios académicos del "Primer Mundo":

> En Sudamérica y en algunos países de Europa estaba evolucionando [durante los años sesenta] una ciencia ficción distinta, más literaria. Frederik Pohl, que por aquel entonces era director de las revistas *Galaxy* y *Worlds of If*, supo de este desarrollo y persuadió a sus editores para que publicasen una revista especial dedicada a esa nueva corriente, *International Science Fiction*. / La nueva revista no fue un éxito. Evidentemente, la *new wave* aún constituía por aquel entonces una innovación. La ciencia ficción literaria todavía debería esperar a que los lectores, acostumbrados a las obras de los *pulps*, escritas por grandes cerebros, se ajustaran a las más sofisticadas obras escritas por grandes corazones.[3]

II. UNA HISTORIA FRAGMENTARIA E HÍBRIDA DE LAS OBRAS, Y DE SU INTERPRETACIÓN

Tal y como ya afirmaron, entre los años setenta y ochenta, ambos prefacios de los compiladores de esa fundacional antología estadounidense citada de nuestra literatura en este género,

---

2 . Isaac Asimov: "Primer prólogo: La Segunda Revolución", en: *Ibídem*, pp 15-21.
3 . Alfred E. Van Vogt: "Prólogo", en: Bernard Goorden y Alfred E. Van Vogt (Comps.): *Lo mejor de la ciencia ficción latinoamericana*. Barcelona (España): Ediciones Martínez Roca (Super Ficción), 1982. Este halagador prólogo fue originalmente agregado en la edición estadounidense de Simón & Schuster en inglés, traducido e incluido en esta edición española.

muchos relatos con premisas y/o tratamientos narrativos de ciencia ficción, o de proto ciencia ficción, se escribieron en países como Argentina, México, Uruguay, Colombia o Venezuela, contemporáneas o años antes que varias de las obras anglosajonas que son históricamente identificadas como iniciadoras modernas del género, incluso desde la etapa del siglo XIX. Con referentes pioneros, puntuales pero innegables, hasta la primera mitad del siglo XX, como los mexicanos Amado Nervo, Juan Nepomuceno Adorno y Juan José Arreola; los uruguayos Francisco Piria y Horacio Quiroga; el ecuatoriano Pablo Palacio; el peruano Clemente Palma, los colombianos José Félix Fuenmayor, José Antonio Osorio y Manuel Francisco Sliger; el nicaragüense Rubén Darío; los argentinos Leopoldo Lugones, Adolfo Bioy Casares, Jorge Luis Borges, Felisberto Hernández y Roberto Arlt[4]; el chileno Ernesto Silva Román, los venezolanos Federico León Madriz (Pepe Alemán), Enrique Bernardo Núñez, José Balza, o el caso especial del venezolano Julio Garmendia[5], entre otros. Y, más allá de los referentes documentales pioneros, su problemática estilística generalizada:

> Mientras que James E. Gunn señala que la diferencia medular entre la literatura fantástica y la ciencia ficción consiste en que la primera proyecta la visión de mundo privado –"La tienda de muñecos", de Julio Garmendia–, mientras que la ciencia ficción

---

4 . Como bien nos historiza el excelente prefacio de: Antonio García Ángel (Ed.): *¿Sueñan los androides con alpacas eléctricas? Antología de ciencia ficción contemporánea latinoamericana*. Bogotá: Alcaldía Mayor de Bogotá-Instituto Distrital de las Artes (IDARTES), 2012.

5 . Algunas interpretaciones, del siglo pasado y también contemporáneas, insisten en colocar a este autor y su relato "La realidad circundante" [*La tienda de muñecos*, 1927], como pionero moderno del género en Venezuela y el continente, incluso ante los escritores angloparlantes. Así como nos han aportado, junto a otrxs investigadorxs como Daniel Arella, a los referentes nacionales, pioneros latinoamericanos del género: Julio E. Miranda: "Prólogo", en: Julio E. Miranda (Comp.): *Antología. Ciencia-ficción venezolana*. Caracas: El Diario de Caracas, 1979. p. 5. Andrea Pezzè: "Paranoia y poder en los trópicos: Recorridos de la ciencia ficción venezolana.", en: *Cultura Latinoamericana. Revista de estudios interculturales*. Volumen 21, número 1, enero-junio 2015. Bogotá: Universidad Católica de Colombia-Fondazione I.S.LA. per gli Studi Latinoamericani-Editorial Planeta. p. 108. https://editorial.ucatolica.edu.co/index.php/RevClat/article/view/1637

proyecta la visión de un mundo público como 1984 o *Un mundo feliz*, de Huxley. En los orígenes pioneros de la ciencia ficción latinoamericana no había distinciones, todo estaba fusionado dentro de la euforia vanguardista por la novedad de las propuestas narrativas y de la exploración arriesgada del modernismo, más cercana a la parodia y la fábula –Felisberto Hernández, Julio Garmendia, Héctor Velarde–, y la ironía o el artificio –Vicente Huidobro, Hans Arp, Borges, Jodorowsky–, que de los temas consagrados por el género.[6]

Cuestionando así la suposición unilateral y automática de la práctica del orden cultural colonialista de imitación tardía de los géneros y temas, desde la literatura latinoamericana, a los centros culturales hegemónicos de Occidente. Colaborando incluso a la consideración de que dicho género se corresponda, en su totalidad y plenitud, con una respuesta artística múltiple o "universal", sensibilidad histórica, "inconsciente colectivo" o una *zeitgeist*, propia a la condición globalizada y desigual de la Modernidad y el colonialismo moderno, desde diversos continentes y países; más que de un género entendido como exclusivamente de origen anglosajón o característico únicamente de la sociedad estadounidense, su principal y más masivo e instituido ámbito de desarrollo.

Me tomaré una licencia atrevida citando, extensamente, el siguiente fragmento de un estudio literario del Instituto Internacional de Literatura Iberoamericana, por resultar muy complejo y revelador sobre el campo literario que nos compete:

> La desconfianza de la crítica latinoamericana hacia la ciencia-ficción tiene larga data y complejo origen. Muchos trabajos tienden a rastrear sus fuentes en la producción anglosajona, subrayando las relaciones con el *pulp*, o buscan las raíces de la ciencia-ficción en lo fantástico (cuando no la confunden o la mezclan con el realismo mágico) como formas de legitimar una modalidad de producción que, a todas luces, no parece ajustarse con claridad a los modelos folkloristas, localistas y/o contestatarios que han constituido buena

---

6 . Daniel Arella: "Prólogo", en: Daniel Arella (Comp.): *Relatos pioneros de la ciencia ficción latinomaericana*. Caracas: Fundación Editorial El perro y la rana, 2015. p. 29.

parte de la producción cultural latinoamericana [...] Tal situación puede ser atribuida a que las preocupaciones capitales de la ciencia-ficción escrita en castellano y portugués rondan temáticas vinculadas con distintos aspectos de las ciencias sociales, en particular, lo sociológico, lo político, lo filosófico (sobre todo, la epistemología) y lo psicológico, adscribiéndose a lo que se ha dado en llamar la tendencia *soft* de la ciencia-ficción, aun cuando tal definición y la descripción precedente sean perfectamente discutibles [...] En este sentido, la tradición de producción más fuerte de la ciencia-ficción latinoamericana rompe con las expectativas de lectura que provienen fundamentalmente del *pulp* y de la ciencia ficción "dura" originados en el mundo de habla inglesa durante lo que se llamó la *Golden Age* de la ciencia-ficción (ca. 1930-1960).

Esto no impide que muchos críticos académicos acepten los mitos fundacionales de la ciencia-ficción producida en castellano y organicen sus agendas de lectura o bien a partir de la emergencia de las revistas más conocidas de la modalidad, como fue el caso de la argentina *Más Allá* (1953-1957), o bien alrededor de la aparente "novedad" de la ciencia-ficción como modalidad de producción, justificados en parte por el crecimiento editorial que se hace claramente visible desde fines de los sesenta, confundiendo problemas de mercado, lectura, difusión y recepción con la historiografía de la modalidad en la región. Si algo puede afirmarse al reflexionar sobre estas cuestiones es que existe una marcada diferencia entre la publicación y producción (así como el consumo) real de los materiales de la ciencia-ficción y la historia de su lectura y de su crítica [...] A pesar de las constantes quejas del *fandom* sobre las zozobras del mercado se han ido generando una serie de hipótesis para indagar sobre la existencia misma de un fenómeno como la ciencia-ficción en América Latina y sobre sus persistentes reencarnaciones en revistas, *fanzines*, publicaciones en la red y en la continuidad de empresas editoriales que siempre encuentran "nuevos" escritores de ciencia-ficción. Como bien demuestra la reciente publicación de antologías, diccionarios bio-bibliográficos, y el incremento notable en el número de artículos en revistas especializadas y en volúmenes críticos, las indagaciones en torno a las problemáticas de esta modalidad no sólo incluyen establecer un siempre cambiante y proliferante corpus de materiales, sino también interrogarse sobre cuáles son las operaciones de la ciencia-ficción y sus relaciones con otras producciones culturales [...] La ciencia-ficción como objeto está generalmente confinada a las carreras de comunicaciones o de ciencias políticas, donde muy de vez en vez se la suele estudiar, o bien como un fenómeno de mercado, o bien como un fenómeno de comunicación de masas, o bien como el lugar de cruce de los discursos sobre la utopía. La ciencia-ficción se presta a todas y cada una de estas lecturas: es un objeto semiótico complejo.[7]

Género literario en un auge actual de su historiografía, interpretación y crítica literaria. Su lectura, recepción crítica e interpretación disciplinaria altamente divergente, tendiente a interconectarse e hibridarse con/desde otros géneros. "Objeto semiótico complejo", requiere de una semiología, una crítica literaria, una interpretación histórica desde las ciencias sociales, acorde con su historia global y local, así como a su contexto de enunciación, como también a sus intenciones estéticas y políticas particulares. Su problemática estilística generalizada: literatura divergente de lo privado antes que de lo público; de manera incidental y experimental antes que constante y sistemática; heterdoxa, fragmentaria e híbrida antes que especializada, insituida y ejemplar; construcción de ordenes subjetivos interiores más que de ordenes objetivos exteriores; donde la ciencia y especulación son más un recurso narrativo que una narrativa en sí misma, ceñida a normas de género; más vanguardista que purista; más desde el arte luchando por ser masivo que desde lo masivo luchando por ser considerado arte.

Para interpretarla y estudiarla, en tanto texto cultural: revisar y describir el proceso narrativo, simbólico y comunicacional de su producción, lectura e interpretación, y su impacto sociocultural; a la manera integral de una *estética de la emisión* (historia, biografía, ideología y modo de producción material y simbólico) y una *estética de la recepción* (comunicación social, antropología cultural y sociología del gusto), como perspectivas metodológicas complementarias, interdisciplinarias y polivalentes para los estudios culturales del género en Latinoamérica. Las cuales

---

7 . Silvia Kurlat Ares: "La ciencia-ficción en América Latina: Entre la mitología experimental y lo que vendrá", en: *Revista Iberoamericana* (edición digital), Vol. LXXVIII, Núms. 238-239, Enero-Junio 2012. Instituto Internacional de Literatura Iberoamericana-Universidad de Pittsburgh. pp. 15-17. https://revista-iberoamericana.pitt.edu/ojs/index.php/Iberoamericana/article/view/6884/7047

se han dado, desde los centros y las periferias culturales, pero de maneras fragmentarias, alternadas o contrapuestas.

Por eso, para introducir la presente obra antológica virulenta, resulta relevante revisar y partir de una genealogía editorial inicial de las obras con estas características (ficción especulativa latinoamericana en castellano), que pueda ser completada y actualizada luego. Considerando las particularidades estilísticas del género, y sus interpretaciones, propias de las literaturas nacionales de nuestras tierras sudamericanas en globalización y "glocalización".

III. ANTOLOGÍAS DE CUENTOS DE FICCIÓN ESPECULATIVA DE AMÉRICA LATINA

Ante una más extensa bibliografía contemporánea de historia, teoría y crítica literaria, aquí inabarcable, pasamos a terminar de referir una provisional genealogía de los principales referentes encontrados de antologías de ciencia ficción de la Abya Yala o Nuestra América, en castellano.

En primer lugar, una mención especial requiere la ya citada edición local de *Antología. Ciencia-ficción venezolana* [1979], pero por su carácter pionero en su fecha de publicación, tratándose de una compilación nacional insólita en nuestro país, donde se asentaron las bases de toda la historización y crítica literaria posterior. Como fundacional, a la compilación continental, la citada antología *Lo mejor de la ciencia ficción latinoamericana* [1982], la cual posee dos prefacios con el más amplio mapeo o panorama histórico y crítico del género en nuestro continente, para la fecha. De la década de los años noventa no encontramos alguna antología, aunque no descartamos la posibilidad de su existencia. A continuación, cronológicamente, apareció *Cosmos Latinos* [2002], otra obra crucial de edición estadounidense sobre literatura en castellano, pero editada por dos compiladoras de procedencia "latina" y con sendos estudios académicos sobre la literatura latinoamericana o *Latin Studies*. Después, se publicó la edición argentina de *Postales del Porvenir* [2006], considerando a dicho país (Argentina) como el principal núcleo histórico, editorial y crítico, de la región. Luego, vino la ya mencionada edición colombiana de *¿Sueñan los androides con alpacas eléctricas?* [2012], la cual volvía al compilado continental de cuentos. Seguida de la edición venezolana de *Relatos pioneros de la ciencia ficción latinomaericana* [2015], otra obra importante y polémica para la reconstrucción de esta historia regional de la ficción especulativa, con un extenso prólogo cargado de documentadas referencias editoriales, literarias y críticas relevantes. Finalmente, nos topamos con señales de la edición española, con importantes aportes feministas, de *Las otras. Antología de mujeres artificiales* [2018], la cual escapa mayormente en autorías a nuestro continente, pero se establece como referente actual del género en castellano. Sin descartar a las otras existentes encontradas, y la posibilidad de que existan más antologías por países, no ahondamos más allá en las compilaciones nacionales, para centrarnos en las pocas antologías continentales. Una vez propuesto este panorama genealógico inicial, podremos después ir completando las ausencias documentales existentes, y preparándonos ahora para comprender cómo se inserta el presente libro, en el 2020, dentro de dicha trayectoria editorial.

IV. UNA ANTOLOGÍA AUTOEDITADA QUE AMPLÍA Y DIVERSIFICA LA GENEALOGÍA

Esta obra antológica trata de un conjunto de cuentos por autor/autora, organizados a su vez por países. Debido a esto, existe la posibilidad latente, en cada unx, de que los conjuntos de cuentos planteen o puedan suscitar interconexiones simbólicas, u eventualmente ocurrir en el mismo universo narrativo, explícita o implícitamente. Con un formato de compilación tan particular, capaz de permitir y estimular en la escritura continuidades o discontinuidades, narrativas, temáticas o poéticas; y una tendencia al minicuento o al microcuento, se abre la oportunidad para el desarrollo, inmediatamente verificable por parte del lector, de la confluencia o alternancia de estilos literarios, subgéneros, críticas sociales y políticas, filosofías, u obsesiones en y de cada autor o autora, dentro de una misma obra, ampliando las interpretaciones estilísticas, como veremos a continuación.

ALEJANDRA DECURGEZ, DE ARGENTINA. Con cada relato va construyendo un universo narrativo coherente en sí mismo, con temáticas alternadas que avanzan ordenadamente desde la realidad inmediata de este año de transiciones históricas globales, que atraviesa la obra completa desde el título, inspirando a un eventual biopunk generalizado: La "peste". Pasando por la ecologista preocupación por la desertificación de la tierra; pasando al ámbito existencial del cuerpo con la temática del cyborg; el horror apocalíptico, y, finalmente, su vinculación con las vicisitudes contemporáneas del sexo-género. Podemos percibir un estilo personal transversal, afectivo y crítico, y aunque no explícitamente, todos sus relatos bien podrían ocurrir en un mismo universo narrativo.

ELIANA SOZA, DE BOLIVIA. Nos increpa con un planteamiento dramático sobre los software de búsqueda de pareja; una versión original y cotidiana del recurrente tema del arribo extraterrestre y supervivencia de la especie humana; o las consecuencias climáticas y desigualdad social junto a un remate inesperado con tema de género; la determinista solución tecnológica a los problemas sociales de la pandemia, la realidad virtual, y una elipsis aterradora final, debido a la ambigüedad del personaje, que se desdibuja de manera sobrenatural entre sujetos y ambientes. Con un énfasis dramático, son cuentos que parecen andar por sus propios senderos narrativos.

LEONARDO ESPINOZA BENAVIDES, DE CHILE. Comienza sus relatos estableciendo un vínculo poco visto: cyborg y religión, el cyborg como intriga identitaria y el tiempo mítico como maldición del control social religioso; luego, tocará puntualmente el tema agrotecnológico; luego, ¿distopía o realismo futurista sobre la progresiva hegemonía tecnológica y global china?; y finaliza con un microcuento donde se cuestiona el lenguaje, la memoria literaria y la hegemonía cultural, muy a la manera internauta actual. Son relatos desenfadados que suceden en momentos temporales imprecisos, pero cuyos tropos no parecen contradecirse mutuamente.

MAIELIS GONZÁLEZ, DE CUBA. Sus historias contagian un intimismo en primera persona y situaciones de padecimiento ecológico, estilo ciberpunk, pero en contenidas y enigmáticas descripciones; sobrepieles infantiles y la mirada extraterrestre; el problema de la memoria extrasensorial y de la consciencia humana sobreviviente; ambiguos mundos arruinados, la escala familiar de los grandes cambios civilizatorios y la melancólica desmemoria; mayormente en primera persona, cuando usa la segunda y la tercera también es centrada en un personaje único y su subjetividad afectiva. En sus cuentos la sensibilidad de la pandemia se asoma de manera tímida y lejana, y solo en su último aparece de manera contundente, denunciando el desborde y sobredimensión global que esta ha tenido como un futuro, ya no distópico, sino de realismo futurista. Historias con muy pocas referencias del contexto o temporalidad, pero cargadas de una subjetividad verosímil.

ERICK J. MOTA, DE CUBA. Sus primeros relatos se enfocan en la ucronía, la "historia escondida" o "el manuscrito encontrado"; una forma de futurismo retroactivo en sus tres primeros cuentos, mientras que en dos de ellos surge la intriga por el viaje temporal y una alteración de la Historia solo consciente para sus perpetradores. Así como una preocupación por la desigualdad social entre los mal llamados "primer mundo" y "tercer mundo", el llamado "subdesarrollo" que nos coloca, como latinoamericanxs, en competencia desigual en una carrera modernista que no elegimos, como es el modelo de desarrollo insostenible. Estas ficciones apuntan a un modelo sostenible y a la legitimidad poética de las identidades híbridas latinoamericanas, aunque no atiendan a la economía de los "recursos" naturales. Sus historias conforman una unidad narrativa y cosmogónica integrada, manteniendo el carácter fragmentario y aparentemente episódico de cada una.

ARISANDY RUBIO, DE MÉXICO. Con el tono del relato de misterio comienza abordando la premisa de la pandemia y el viaje o existencia interdimensional, con una magistral elipsis final; luego, a partir de la pandemia, desarrolla una distopía que por carecer de un giro argumental trágico (más sí filosófico), concluye más bien como una utopía sospechosa; también propone una tecnología fantástica que viola las leyes de la Física, pero que amplía la crítica con respecto a las soluciones desesperadas durante la pandemia, así como el horror corporal y la nanotecnología; igual que sucede con su último cuento, el cual lleva al extremo el terror pandémico distópico. Sus relatos, están conectados por el mentado contexto del 2020, y aunque lo aborden desde distintos puntos de vista: "pudieron pasar" en un mismo universo.

MARY CRUZ PANIAGUA, DE REPÚBLICA DOMINICANA. Inicia sus historias con el intimismo de la fábula y la mirada infantil, una subtrama de misterio y un clímax con enigmática elipsis; después, aborda el género policial de ciencia ficción médica con el pánico de la infección máquina-humano, un magistral cierre narrativo y de arco de personaje para un minicuento tan corto; después, en vez de una pandemia viral, nos enfrenta a una enfermedad evolutiva masiva, cuya solución tecnológica resulta peor que la enfermedad, en una inevitable deshumanización que recuerda a la pandemia silenciosa del trastorno depresivo; concluye con otro relato que también apela a las realidades distópicas del micromundo, pero con un gran enigma. Sus cuentos parecen habitar mundos diferentes y no necesitar de una interconexión narrativa o simbólica.

ÁLVARO MORALES, DE URUGUAY. Comienza sus cuentos con la primera distopía de expansión galáctica, donde nos confronta con un existencialismo interplanetario que cuestiona la legitimidad de los mitos o el origen religioso de todo apocalipsis; luego, una interesante reflexión sobre la política farmacrática auto esclavista que prematuramente auguraba Aldous Huxley; finaliza con dos cuentos que innovan en formas inesperadas del contacto extraterrestre, una por su angustiosa imposibilidad y la otra por el giro de perspectiva de la narración. Sus historias bien podrían coexistir en una línea temporal, pero el autor parece preferir desarrollar premisas puntuales que nos aporten una episódica experiencia intensa de reflexión e incredulidad.

AVE (ANNIE VÁSQUEZ RAMÍREZ), DE VENEZUELA. Conjunto de microcuentos con una redacción poética minimalista y juegos de serialismo de sus frases, cierta rima y el uso de la puntuación, que parecen interpelar enigmáticamente a la ciencia y a la religión al mismo tiempo; repite el formato en su segundo relato, pero esta vez no solamente asoma tímidamente la temática distópica del zoológico humano y la ingeniería genética, sino que el mismo uso del lenguaje y la puntuación hacen referencia a las inteligencias artificiales y el lenguaje de programación informática. Su intencionada brevedad y parquedad nos parece digna de poemas haikus narrativos y sin métrica, o con una métrica tan íntima que resulta en una pareidolia literaria; acertijos o *kōans* para una subjetividad que medita cada palabra hasta extinguirlas en prolongados silencios, cual contemplación Zen.

CRISTIAN SOTO, DE VENEZUELA. Inicia sus cuentos con un enigmático realismo del presente, que se desvela en una premisa especulativa del futuro más inmediato imaginable de las inteligencias artificiales, con cuidadoso detalle; después, el profesor de la distopía postpandemia, cargado de ironía, nos muestra cómo el sistema capitalista corporativo modelará cualquier realidad global a su beneficio. En otro cuento, mantiene la distopía sobre la pandemia exagerando el curso e incorporando un elemento inesperado: el terror filosófico de las diferencias antropológicas en las sociedades humanas; finalmente, nos imbuye en la ironía del *marketing* político distópico, siempre en la postpandemia. Sus historias parecen contar perspectivas diferentes de un mismo tiempo histórico coherente.

OBITUAL PÉREZ (OSVALDO BARRETO), DE VENEZUELA. Desde lo más intimo, la intimidad más solitaria del "Siendo", y aparentemente fuera del género, irrumpe de manera repentina en unas premisas especulativas inabarcables, excepto por la imaginación lectora tras sus elipsis. Tras el recurso crítico de las "comparsas", en todos los títulos, hilvana los cuentos partiendo de la misma premisa anecdótica pandémica con la misma frase exacta, planteando realidades individuales divergentes, pero que podrían habitar el mismo universo o momento histórico; ficcionando premisas especulativas realistas o neorrealistas, como metáforas de etapas psicológicas... o sociales. La pandemia, el tiempo, la contemplación de la naturaleza, la ecología, el rompecabezas, el sueño; finalmente cierra su serie de cuentos deliberadamente interconectados *a priori* con una reflexión espiritual sobre la condición de cuarentena, con un clímax sorprendente, y la posibilidad patente de que todos los relatos coexistan narrativamente sin contradicción. Pudiendo cambiar de narrador, siempre en primera persona, cuyos nombres o perfiles de personaje nunca se nos muestran, pero cuyas atmósferas existenciales nos envuelven y desafían.

WILD PARRA, DE VENEZUELA. Su primer cuento pone sobre la mesa de manera sutil los resultados atroces de políticas postpandémicas, haciendo referencia al terrible caso de experimentación inconsulta en humanxs racializadxs conocido como el Experimento Tuskegee; luego, una interesante preocupación sobre las tecnologías del desastre ecológico, con una variante ingeniosa del conocido tópico de horror "el humano es el alimento"; así como otro relato sobre las posibilidades de la inteligencia artificial y el respaldo de la consciencia humana en el marco del autoritarismo tecnológico; finalizando con una especulación sobre las compulsiones humanas actuales, asistidas por la tecnología actual y futura, por medio del famoso caso del caníbal venezolano.

Para terminar, resulta importante destacar el cuidado gráfico de esta obra. Las ilustraciones de Omau que encontrará la lectora y el lector, especialmente realizadas para representar e identificar a cada autora y autor, en páginas dobles de portadilla, condensan tropos narrativos, símbolos, y alegorías combinados de cada conjunto de relatos compilado. Que nos introducirán en estos imaginarios angustiantes estimulando la sensación visual de una unidad temática y de estilo para cada unx de estxs escritorxs de la América Latina actual, representando un panorama literario. Dentro del característico estilo artístico del propio ilustrador, que combina recursos dramáticos surrealistas y expresionistas impactantes. Todo sea por convertir este confinamiento forzado y atemporal en materia fértil para la consciencia especulativa, crítica y existencial, de un mundo cada vez más complejo.

JOSÉ LEONARDO GUAGLIANONE

ALEJANDRA DECURGEZ

Dice mi mamá que la Pacha se fue alejando de a poco. Fue dando avisos pero nadie quiso verlos. Se fue como se van los decepcionados: una noche, de puntillas. Así contaba mi mamá, mientras clavaba la pala en la tierra gris y fría del pastizal. Por eso colgaron esos satélites de mierda, decía. Porque era eso o nos moríamos.

Contaba que los de antes hacían rituales parecidos, pero que ahora para qué iba a querer La Mama embriagarse de alcohol y cigarro. Hay que ir hondo, decía mamá, porque ahí donde está más oscuro es donde la luz más brilla.

Yo me sentaba, la miraba y no sabía si ayudarla o decirle basta. Era horrible verla escarbar la tierra imaginando cómo la peste escarbaba también en mi madre.

A mi mamá no le habían ofrecido lo de ponerse parches para ser mitad carne y metal. No quieren, dijo, cuando salió del laboratorio. Para ellos soy un peligro.

A mí, al principio, me gustaban los satélites que controlan el clima, los colgaron una noche. Están ahí arriba, plateados como si los lustraran a cada rato, como un móvil sobre una cuna. Mi mamá extraña lo de antes: la sorpresa de una lluvia fría después de días de calor rojo, el granizo, el viento que volaba las faldas.

El clima debe ser libre, dice mamá, y hunde la pala en el polvo mientras sostengo la semilla ancestral que es como un ojo resguardado por mil párpados. Ella me la dio para que mis manos la entibien. Dice que a los niños, La Mama todavía puede escucharlos. Para ellos tiene un oído y un corazón dispuesto.

Yo ya estoy perdida, dice y escarba, se agita, se asfixia pero sigue.

Ya me explicó qué tengo que hacer cuando la peste termine de comérsela por dentro: "Hundí la semilla en mi ombligo, hundime en La Mama, encendé la semilla y que arda. Pedile a La Mama y esperá. Ella escucha a los niños, vos pedile que vuelva".

PARE DE SUFRIR

ALEJANDRA DECURGEZ

Se preguntará qué hago en su pantalla esta mañana mientras toma su café. ¿Isidore, en la tele? ¿No había...? Creyó que sería uno más, que la peste me vencería, ¿verdad? Isidore, galán de la tarde, devorado, derrotado, otro de tantos, lo sé. Pero déjeme decirle que no, que estoy aquí, ¡y míreme! Soy más fuerte y más feliz que nunca.

Usted se prepara para salir, tiene que mantener a los que ama y no sabe, usted es consciente, ¿verdad? Usted no sabe si volverá sano. No sabe siquiera si la peste ya está en usted y tampoco sabe si ha contagiado a su familia. Usted no sabe, ¿cómo podría saberlo? ¡Yo mismo no lo sabía!

Déjeme ser sincero, es lo que todos necesitamos en este momento, que nos digan la verdad, ¿no es así? Y la verdad es que un día estaba en escena y al siguiente estaba tendido en un galpón, uno más con un tubo en la garganta y el peso de mil elefantes sobre el pecho.

Tuve suerte, voy a serle honesto, tuve mucha suerte de ser quien soy. Me ofrecieron ingresar al Programa Patchwork porque era el galán de la tarde, no voy a mentirle.

Pero ahora esta oportunidad también puede ser suya. Por eso estoy aquí esta mañana, porque usted también puede formar parte de la más osada aventura de la historia moderna. El Programa Patchwork pone ante usted la posibilidad de una salud y una fortaleza inigualables, de la solidez y la confianza del metal sin perder su esencia humana.

¿Quiere volver a los días felices? ¿Quiere regresar a su casa y compartir con su familia sin temor a transmitirles la muerte? ¿Quiere paz? Solo el metal puede dársela, créame, sé lo que le digo. El Programa Patchwork introducirá metal de primera calidad en su anatomía, y le devolverá la seguridad y la esperanza. Míreme: soy prueba irrefutable de que la vida que usted merece está a su alcance.

Solo tiene que llamar al número en pantalla.

A PUNTO

R790 desgrana la tierra, en las grietas se ocultan monedas y trozos de pantallas plásticas que tantos usaron creyendo que se salvarían. Las nubes compactas son un toldo y en el pastizal el aire es viscoso e irrita. R790 busca tierra viva, capaz de ser potencia, y siente las partes orgánicas de su cuerpo calientes.

Se acercan Centinelas en su ronda de la tarde. R790 permanece inmóvil, que el metal no refleje, que no emita ni un destello, que no rechine. Ellos se van, él sigue cavando. La tierra se convierte en polvillo cuando la remueve, se desintegra al contactar con el aire. R790 siente tensión en los retazos orgánicos, sus articulaciones metálicas crujen con el movimiento, pero no tiene sed, tampoco hambre. Desde que la peste lo carcomió, esas sensaciones ya no existen porque está "a punto", tal como prometía el comercial.

Pero sí siente la gravedad, que hala.

Busca tierra húmeda, trabaja como un partero extrayendo recuerdos ajenos, vivencias y porquerías enterradas en ese pastizal, esa necrópolis de objetos roídos por la peste que empezó devorando los cuerpos.

Oscurece y la tierra se desliza entre sus dedos, fría. Como la noche fría. Ya no aparecen pedazos ni monedas, empieza a imaginar un futuro húmedo. Cierra los ojos, sus dedos perciben la hondura y la tibieza del suelo. Cava como un ciego tantea el sendero de regreso.

Antes de la primera ronda Centinela de la mañana se acurrucará en el foso, se tapará con una manta de tierra negra. No lo verán dormir. La tierra, sus manos y su anatomía serán una continuidad orgánica, también cósmica, retoños una del otro. Se fusionará con el humus y se hundirá, navegará mientras sueña, y su conciencia será resplandor, hálito de luz que no se extingue.

Tal vez tenga suerte, y renazca. Ya no un ridículo *patchwork* de metal y vísceras. Ya no "a punto", sino imperfecto.

Cava hasta el fondo buscando el cosmos. Cava como un ciego.

POTENCIA

ALEJANDRA DECURGEZ

En plena emergencia, el metal sirvió para reconstruir las cavernas que la peste había escarbado en los pulmones. Pero ahora, el metal había ganado terreno. Solo quedaba lo indispensable, lo irremplazable: el sistema nervioso, las cuerdas vocales y la musculatura gesticular del rostro. Apenas eso. Solamente eso.

Todo el resto, metal.

El balance entre los componentes es precario y el trabajo de integración, minucioso. Por eso hay que acondicionar los retazos orgánicos y también preservar las articulaciones metálicas de la oxidación. Por eso, cada dos días, las *patchwork* metal y carne ingresan al cubículo de lubricación.

Ellas relucen bajo la llovizna oleosa, estiran sus brazos y sus espaldas crujen como goznes. Los labios apretados y los entrecejos fruncidos develan incomodidad humana pero sus anatomías son compactas y sin curvas, en serie. Pronto sus expresiones se distienden y se escuchan sus voces alegres, como de adolescentes en un vestuario. Juegan con el líquido, chapotean y ríen.

CWhite23 observa los remolinos de espuma oscura y residuos en las rejillas. Había elegido el Programa Patchwork por el pavor a lo efímero y también a lo permanente. No quería morir y tampoco, crías. Y ellos habían prometido que cuando su nivel *patchwork* fuera 80% metal y 20% carne, el sufrimiento mensual (todo sufrimiento, toda preocupación) terminaría. Pero ya era una 80-20 y el calambre en el bajo vientre insistía. Serían los circuitos, decían ellos, ahí abajo hay solo bombas y cablerío. Un resabio, explicaban, una reverberación antigua de lo femenino, como el miembro fantasma o el sueño arquetípico.

Las *patchwork* salen del cubículo saturado de vapor. Antes de que CWhite23 diera el primer paso, nadie había notado la sangre que le corría por la pierna.

Entonces una señala, chillando:

—¡Re-gla!

Las otras observan, incrédulas. "No puede ser, si abajo hay metal, somos metal, bombas, cablerío". Una grita "¡No!, ¡no!" Algunas se cubren la boca, otras la nariz, todas retroceden apretándose el vientre. En sus rostros ahora hay repugnancia, odio, lástima.

Miedo.

—¡Qué difícil enamorarse en la pandemia! —afirmaba el abuelo—.

Si no era la cuarentena, que no te dejaba salir de casa; eran los barbijos, los lentes, las mascarillas, los trajes de bioseguridad, que no te dejaban saber si con quien te cruzabas era hombre o mujer.

Después de cuarenta años, los científicos y la tecnología solucionaron la necesidad de emparejarse de las personas, al crear el mayor invento para encontrar a tu alma gemela: Aeternum, un complejo sistema de citas computarizado. No era necesario conocer a alguien por azar del destino, empezar a salir, si había química entablar una relación y esperar que todo saliera bien.

Para los solteros, este servicio facilitaba las cinco mejores opciones de pareja que vivieran en el mismo país. Más importante aún, daba la opción de ver cómo sería el futuro con esa persona a través de la realidad aumentada.

Muchas mujeres casadas, como yo, probaban el sistema para identificar a las cinco parejas ideales y ver cómo habría sido su vida; sé que suena a tortura, pero la curiosidad era mayor. La mayoría comprobaba que el matrimonio con otro u otra hubiera sido incomparable, aunque también había excepciones.

Casada durante quince años, con un dinero extra que gané, decidí saber de lo que me había perdido. Cuando estuve con los lentes puestos y me mostraron mis cinco alternativas, ninguna fue mejor que la que tenía. Me sentí tan afortunada y más enamorada de Gabriel. Volví a casa, preparé una cena romántica, estaba decidida a recuperar la pasión y romance en mi relación.

Veinte años después, cuando Gabriel estaba a punto de morir me confesó que, con nuestros ahorros, había sobornado a un *Hacker* para que me mostrara lo que vi. No pude más que besarle antes de su último aliento.

Transcribiré palabra a palabra lo que me dictaron. Solo soy el traductor de este texto, el que estuvo ahí para escuchar la historia.

"Mi nombre es AXTL, vengo del exoplaneta Ummo, planeta en órbita alrededor de la estrella enana roja Wolf 424. Por tanto, deseo que se me reconozca como una ummita. Llegué a la Tierra en medio de la pandemia del COVID-19; fui enviada por mis líderes para investigar la causa del virus. Aquí, debo aclarar que los estamos observando desde hace mucho tiempo y nos pareció peculiar la estrategia de aislamiento de su gente.

Como investigadora calificada, esperaba que fuera un viaje rutinario que no tardaría demasiado. Ahora, después de quince años luz, a la espera de mi desintegración quiero dejar constancia de mi experiencia y mis claras conclusiones sobre el posible futuro de la humanidad.

Dejé en casa a un compañero y dos descendencias, imagino que todavía esperan mi regreso; siento haberles fallado, pero no podía volver. Los de mi especie vivimos largas temporadas que no se pueden medir con el tiempo terrestre, la sabiduría que acumulamos la compartimos a través de ósmosis. Así pude dejar este escrito y mis conocimientos a un hombre, que podrá con ellos trasladar un número reducido de parejas a Ummo para su sobrevivencia y para luego después pensar en repoblar la Tierra.

Me enamoré, sí, de él, que es el mismo que tradujo estas notas. No debimos continuar, pero este sentimiento, que me lo explicó en varios idiomas y que lo sentí en el calor de su piel, el aroma de su aliento, la protección de sus brazos y que ahora, antes de la desintegración, lo comprendo mejor. Es la mayor razón para que algunos humanos deban sobrevivir, borrándoles la memoria y preservando el amor, hay esperanza para la Tierra".

Tengo los pies y el cuerpo entero congelados. El cuarto en el que vivo hace más de diez años no era tan frío al principio, por eso lo alquilé. Mientras fue pasando el tiempo los inviernos se tornaron más crudos. No pude prevenir nada, la falta de trabajo hizo que mi pobreza, esa, sí continúe sin ningún cambio.

En las largas noches que no puedo conciliar el sueño, por mi imposibilidad de calentarme siquiera un poco, pienso que fue correcta la decisión de no haber tenido hijas. No podría brindarles algo de abrigo, porque ni siquiera me alcanza para comprar una mejor frazada. Tal vez, el fin de la humanidad se acerca y a nadie le importa.

No es porque el poco aire puro que podemos respirar solo se encuentre en jardines privados de mujeres adineradas y que nosotras tengamos que andar con barbijos por la calle. Tampoco, que hayan desaparecido las verduras y frutas orgánicas, y debamos comer estos reemplazos que inventaron las científicas, que no tienen sabor. O que el agua que tomamos tenga ese gusto raro porque el potabilizador en polvo que usamos, desde hace unos años, sea la única forma de contar con líquido potable.

Es el frío, ése que cala segundo a segundo, que entumece mis manos, el que no me deja respirar, porque siento miles de agujas entrando por mi nariz, el que se cuela por mis sábanas raídas y las frazadas gastadas. Ese será el que deje apenas unos despojos en esta cama; que pronto ya no será mía sino de otra que alquile este cuarto y se convierta, para ella también, en un purgatorio, el que fuimos creando las mujeres desde que hicimos desaparecer a los hombres.

En el avión, Carlos podía sentir que la esperanza se apoderaba de su alma. Su compañero de viaje lo miraba curioso y, queriendo entablar una conversación, preguntó:

—¿Negocios o placer

—Negocios, gracias al cielo ya terminaron.

—Potosí puede ser una ciudad agobiante, por el frío y el misterio que encierra.

—Un hombre tan escéptico como yo, escapando, es incomprensible.

—¿Escapando? Ahora tendrá que contarme la historia completa.

—Llegué hace unas semanas junto a tres compañeros. La Gobernación nos contrató para implementar una estrategia tecnológica para impulsar el turismo.

—Golpeado por la cuarentena...

—Por eso utilizaríamos tecnologías innovadoras: la holográfica. A través de los lentes Hololens, conectados a una red WiFi, que permitiría a la gente visitar templos, museos y las calles coloniales, en la noche, mientras escuchara y viera las leyendas en imágenes tridimensionales; incluso podría observar a los fantasmas, protagonistas de los mitos.

Llevamos quinientos lentes e implementamos el *software*. Funcionaba correctamente, hasta que hicimos el experimento por la noche. Nos pusimos los Hololens y otro equipo monitoreaba. A los minutos, alguien empezó a gritar como loco y le siguieron los demás. Apenas pude quitarme mis lentes defectuosos... Los encontré a todos muertos, con los ojos desorbitados. La autopsia determinó que un ataque cardiaco los fulminó. Revisé las imágenes y los fantasmas no eran los que diseñamos, sino otros, con rostros deformados, que atacaron ferozmente a mis compañeros. Cuando fui a mostrar las imágenes a las autoridades, estas habían desaparecido. Así que con una generosa indemnización, y la promesa de mi silencio, vuelvo a España.

—Aterradora historia.

—Solo quiero olvidarla.

Al aterrizar en Buenos Aires, el acompañante de Carlos se despidió así:

—Recuerde que uno puede llevar encima, sin querer, una compañía indeseable a casa. —Los ojos del hombre se iluminaron de un rojo infernal.

HOGAR DEL CYBER CRISTO

Y él dijo:

—Bienvenido al hogar, al Hogar del Cyber Cristo. Adelante, mi amigo.

Mendigo, más bien, qué más da, pensó.

—¿Es por aquí?

—Pues, sí.

—¿Y hay comida?

—También.

El dintel de la puerta de entrada era una mezcla de concreto y cerámica rota. No había luces de neón, como le habían contado. Era solo una casa vieja en Recoleta con intenso olor a piel, humana y al natural.

—Tu ojo —le dijo al rato—, ¿es real?, el izquierdo.

—Tus muñecas —fue la respuesta—, ¿me las muestras?

Las alzó, obediente; ventral hacia el cielo: tenía pápulas por todas partes y surcos diminutos, como pequeños caminitos blanquecinos por donde el Cristo tuvo sus clavos.

—Tienes sarna.

—Y cómo no.

—Tenemos ivermectina, estarás bien.

—¿Y comida para mí? —insistió.

Ese ojo izquierdo, concluyó, era sin duda artificial. Tampoco de neón, pero sí medio rojo. Parado ahí, no lograba divisar cruz alguna. Debían estar allá adentro, con los computadores.

—¿Tú eres el cura de aquí?

—Claro.

—¿Robot? Ya nunca se sabe.

—Solo unas partes —precisó—, ¿cyborg no le dicen?

—Cyborg jesuita, qué se yo —respondió.

—Por favor, adelante. Estás en el lugar indicado.

—Espera —le dijo—, tengo una duda: ¿cuánto tiempo es que hay que estar en internet revisando esas cosas que dicen?

—Los pecados —dijo el cura—, y entre todos los iremos perdonando.

—Bueno, eso, ¿cuánto tiempo?

Y el cyborg cristiano rio:

—Eso tú ya lo sabes.

Era normal encontrarse con huasos santacruzanos en medio de las plantaciones de choclo. Con los de metal, claro; los más cariñosos de todos. Lo que no era para nada normal, sin embargo, era encontrarse con la cabeza de uno de ellos, en el suelo y apagada. Cuando Manuel la tomó entre sus manos, sintió un atisbo de culpa al ver el óxido cubriendo sus párpados artificiales. Cerrados. "¿Eres tú?", le preguntó. Y, una vez más, solo tuvo silencio de respuesta.

GUÍA del USUARIE de PENGSHU
3ª EDICIÓN (FRAGMENTO)

Capítulo I-b

Comenzando:

¡Felicitaciones y bienvenide! Con los soportes ya instalados, te encuentras a tan solo un par de pasos para comenzar a disfrutar de tu nueva biblioteca Pengshu. Recuerda que, una vez activado el sistema, podrás darle la forma y el tamaño que desees. ¡Siéntete libre de experimentar!

En nombre de toda nuestra familia lectora y consciente del progreso responsable y sustentable, te extendemos nuevamente un agradecimiento sincero. Tu confianza nos permite continuar mejorando cada vez más nuestra tecnología para que todes sigan disfrutando de sus libros favoritos acorde a los tiempos modernos. Nuestro compromiso es contigo, con nuestro mundo, con nosotres mismes: con la esencia de tomar un libro y sentirlo.

Los siguientes capítulos de esta breve guía te familiarizarán con las características y funcionalidades de tu biblioteca Pengshu y sus libros holográficos tangibles. Es posible que algunas propiedades no se encuentren disponibles en tu región. Para más información sobre potenciales restricciones en tu área visita www.pengshu.com/global-support.

Activar tu Pengshu:

Continuando con los pasos realizados al final del capítulo I-a, puedes iniciar la sincronización del usuarie definide con tu nueva biblioteca Pengshu. Recuerda que podrás configurar la apariencia de esta y sus libros respectivos tanto desde tu computador personal como desde tu teléfono móvil. Consulta las secciones *Configurar mis libros* y *Rangos de alcance según red y energía* para obtener instrucciones avanzadas.

Si has realizado los pasos correctamente, recibirás el siguiente mensaje:

PENGSHU

碰书

Touch the Book

[Acceso 100920 –L.E.B. #17991846]

LEONARDO ESPINOZA BENAVIDES

"Please, could you just shut it? I'm trying to figure this out." It had been a simple, innocent mistake; yet brilliantly executed. A majestic event allowed by the absurdist stars. All of them—wiped out. "I'm getting fired," ve said, "what a mess." Some giggles came back, a little nervous—not much. Then, a final glance to vis hand in space. Some said the book's worth it, but still: "Never mind, mister Quixote. You're too long anyway." And out it went, thrown away to the black, cold, ever-laughing void. Again.

(Y una Mancha, también, de apellido, lugar y papel: ¡despedidos!)

SOBREPIEL

MAIELIS GONZÁLEZ

Mamá cubrió mi cabeza con la sobrepiel y palpó el lugar donde se hubiera encontrado mi cabello. A mamá siempre le gustó mucho mi cabello. Me lo dejaba crecer hasta los hombros, lo peinaba por largo tiempo mientras veíamos las noticias de las ocho. Con cada cepillada mi cuello se erizaba un poco y me entraba ese adormecimiento que ahora vuelvo a experimentar cuando ella pasa, melancólica, la palma de su mano por mi cráneo rasurado. Lloró el día que tuvo que cortármelo, pero era necesario para usar la sobrepiel. Todos tuvimos que raparnos.

Cuando mi madre terminó de cerrar el zipper que adhería con eficiencia la sobrepiel a mi cuerpo, me entregó la mochila y abrió la puerta de casa. Habíamos practicado durante todas las vacaciones para cuando llegara este día. Cada mañana usaba la sobrepiel unas horas para irme acostumbrando a estar dentro de ella; para adaptar mi respiración al nuevo ritmo que imponía la apretazón del latex sobre mi tórax. Pero aún así, fue muy incómodo traspasar la puerta envuelto en mi nueva piel, que era al mismo tiempo, la nueva piel de todos los habitantes de la Tierra.

La escuela quedaba cerca. A mi lado pasaban otros con sus mochilas y sus sobrepieles. No nos saludábamos porque no nos reconocíamos. Tomé un atajo para ir a solas con mi incomodidad y entonces vi al niño sintecho. No llevaba más piel que la suya; esa con la que nació. Me miraba como se mira a un *alien* recién desembarcado de la nave nodriza. Di un paso en su dirección, pero echó a correr y lo perdí de vista. La mochila resbaló por mi hombro y cayó al suelo.

No entendía. ¿Por qué aquel niño no estaba muerto? Mi mamá me había mentido.

NOMBRAR LAS COSAS

MAIELIS GONZÁLEZ

Adam se separó de la página y observó con detenimiento su caligrafía. Había quedado perfecta. Parecía un leve encaje sobre el papel. Sopló para acelerar el secado de la tinta y un instante después comenzó a guardar sus instrumentos. Cerró con un golpe seco el álbum que, de tan grueso y pesado, casi le costaba trasladarlo de un lugar a otro del apartamento.

No sabía de dónde le venían las palabras, quién se las dictaba. Pero había dejado de preguntarse el por qué de las cosas. Esa era su vida ahora: comer, dormir, bañarse a veces, y trabajar en el álbum.

Ya no recordaba cómo había adquirido las cajas y cajas de postales del mundo que guardaba en la habitación pequeña del apartamento. Sin embargo, aquello no era lo más extraño. Una vez frente a la página, para escribir una descripción de la postal de turno, Adam era capaz de aducir datos que primero no pudo otra cosa que pensar, nacían de una desbordada e insospechada imaginación. Luego, ya no estuvo tan seguro. Cuando trabajaba en el álbum, entraba en una especie de éxtasis que lo hacía pensar y decir, a través de las palabras, cosas que él nunca había aprendido, que no tenía manera de conocer. Sin embargo, allí estaba su pequeña obra, creciendo por día. La síntesis del mundo que fue y al que ya nunca más tendrían acceso los hombres, como no fuera a través de la memoria o la imaginación.

Nadie sabe qué clase de embeleso posee a nuestros padres cada día a las nueve de la noche. Muchos hemos preguntado, pero no recibimos otra cosa que silencio. Al principio, cuando aún éramos niños, los imitábamos; copiábamos sus movimientos porque aquello era lo natural, lo lógico, incluso lo correcto. Con la pubertad, llegó la rebeldía de muchos y la puesta en evidencia de que aquella actitud de nuestros progenitores no tenía sentido. Pienso, ahora que yo mismo soy un adulto, que tal vez para ellos sí lo tenga; que quizás hubiera sido necesario haber vivido lo que ahora se niegan a contar. No creo que estén locos, simplemente creo que nos volvimos demasiado diferentes.

Pero la madurez hace que te reconcilies con tus padres, que los entiendas o al menos, que los aceptes. Llevo al mío del brazo mientras caminamos por las calles sobresaturadas del centro. En la pantalla traslúcida, que mantengo permanentemente desplegada frente a mi rostro, se me indica cuál es la mejor ruta para llegar a la residencia de ancianos y devolver a mi padre a su mundo.

No me doy cuenta de cuán tarde se ha hecho. Nos entretuvimos en su restaurante favorito. Las nueve de la noche nos sorprende a mitad de un bulevar y mi padre, como si supiera qué hora es exactamente por medio de un dispositivo que nunca me fue dado a conocer, comienza a aplaudir eufórico. Da palmas con más fuerza de la que sospechaba que tuviera. No baja la intensidad, su cara adquiere esa familiar expresión ausente. La gente a nuestro alrededor lo ignora. Pasado un minuto, sale del trance como quien despierta de una sesión de hipnosis y continuamos nuestro camino sin decir palabra.

En lo primero que piensas es en tu hermana del otro lado de la puerta. Antes de entrar a la sala te abrazó y prometió que todo iría bien. Pero la voz del juez, emitida por los altoparlantes en cada esquina del juzgado desierto pronunció "culpable". No sabes qué pasará ahora. Supones que vendrán a buscarte y te llevarán a algún sitio, lejos de la sociedad para la que eres un peligro mortal.

A tu hermana le irá bien sin ti. Quizás, esto sea lo mejor para ella; siempre te has sabido una carga desde que quedaron huérfanos. Ahora lo continuarás siendo, pero para el Estado; y el Estado lleva mucho tiempo practicando cómo deshacerse de sus cargas de la manera más eficaz posible.

No tuviste abogado defensor. No hubo jurado, ni fiscal. Así funciona ahora: todos los juicios por causas como la tuya son sumarios. Nada tuviste que hacer salvo quedarte en silencio y esperar el veredicto. Todo se sabía de antemano... ahora entiendes. Cada cámara de aquella plaza totalmente vacía captó tu crimen y cada ciudadano te condenó antes de que el juez pronunciara "culpable".

El juzgado huele a lejía y desinfectante, como huele absolutamente todo desde hace años. A través de la fibra de tu máscara nasobucal, las moléculas de esa insoportable emanación penetran e irritan tus mucosas. Volverá a ocurrir y no será el olor fresco de los árboles de una plaza vacía los que te hagan estornudar con estridencia. Otra vez apartarás la máscara de tu cara antes de hacerlo y esparcirás, a dos metros a la redonda, la muerte. Las historia se repetirá, pero ahora por venganza, no por nostalgia. Y desearás, con toda la rabia que te permiten tus doce años de edad, infectar a alguien... como el criminal que eres.

ÚLTIMAS NOTAS del *DIARIO* de VIAJE del ALMIRANTE CRISTÓBAL COLÓN

ERICK J. MOTA

Jueves 11 de octubre, 1492.

Navegó al Güesudeste. Tuvieron mucha mar. Más que en todo el viaje habían tenido. Vieron los de la carabela "Pinta" un palo flotando en el agua, otra yerba que nace en tierra y una tabla. Los de la carabela "la Niña" también vieron otras señales de tierra y se alegraron todos. Después del sol puesto navegó a su primer camino al Güeste. Andarían doce millas cada hora. La carabela Pinta era más velera e iba delante y justo cuando el vigía dio la voz de tierra apareció el primer leviatán entre la Pinta y la Niña. Era como de cien varas de largo y tenía cuerpo de serpiente marina. Devoró a la Niña en menos de una hora mientras la Pinta seguía su curso rumbo a tierra y la nao capitana, la "Santa María", lo bordeaba. Les persiguió cosa de una milla o dos en dirección a la costa.

Pronto el leviatán perdió interés, o la proximidad de la costa hacía el agua menos profunda y el monstruo no podía acercarse. Justo antes de desembarcar, el vigía de la Pinta, un marinero que se decía Rodrigo de Triana, divisó a dos leviatanes más en lontananza que, o bien peleaban por su vida, o eran hembra y macho en cortejo. Eran más grandes que el anterior y las olas que formaban con sus cuerpos rompieron en la costa y volcaron la Pinta, haciendo encallar la Santa María.

Así dio el Almirante orden de desembarco y una vez en tierra todos dieron gracias y dijeron la Salve, que la acostumbraban a decir y cantar, a su manera, todos los marineros.

Y desde la costa pudieron ver que eran animales de agua profunda, grandes como montañas y ponzoñosos como las alimañas del infierno. Y fueron muchos los que vimos en las aguas de este mar, preocupándonos el viaje de regreso.

Nota: El original, encontrado en 1514 por el cacique Agüeybaná, en Guanahani, actualmente se conserva en el museo de historia de Borinquen.

FRAGMENTO de la *CARTA* de ALEJANDRO de HUMBOLDT a J. C. DELAMETHRIE

ERICK J. MOTA

Cumaná, en la América meridional, 18 de julio 1799

Hace solo tres días que he llegado a esta costa de la América meridional y ya se presenta una señal favorable para apresurarme a decirle que mis instrumentos de anatomía, de física y de química no se han alterado. Que he trabajado mucho durante el vuelo sobre el Caribe en la composición química del aire y su densidad por encima de las nubes. El bergantín aéreo procedente de Borinquen realizó un vuelo preciso y directo. Salvo por una nube de tormenta, de esas que los indios llaman huracanes.

Hubo una discusión en el puente de mando entre el capitán y su primer oficial. El primero insistía en eludir la tormenta y salvar la nao. El segundo aseguraba que la tormenta no era muy intensa y que el bergantín podría atravesarla. El capitán acusó al primer oficial de buscar la ciudad perdida de *Guatquirá*. Finalmente el capitán impuso su deseo y la cuestión quedó zanjada.

Apenas llegué a Cumaná me he informado sobre el nombre de *Guatquirá*. Resulta que procede del idioma muisca y literalmente significa "Ciudad del Cielo". Al parecer, se trata de una leyenda común en tierras muiscas. La leyenda en cuestión, habla sobre una ciudad de los tiempos anteriores a los mexicas, toltecas y mayas. Cuenta sobre la capital de un imperio que regía toda la América meridional. Una ciudad construida sobre un mineral con propiedades levitatorias.

Los guías indígenas me han llevado a los restos que han caído en el pasado. He visto las estatuas antiguas del dios de la serpiente emplumada. He observado el viejo mineral. Ha perdido propiedades pero, al parecer, cuando cristaliza se vuelve rocahelio. Poca es la información que he obtenido de mis instrumentos. En efecto, este mineral posee helio e hidrógeno en su interior. Pero sus propiedades físicas son únicas. Es laminoso y semitransparente en los bordes. Usted verá las observaciones que yo le he enviado junto con una memoria astronómica y notas sobre la anatomía de un leviatán del Caribe.

SARAJEVO, 24 de DICIEMBRE

ERICK J. MOTA

Comenzaba a nevar cuando el tren imperial llegó a la estación. Tres autos imperiales aguardaban al archiduque Maximiliano y a su esposa. En los países que se autoproclaman imperios suele pasar esto. Hay trenes imperiales, autos imperiales y hasta dirigibles imperiales.

La comitiva avanzó por la calzada rodeada de entusiastas que agitaban pequeñas banderas de Austria-Hungría.

La situación era asombrosamente similar a la descrita por la máquina analítica. Imaginé ambas líneas temporales como si fueran dos series numéricas. La nuestra y la mostrada por el ingenio diferencial. Si vemos cada evento como un número de la serie, la historia misma es como una serie de eventos consecutivos que se van sumando hasta llegar a un resultado. A un hecho histórico concreto. Una Guerra Mundial, en este caso.

El asesino con pistola aparece junto al segundo auto. Se acerca al auto imperial y saca una pistola. El archiduque lleva un chaleco antibalas de seda. Hasta 30 capas de seda que pueden detener las balas. A menos que el disparo sea en la yugular, como fue el caso de la serie alternativa. El extremista dispara y la bala le da en el pecho. Los agentes navajos disparan a la guardia personal que intenta bajarse de los demás coches. Yo entro en escena y disparo. Esta vez acierto en la yugular del archiduque Maximiliano.

He hecho la corrección necesaria para que la serie numérica converja.

He provocado una guerra que devastará Europa.

Pero he salvado a toda América, desde Alaska hasta la Tierra del Fuego, de la invasión combinada de todos los imperios industriales. Imperios colonialistas y racistas que no se abstendrán de violar mujeres negras, ni se detendrán ante niños pieles rojas.

Morirán miles pero se evitará el genocidio previsto por la máquina analítica.

Me pierdo entre la multitud que corre.

Los agentes navajos hacen lo mismo.

Comienza a nevar sobre Sarajevo. El infierno es un lugar frío.

Camino entre la gente que corre. Pero, por más que trato, mi conciencia no deja de gritar: ¡Asesino!

ESTACIÓN GUATQUIRÁ.
ESPACIO SUBORBITAL TERRESTRE

ERICK J. MOTA

6 de diciembre de 1968.

Las nubes sobre el mar Caribe siempre son blancas y cuando se esparcen suele confundirse el azul del cielo con el del mar. Desde lo alto de la Estación Guatquirá hasta las estelas que dejan los leviatanes a su paso, se antojan como pequeños surcos de espuma en un azul intenso. La antigua ciudad de los dioses parece flotar entre las nubes como un islote en medio de un mar espumoso.

La ciudad de los cielos que gobernó la civilización Muisca pertenece ahora a los Estados Antillanos. La caldera de gas helio construlda por los toltecas la mantuvo funcionando incluso después de la caída del imperio Muisca. Como consecuencla, aumentó la temperatura atmosférica en los alrededores de la ciudad creando un ciclón perpetuo a su alrededor.

Cuando el primer explorador quisqueyense se bajó del planeador, luego de atravesar el huracán eterno que la rodeaba, su barómetro marcó varios milímetros de mercurio por debajo de lo normal. Pero apenas Juan de la Cruz apagó la caldera en el corazón de *Guatquirá*, los vientos huracanados desaparecieron y la flota de dirigibles consiguió aterrizar en la ciudad flotante.

El Proyecto Chía, nombre con que la civilización muisca llamaba a la Luna, proponía usar Guatquirá como plataforma de lanzamiento de cohetes estelares. El plan era aprovechar un emplazamiento natural para crear una estación gemela a la Estación Valhala que flota sobre Hamburgo. Así fue como llegamos a construir nuestra Estación Pachamama, en órbita sobre la Tierra primero que los prusianos.

Hoy es un gran día, por lo que me levanté temprano y me senté en uno de los balcones antiguos, justo en el borde de la ciudad vieja. Hoy partiré hacia Pachamama, donde me espera mi nave estelar. Hoy llegaré más lejos que el abuelo Matías Pérez. Hay informes de que los alemanes también preparan un módulo en la Estación Asgard.

Pero a mí no me preocupa.

Yo llegaré primero.

—¡Ey, anciano! Tienes visita.

La señorita Méndez entró a la celda haciendo eco con sus tacones.

—Leopoldo de la O, solo tengo media hora, así que me saltaré las palabras de cortesía e iré al grano. Durante la pandemia del 2019 y 2020, ¿dirigió la brigada que buscaba una vacuna para el SARS-CoV-2?

—Sí.

—Uhm. —Méndez carraspeó sorprendida, aquel hombre nunca había respondido preguntas—. Dígame... Dígame, ¿por qué nunca la encontraron?

—En medio de las pruebas nos comunicaron la situación real: era tarde. El virus ya había causado la muerte de cinco mil millones de personas. De los ocho mil millones que éramos, la mitad se pudría en fosas comunes.

—Sin embargo, usted y yo, y dos billones de personas están a salvo. ¿Qué paso?

—Fuimos enviados a un nuevo equipo. Éramos virólogos, bioquímicos, ingenieros en Biogenética y todo tipo de especialistas en Medicina, cuidando a un puñado de eruditos que construyeron una máquina con la que rasgaron los límites de nuestra realidad, lo que nos permitió pasar al universo paralelo donde la enfermedad no existía.

—Está condenado a cadena perpetua, ¿fue por los que murieron desmembrados en el vórtice?

—No. Yo maté al equipo de investigadores y destruí la máquina junto con los documentos de información.

—¿Por qué?—Intentaron abrir otros portales.

—¿Y?

—En uno de ellos 2.000.000.000 de cuerpos se pudrían bajo el sol mientras los científicos abrían un vórtice tras otro.

—¿Siente remordimiento por sus acciones?

—Nunca me arrepentiré del acto valeroso y misericordioso que realicé.

—¿Por qué se calló esto?

—Si lo decía antes de hoy, esta habría sido la realidad donde un infectado causaba la muerte de todos los restantes.

—¿Leopoldo, conoce más realidades?

—Señorita Méndez del *Diario Nacional*, ya se acabó el tiempo. Adiós.

PERPETUIDAD

ARISANDY RUBIO

La Revolución Industrial constituyó el gran florecimiento tecnológico y quizá, solo fuimos testigos de uno más, gracias a la Gran Pandemia del siglo XXI. Mediante una economía basada en el encierro, surgieron portales transportadores, novedosos dispositivos de comunicación y empezó el trasplante de mentes, que si bien, ya tenía condiciones para realizarse, nunca había sido aplicado en masa.

Fue aceptado fácilmente, nadie quería morir. Además era un procedimiento sencillo, realizado por el infectado en los primeros días de incubación viral. Consistía en reservar una cita en su hospital de confianza donde elegía un nuevo cuerpo de pago o subsidiado.

Una vez seleccionado, el organismo recibía un tratamiento de reanimación celular y se comprobaba la inmunización al 99% de virus, bacterias y hongos, lo que aseguraba una satisfactoria vida de ochenta a ciento veinte años.

Si el proceso carecía de eventualidades, la persona pasaba a un gabinete aséptico donde su mente era transferida a un módulo de almacenamiento, a fin de verterla en el recipiente electo durante las siguientes cuarenta horas.

Todo lo anterior, ocurría bajo los más altos estándares de seguridad e higiene, y las personas contaban con una fabulosa garantía bimestral para probar el cuerpo o constatar la integridad de sus memorias. Conjuntamente, con el programa "Mano Amiga", se podía entregar el contenedor moribundo y enfermizo al nosocomio, lo que confería un descuento hasta del ochenta por ciento (según sus características), modalidad que aseguraba el envío del organismo a un país extranjero en el que su dueño original nunca se lo encontrara.

Han pasado varias décadas desde entonces. El trasplante ha cambiado, ya nadie recuerda su fisonomía original. Algunos hemos olvidado nuestra edad. Hoy, la enfermedad es un mito y se fabrican cuerpos sin alma para un mercado de gente que quiere vivir eternamente joven.

DIMINUTO

La milésima parte de un milímetro recibe el nombre de "micrómetro". Mil nanómetros construyen un micrómetro. Mientras la mayoría de patógenos oscila entre las cien y trescientas unidades nanométricas, el virus causante de la enfermedad COVID-19 tiene un tamaño de quinientas. En efecto, es un agente diminuto, pero también gigantesco.

Para la humanidad, el descubrimiento de esta cepa altamente contagiosa supuso un colapso mundial nunca antes visto. Sin embargo, Ernesto Aguilera lo asoció con el trabajo arduo. En tanto los hospitales colapsaban, él daba vueltas en su laboratorio, sosteniendo un cuaderno lleno de notas sobre física cuántica y datos del virus en cuestión. Por fin, se detuvo, respiró profundamente, buscó una página vacía donde escribió "Prueba 26" y exhaló con lentitud.

En la mesa del fondo, un aparato lanzaba destellos dorados. Ernesto pulsó un botón rojo ubicado al costado izquierdo de la máquina, que emitió ruidos desde el interior. Al frente, en una bandeja, cinco naranjas emanaban su perfume dulzón. Aguilera enfocó la fruta mediante un lente aumentado, centrándola, y por último, cerró los ojos antes de accionar dos manijas de color negro.

Durante algunos segundos la estancia se iluminó con una luz verdosa que desapareció sin dejar muestras de su existencia, no obstante, Ernesto podía comprobar que había sido real: puso los ojos en la mirilla de un microscopio y este, apuntado hacia donde estaban las frutas, le reveló que seguían ahí, con el increíble tamaño de seis micrómetros. Por supuesto, probó decenas de veces con piñas, ratones y conejos.

Tras ejecutar las pruebas con éxito, proseguía adquirir permisos y buscar un ejército que se sacrificara yendo a destruir el virus en su terreno natural, pisoteándolo como quien aplasta a una despreciable cucaracha. Aunque los enviados no pudieran regresar, los seres humanos obtendrían la victoria.

LOS NIÑOS DE LA PANDEMIA

ARISANDY RUBIO

Una vez que apareció ese terrible virus en el mundo, las cosas cambiaron por completo: trabajábamos desde casa, nos abrazábamos en vídeo llamadas, hacíamos pagos mediante el móvil y los adultos mayores morían como moscas rociadas de insecticida.

Entre todo aquel horror, los científicos, de buenas a primeras, dejaron de buscar una cura al enterarse de que las características del virus lo harían endémico y entonces comenzaron a poner en marcha la "preparación neonatal", es decir, inocular a mujeres gestantes con dosis puras del nuevo coronavirus para que experimentaran la enfermedad en las últimas semanas del embarazo. De ese modo, si las madres sobrevivían a la enfermedad, quedaban inmunizadas junto a sus hijos. Si por el contrario, no lo soportaban, cada bebé pasaba a la tutela del Estado sin la preocupación de que pudiera contraer el virus jamás.

¿Cuántas muertes se debieron al brote epidemiológico y cuántas fueron producto de la preparación neonatal? solo los expedientes de la Secretaría de Salud lo saben. Pero nadie podría siquiera pensar en investigarlos, pues el 87% de la población se ha convertido en montañas de ceniza cerca de los crematorios; y los que aún resisten, sea por inmunidad o protección, se hacen cargo de miles de bebés que requieren atenciones las veinticuatro horas del día.

VIAJE

MARY CRUZ PANIAGUA

Ma Gua me enseñó a ponerme pantalones. Iba a su casa en cuerito y me decía que no me daría comida hasta que no tapara mis féferes. Ma Gua tenía los nudillos abultados y de color diferente al resto de su cuerpo. Preparaba mi comida favorita cuando me portaba bien. Cuando me portaba mal, se limitaba a extenderme el platito con comida que yo engullía asustado.

De camino a casa de Ma Gua, veía en el pavimento un hoyito azul que parecía el reflejo del cielo. Al principio lo miraba de lejos, luego me fui acercando y me percaté de que realizaba un movimiento.

Se lo comenté a Ma Gua, y mirándose las manos, dijo algo que no entendí. "Límite tiempo", repetía sin advertir mi presencia. De regreso a mi cueva de cartones, me detuve en el hoyito. Asomé mi cabeza que casi toca el azul que no dejaba de moverse como juego de *pinball*, pero sin bolita impulsada. Me alejé conforme el movimiento se agitaba, pero la curiosidad me hacía voltear, y veía el azul salir del hoyito salpicando el pavimento.

Al día siguiente, me sorprendí. Viviendas, calles, árboles, todo el barrio tenía ese azul moviéndose. Fui al lugar del hoyito, resultó difícil por el movimiento debajo de mis pies, pero no estaba. El pavimento era liso, ni rastros de agujero. Corrí como pude a la casa de Ma Gua. Mi impresión fue tanta que frené de golpe, mis pies se enredaron y caí de boca. En lugar de su casa, encontré una enorme piedra azul.

No me había equivocado, conocía ese camino perfectamente. Pensé que quizás los eventos de los últimos días habían sido mi invención. Caminé aturdido hasta donde repetidas veces vi el hoyito, para terminar de enloquecer, allí me esperaba el platito con mi comida favorita.

PUTAS ELECTRÓNICAS

MARY CRUZ PANIAGUA

Su frío pecho y sus pupilas plateadas confirmaron la infección en última fase.

—Doctor Booz, ¿le inyectamos Taclirinina?

Escuché la voz de la enfermera como si estuviera en otra habitación. Mi mente estaba en aquella conversación con Rut. Habíamos terminado de tener sexo y me había preguntado si los robots pueden transmitir enfermedades. "Lo dudo", le dije, y se anidó a mi cuerpo quedando dormida. Luego se supo, ella fue el primer caso del virus metálico.

—No —dije a la enfermera—. Aislémosle. Usaremos la Taclirinina en casos con probabilidad de vida.

El virus surgió por una falla en el sistema operativo de las putas electrónicas, las tan admiradas por el placer sexual que ofrecen. Nunca me interesaron, aunque admito que su diseño es llamativo.

—Doctor. —Nuevamente la enfermera—. Ayer llegó otro infectado. Dijo que había estado con una de las putas electrónicas de la Calle Moab.

—¿La Calle Moab, dijo?

—Si.

Mis manos temblaron. Desconocía la existencia de las putas en esa zona. Corrí a los laboratorios, empujé la puerta y encontré a Lise rodeada de tubos de ensayo holográficos.

—¿Otro caso? —preguntó asustada.

—¿Dónde encontraron a Rut cuando la infectaron? —pregunté.

—A una esquina de la Calle Moab. —Reanudando su trabajo—. ¿Por qué?

Regresé al consultorio sin responderle. Todo encajaba. Rut me mentía, no asistía a ningún teatro en la Calle Moab, iba a verse con la famosa Mara.

—Son las 8:00 pm, ¿no irá a ver a su paciente personal? —dijo la enfermera mirando el reloj.

La verdad era que a esa hora salía a buscar putas, preguntaba sus nombres esperando encontrar a Mara, maldita puta electrónica que había infectado a Rut. Quería aniquilarle, pensando que había abusado de ella; ahora que sé la verdad y dónde encontrarla, no me importa.

—No es necesario —respondí—, el paciente murió.

Para el 2033 una alta tasa de la población en todo el mundo se vio afectada por una nueva enfermedad. Una Ataxia severa, a la que pronto nombraron Ataxia33. Esta condición era causante de la descoordinación del movimiento e inestabilidad motriz, y obligaba a los que la padecían a mantenerse acostados, generando una nueva problemática a la economía, ya colapsada.

V&T-A Corporation, compañía dedicada a la creación de nuevas tecnologías, junto a la empresa de belleza EstheTIC, lanzaron al mercado lo que según ellos, sería la solución. El *"Live"*, un dispositivo del tamaño de un gandul, económico y de simple uso. Solo debías sostenerlo en tus manos y pensar en la persona que siempre deseaste ser. En segundos, tu *#YoDeseado*, figura dotada de la apariencia física y emocional que deseas tener, se presentaba dispuesto a realizar tus actividades y deberes, mientras permanecías acostado viendo y sintiendo todo nítidamente.

Los *#YoDeseado* ocuparon los hogares, las escuelas, los puestos de trabajo; permitiendo que el mundo volviera a la normalidad. La cura a la Ataxia33 no produjo una conmoción como lo hizo la nueva actualización de El *Live*, con mejoras en el *software*, dotando a los *#YoDeseado* de movimientos inhumanos.

El dispositivo se hizo esencial y las ciudades se vieron plagadas de ellos. Hasta las personas que lograron recuperarse, y las que no se vieron afectadas por la Ataxia33, los adquirían. Se quedaban acostados todo el día, mientras sentían y veían a sus *#YoDeseado* trabajar, reír, llorar, salir a vivir por ellos.

EL PEREGRINO

MARY CRUZ PANIAGUA

En las puertas de Ortula, nanoplaneta habitable pero de acceso prohibido, apareció un hombre sin gabardina. Sí, sin gabardina he dicho. Ortula había cerrado sus puertas doscientos años antes, nadie salía ni entraba de allí.

El desconocido no articulaba ni una palabra. Se mantenía inmóvil, una figura esbelta de extraña vestimenta, como una estatua de ojos dilatados erguida frente a la entrada.

Los dirigentes no sabían cómo proceder. ¿Qué buscaba aquel hombre? El pánico y las teorías conspirativas invadieron el lugar. Unos decían que había llegado para robar los Droakus, que por años habían recolectado en los sembradíos del Norte. Otros, que era un doctor de algún planeta interestelar que venía a tratar los casos de disnea persistente, o un científico enviado por alegados problemas en el método anaeróbico. Sea quien fuese, no le estaba permitido entrar.

Aunque a simple vista el extraño no presentaba ninguna amenaza, los Ortulanos estaban desesperados. El rumor trascendió, y para el medio día, todos habían recogido sus pertenencias, firmes en salir de Ortula.

El infundio que desató la histeria era el siguiente: si las puertas no eran abiertas antes del anochecer, el nanoplaneta se vería sumido en una peste que les dejaría mudos. Ese silencio terminaría por enloquecerlos a todos.

Las puertas fueron abiertas debido a la presión de los habitantes que en avalancha salieron desaforados al espacio, procurando no tocar al inerte extraño.

Después de unos minutos Ortula quedó en total silencio. Vacío, excepto por los caídos en la estampida.

Silencio. Silencio y luego las pisadas del hombre que ahora entraba a Ortula, caminando en medio de los cuerpos sin vida, despacio, y sin gabardina.

ÁLVARO MORALES

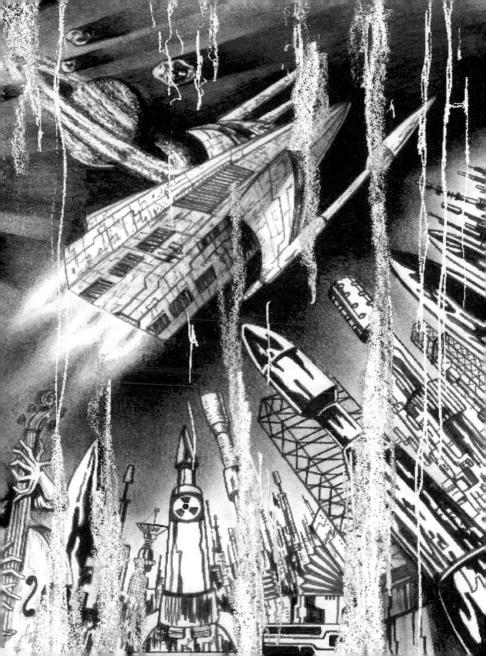

FUEGO EN EL CIELO

ÁLVARO MORALES

Fuego cayendo del cielo, plagas variadas y oscurecimiento repentino en pleno día, son inexplicables sucesos que han sido detectados en varias ciudades al mismo tiempo. El 2 de enero el fuego cayó sobre Demeria. Pocas horas después, el 3 de enero el fenómeno se repitió sobre Visdav y Temondeum. El 4 sobre Neuma y Kaptz. La destrucción ha sido total y es de temerse que no haya sobrevivientes. Si tenemos en cuenta que todas las ciudades están en planetas diferentes, deberíamos creer que comparten el sistema y que el evento catastrófico es el mismo. Pero lo asombroso es que las ciudades están separadas por distancias siderales y que no hay dos que pertenezcan al mismo sistema, o que siquiera estén cerca. Con respecto a la sucesión de los días, 2, 3, y 4, cabe recordar los principios elementales de la relatividad del tiempo. Teniendo esto en cuenta, es deducible que todo ocurrió en un único y singular momento.

La noticia fue destacada esta mañana (hora de Moira) por la agencia Infonemus del canal 8 de Moira. El agente responsable declaró: "¿Será posible que la protervia otra vez alcance a nuestros indefensos pueblos esparcidos por la galaxia? ¿Es posible que ese criminal, destructor de mundos, enemigo del hombre y de todas las especies y razas, esté otra vez libre? ¿Será posible que la ineptitud de las autoridades sea tan rutilante? Estas son la preguntas que todos nos hacemos. ¿Otra vez se les ha escapado ese demente que se hace llamar Dios?"

ESPLENDOR

ÁLVARO MORALES

—Consumí Crac Azul en la luna verde de Fassa; Morfeo Rojo, en un tugurio céntrico de la plaza principal de Napalm City; Rastrillo, en un bar del casco viejo, con un tango de Piazzola sonando de fondo, interpretado en forma excéntrica por dos xenoformos con veinte veces más dedos que manos. Para despertar, me di unos saques de Huesos, y para la hora en la que se suponía debería activarse mi apetito, un chupito de Selvavas, que permitió que tomara las píldoras alimenticias. El dolor de cabeza lo suprimí desde mi chip de rastreo, y el de espalda (que me viene siempre después de cada cena) con un relajante de Neuroflex. Los nanobots de Seix se encargan de regular todo mi organismo en este preciso momento, y me hacen un veinte por ciento de descuento porque el último pago lo hice antes del seis. De modo que ya estoy listo para más Morfeo Rojo y más Rastrillo. A propósito, déjame una bolsita de Huesos para más tarde; que la modorra me entra apenas se oculta el segundo sol. Todo me ha ido tan bien con esto del gobierno totalitario que he decidido probar algo nuevo. ¿Has escuchado de eso que están hablando todos? El Esplendor.

—¿El Esplendor, la nueva sustancia que fabrica el Estado?

—Eso mismo.

—Sí, claro. Es cara, pero aquí la tengo.

—Increíble. ¿Y cuál es su efecto?

—Te restaura al estado original, antes de haber probado nada, como cuando eras niño.

—¿Y cómo se siente?

—No lo sé... Uno se siente normal...

—Maravilloso. Déjame dos. Ah... y un Saca Chispas Roseball, por las dudas de que no lo soporte.

SOLEDAD

ÁLVARO MORALES

Estamos yendo. Véanos. Somos nosotros. Los mismos de los que hace tiempo que ya han estado hablando. Ya nos conocen. Y nosotros los conocemos a ustedes. Ahora, estamos yendo. Es hora de que nuestra hermandad sea un hecho.

La inmensa nave se asoma detrás de Plutón.
Se venden todos los telescopios.
Las escuelas místicas agotan sus localidades.
Las autopistas se convierten en estacionamientos.
Los trenes parecen no tener fin.
En el cielo, solo las aves vuelan.
Se venden todas las armas.
Los seguidores de sectas extremas se multiplican de forma exponencial.
Las reservas de alimentos básicos se extenúan.
No hay agua a la venta en ningún lado.
Todos los que tienen deudas exigen saldarlas.
Nadie salda una deuda.
Todos los cañones apuntan al cielo.
Antes se han vaciado en sus enemigos.
Las inmensas moles de cemento gimen y se retuercen.
Luego enmudecen.
La nave se detiene al llegar a la órbita de Saturno.
Retorna su curso y se pierde en la inmensidad del cosmos.

Otra vez estamos aislados y solos.
Por suerte.

ÁLVARO MORALES

—¿Eso en la sien es un ojo?

—No. No es la sien.

—¡Dioses!

—¡Y tiene dos!

—¿Dos sienes?

—No. Dos ojos.

—¿Eso del otro lado también es un ojo?

—Eso creo. ¿Qué es lo que hay en medio?

—Déjalo ya, es inútil... Antes que despierte.

Y se desvanecieron.

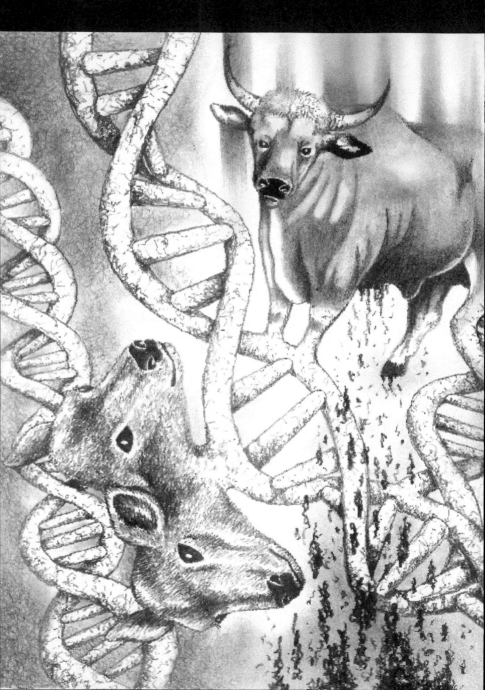

Ah! Experimentaron la conservación
No! Necesitan carne
Ah! Cuernos inmensos los humanos
No! Negro o marrón tu padre extinto años antes
Ah! Lleva tu nombre tatuado en su piel
No! Partiste dos días después de nacer
Mala leche

SOLILOQUIO EN EL ZOO CONGELADO

ACT— Tengo la muestra 319, padre extinto en 1980

Ban — 20 02 capicúa

ACT— Voy a implantarla en una especie diferente

Ban — De las montañas al cautiverio

ACT — Clonado por partida doble, uno sano otro enfermo

Ban — No me joroben ni me den bambú

PRELUDIO CREMONA

Predices premios
Prometea prendida
Probeta predios

Negaste la muerte trayendo las mismas manchas en el Alma.

CRISTIAN SOTO

En todas las Américas, cientos de telepantallas en las plazas centrales, transmiten en directo el espectáculo. Afuera del hemiciclo, los suecos arden de optimismo, como el hábito del diciembre invernoso. Adentro, el silencio se hace en absoluto, sin que nadie lo pida. El maestro de ceremonia, un anciano en su frac y gafas autofocales, aguarda acérrimo desde el podio. El borde del escenario está cubierto, una vez más, con las flores viajeras de Sanremo, y en sigilo, esperan los medallones a ser conferidos a manos vitalicias.

Desde el foso, la filarmónica, anuncia con trompas y clarines la entrada de los reyes. La Familia Real, con sus mentones perfilados, desfila al completo por un lateral del estrado. Como la tradición manda se disponen pues en sus sillas imperiales. Incorruptos e impolutos. Al frente, le antagonizan los asientos burdeos aun vacíos de los galardonados. Una vez el Rey en sitio, comienza el *Allegro* en Do mayor, los espectadores expectantes responden poniéndose en pie. De la nave central, se dejan ver entonces los honrados del año, en una marcha ensayada que recobra más de siglo y medio de solemnidad.

Pero la caravana de aplausos calculados pierde academia con la aparición del último eslabón del cortejo. Se deslavan los vitoreos ante la aparición de Georgie, que rodaba por aquella Sala de Conciertos de Estocolmo, con la virtud de ser el primer ordenador en marcarse el palmarés, después de conquistar el Geneplore y reclutar el alma perdida del soñador argentino. Las consignas alrededor del mundo contra la informática creativa, no estorbaron para que el comité le eligiera, aunado al epígrafe ese: "Por inclusivo y natural en su arte en miniatura".

Ante la algarabía, se suspende Georgie en la N omnipresente de aquella moqueta azul. Se hacinan los *flashes* de los fotógrafos capturando la historia. En el centro del escenario, al fondo, atestigua icónico el busto de Nobel en su eterno sitial presidencial.

COROLARIO DE UN PROFESOR

CRISTIAN SOTO

Estimado Sr. Ministro:

Le dirijo estas atrevidas formas, con permiso de la confianza que tenemos, para responder con encomio a su fugaz misiva. Agradezco, de antemano, los grandes esfuerzos de su comitiva por dotarnos de increíbles presupuestos e innovaciones, que nos sumergieron en el extranjero universo de la teleducación. La enseñanza ha cambiado su ruta para siempre, y me honra ser parte de este nuevo orden educativo.

Si supiera usted, lo que he disfrutado con las realidades mixtas y extrasensoriales, con las dystoclases, las eRúbricas, los holoportafolios, telecorrectores, los fotoapuntes, con la ciencia de las imágenes mentales y, desde luego, con el lectoemociones. Agradezco también la propedéutica para ilustrarnos, y el estudiado protocurrículo del cual somos pioneros ante el hemisferio.

Le confieso, que me aterra un tanto el contrato social que ahora es mayor; mis enseñanzas ruedan infinitas por las borrascas internáuticas y ser teleprofe no es oficio fácil, pero, lo asumiré sensato... ¡Me comprometo con anarquía! Además, acá entre nos, me entusiasma el estatus de celebridad que naturalmente he de adquirir, y también husmear las pugnas entre mis colegas por el número de reproducciones... ¡Fascinante!

Sirva toda esta experiencia maravillosa, que atesoro en mi profesión, para poner en contexto mi respuesta ante esa desconcertante consulta suya, que recibo con displicencia. Si aún no he sido claro, he de responderle con una reflexión que espero le sea formidable: Hoy más que nunca, resulta insignificante e imprudente, el regreso al aula presencial. Ya no estamos cualificados Sr. Ministro, para mirar a los ojos, preferimos la ventura de nuestra sofisticación.

Vitalicio agradecimiento a nuestro Sistema, por sembrarnos certidumbre cuando más perdidos estábamos. Tenía usted la boca llena de razón en sus otrora tesis: solo faltaba comprender que el internet del todo es nuestro más instantáneo y eterno.

Saludos afables desde la distancia.

AMÉRICA FUE UNA VEZ

La primera vez, flechas gigantes atravesaron el holograma. Aquellos animales habían reaccionado histéricos ante lo que creían era un dios o una amenaza. El horror los replegó de nuevo al misterio de la selva. Desde las cámaras de observación, doctos y corresponsales bufonearon de aquellas reacciones primarias de los salvajes. Intuí, entonces, mi error. La noche siguiente, aquel que asumimos como el chamán de los Flecheiros se apersonó y enfrentó osado a nuestro MATD 3D. Y es que cuando la inmunidad a los SARS arribó al mundo, fue demasiado tarde. Corubos, Toromonas, Mariposas, Yanomamis y otras tantas, habían colapsado a la procesión de pandemias. Solo una veintena de Flecheiros sobrevivían en el Valle de Javari, y el último recurso utilizado por estas ONG fue proyectar un aborigen semejante a su etnia, para seducirles a nuestro mundo y consensuar anticuerpos. Yo, valiente idiota, fui el lingüista que dotó de gramática a aquel espectro.

El encuentro se dio en la antigua franja del área protegida de la FUNAI. El selvático, rostro de jeta feroz y cuerpo, lienzo de *annatto* que lucía claramente enfermo. Sus pupilas, sospecho, habían perdido su capacidad de asombro; pues, porfiado, se acercó a la proyección y lentamente... la atravesó...

...entonces, nos encontró escondidos tras la hierba. Inertes nos quedamos ante sus ojos. Él, respiró profundo y observó de lado a lado el espectáculo. Allí estaba él con su desnudez, nosotros ataviados con trajes EPI, él con su antorcha, arco y flecha, nosotros con escritorios científicos, drones y proyectores. A nosotros nos protegían las nuevas leyes, a él la ley desnuda del origen. Entonces, después de un pavoroso silencio, el hombre, con calma autocomplaciente, sentenció:

*Si hemos de morir, moriremos. No quiero su mundo, ni su inmunidad.
Si acepto su inmunidad, entonces dependeremos de usted y...
preferimos ser libres.*

Con aflicción, traduje yo sus palabras. El humano atravesó de regreso el holograma y se extravió en los confines del bosque.

Semanas después, se viralizaron las noticias. Aquellos inconquistados habían enfermado de emociones. Me acurruqué en mi cama y lloré. Eran los Flecheiros, la última tribu perdida del mundo, y con su desaparición, se acabó para siempre la libertad.

EL REBAÑO

CRISTIAN SOTO

Diputado 1: Garantía Ejecutiva √, Garantía Legislativa √, Garantía Judicial √, Garantía Farmacéutica√, Garantía Militar√ y por último le presentamos...

Diputado 2: ...a RATIO. ¡La garantía comunicacional!

Diputado 4: ...Esta aplicación de *Big Data* estará, desde la próxima quincena, decretada por el supremo tribunal en todos las pantallas y móviles del país. Impulsaremos en publicidad programada y exterior.

Diputado 1: RATIO tiene de consigna la veracidad informativa. Fluiremos en ella titulares *clickbait*, información pasiva, bulos, clústeres y datos contubernio. Tenemos un ejército de bots para las faenas controladas. Hoy, la conexión a la Nube es intermitente y el respeto por RATIO surgirá en breve. Habrá dependencia en un 96%, casi.

Diputado 5: Clonaremos *sites*: BBC, CNN, OMS... ¡Las que haga falta!

Diputado 3: ...y tal vez ni haga falta. ¡Vamos... que la gente creerá en la primera cadenita de WhatsApp que ruede!

Diputado 1: Poco a poco, nuestros desocupados lectores, diría Cervantes; ¡infoxificados lectores, les rebautizo yo!, depositarán su fe en RATIO...

Diputado 1: ...y saltarán como antílopes, al encuentro de anticuerpos que ya RATIO habrá hecho el menester de vulgarizar...

Diputado 3: ¡Ya sabe, con que uno mueva la cola, mueve la cola la manada!

Diputado 6: ...además, ¡precio popular!

Diputado 7: ¡consumo masivo!

Diputado 8: ¡lavamos los ingresos y financiamos las elecciones, Señor!

Diputado 9: Convenimos con chivos expiatorios y por los anticuerpos no recele usted. Se trata de un placebo que no obra efecto secundario...

Diputado 10: ¡al menos no físico directamente, eh! ¡¿Qué si habrán otros?! ¡Los habrá! ...histerismo, vandalismo... ¡Qué sé yo!, pero...

Diputado 1: ...pero tenga usted muy claro, Señor, ¡que son ellos quienes nos han acordonado! ¿El mundo, necio, quiere inmunidad de rebaño? ...nosotros, sabios, les daremos mentalidad de rebaño.

Diputado 11: ¡Y ganamos todos!

Diputado 3: ¡Ahora, discúlpenos! Nos han dado tres minutos para resumirle la situación, pero llevamos en realidad doce horas de asamblea, los doce partidos tenemos consenso. Sudamos como puercos, tenemos hambre de musaraña y queremos ir a dormir como pitones. Solo urge su apruébese.

Diputado 1: ¿Qué dice, Sr. Alcalde? ¿Que se haga rebaño?

Alcalde: ¡Hagamos rebaño!

Por las calles desoladas deambula un virus, la muerte lo secunda con fervor; angustia y miedo también conforman esta comparsa del silencio.

Mientras tanto, en mi casa, resquicio de tranquilidad, me entretengo con una cámara fotográfica equipada con un portentoso teleobjetivo que compré a buen precio en la última feria que se celebró en esta ciudad, antes de que decretasen el estado de cuarentena indefinido, obligatorio y democrático.

Lo que hago es fotografiar aves. Descubrí que tengo paciencia para la ornitología, aunque hoy por hoy, todos han descubierto que tienen paciencia. Apostado en mi ventana como un francotirador, mantengo en la mira la rama de un araguaney ubicada a unos 396 metros, según indica el medidor de la cámara, en la cual anida una especie de ave que jamás había visto en estos nueve años que tengo fotografiando plumíferos. Aunque la otra noche, tratando de registrar un ave nocturna, fotografié por error un murciélago… Bueno… Cosas que pasan…

Tan en serio me he tomado esta actividad, que cumplo un horario estricto de ocho horas diarias. Solo paro para comer y hacer una rutina de ejercicios que tonifique mis adormecidos músculos.

Lo bueno es que tengo novecientas horas de música selecta en MP3, porque también soy melómano. Sobretodo gusto de la música donde hay músicos humanos ejecutando instrumentos, me declaro muy conservador en ese aspecto; la música neoposmoderna, esa en la que no hay músicos, donde una IA genera logaritmos *ad infinitum,* no es algo que logre digerir.

¡Santo Dios! Tengo al pajarraco en la mira, se ha posado como si posara para mí. Abre sus alas, abre su pico, hace movimientos estroboscópicos, despliega unas antenas, su cola gira como un radar, los ojos despegan de sus orbitas a manera de micro drones. ¡Por fin! ¡Lo tengo! ¡Lo tengo! ¡Lo tengo!

COMPARSA PRAGMÁTICA

OBITUAL PÉREZ

Por las calles desoladas deambula un virus, la muerte lo secunda con fervor; angustia y miedo también conforman esta comparsa del silencio.

Mientras tanto, en mi casa, reducto de sosiego, me entretengo en un pequeño conuco que comencé hace años cuando inició la cuarentena permanente y humanitaria, bajo régimen militar, decretada por la OMS.

Yo tenía un jardín con plantas ornamentales y las quité para hacer el huerto. En él, produzco alimentos como tomates, papas, zanahorias, ajíes y plantas medicinales; albahaca, yerbabuena, menta, toronjil, limonaria, entre otras... Trato de rotar el cultivo.

Elaboro un buen fertilizante con las vitaminas que distribuye el Gobierno para la salud de la población. Como se difundió el rumor de que procedían del mismo laboratorio chino del cual salió el virus, prefiero no arriesgarme y usarlas de otra manera, porque hoy en día no se debe desperdiciar nada, ya que los sistemas de producción han venido colapsando a raíz de la pandemia y el planeta necesita con urgencia un aprovechamiento de los recursos más consciente por parte de la ciudadanía. Lo bueno es que ya hay gobiernos que están aplicando medidas en esa dirección. Por ejemplo: los chinos, están haciendo abono con los cadáveres que va dejando la pandemia. A muchos les parece cruel, pero es algo que otros países están implementando (Alemania, Suiza, Inglaterra, Francia). Si sacamos la cuenta, somos 36 mil millones de personas en el mundo; el virus mata semanalmente 3 millones, pero los índices de natalidad hablan de medio millón al día; creo que algo hay que hacer con tanta materia orgánica.

En Latinoamérica, resulta difícil la desacralización de las ritualidades fúnebres; nuestra concepción de lo sagrado y nuestra cercanía al mito nos alejan de tales pragmatismos. Pero les digo que el abono chino es buenísimo, ¡he cosechado tomates súper jugosos!

Por las calles desoladas deambula un virus, la muerte lo secunda con fervor; angustia y miedo también conforman esta comparsa del silencio.

Mientras tanto, en mi casa, lugar favorito de mi existencia, me entretengo con un puzle de 90.000 piezas.

Sí, leyeron bien, noventa mil. Es único en el mundo y armarlo es el principal objetivo que tengo en la vida. Fue el regalo de una amiga dueña de un estudio de diseño gráfico bastante exitoso antes del decreto de estado de excepción con cuarentena indefinida promulgado años atrás. Ella misma lo ilustró con un motivo de zombis. Se trata de una muchedumbre putrefacta hacinada de tal manera que no se logra ver el fondo. Un amasijo de carnes trepidantes, un festín de iracundos carroñeros, una turba pestilente tratando de imitar la vida; pero al carecer de pasiones, sueños o ideales, y deambular con su hambre falaz, sin razonamiento alguno, solo logra ser una mueca sórdida carente de todo sentido.

Despierto cada día ansioso por encajar una pieza, estoy realmente obsesionado, a veces me absorbe tanto que me descubro cabeceando a altas horas de la madrugada. En una ocasión creí ver a un zombi parecido a mí... Qué tontería, otra ilusión provocada por el sueño...

La otra noche soñé que ese ejército de zombis me perseguía, y yo sabía que estaba soñando; la pesadilla se tornó cruel cuando el puente por el cual corría acababa de forma abrupta con un letrero que decía: "Obra clausurada por falta de presupuesto". Pensé en tirarme al río pero este se había secado, giré para hacerle frente a la estampida famélica, pero al voltear me vi a mí mismo corriendo en sentido contrario. Entonces comencé a perseguirme, por suerte un zancudo se metió en mi oreja, haciendo retumbar su zumbido en mi cavidad craneal.

Por las calles desoladas deambuló un virus, la muerte lo secundó con fervor; angustia y miedo también conformaron aquella comparsa del silencio.

Desde aquel entonces, en mi casa, sepulcro de mis pasiones, entregado al abandono, observé cómo las cosas se fueron deteriorando lentamente adquiriendo esa belleza ruinosa que evoca el retorno al paraíso. De las paredes, otrora blancas, brotaron hongos de colores alucinantes, los papeles con el aviso de cuarentena yacían marchitos por el suelo y se movían caprichosamente con la brisa.

Yo, en cama, con la piel ceñida, una inquietante sonrisa y los ojos perdidos en la oscuridad del embeleso.

Antes de dormirme dejé abierta la puerta principal, porque ya nada me preocupaba, todo debería ser bienvenido, y recibí visitas muy agradables. La primera, fue un colibrí que tuvo el simpático gesto de posarse en mi cabeza y picotear mi nariz como si me saludara. Meses después, entró un venado, suelen ser muy tímidos, pasó a la alcoba y se echó en la alfombra donde le daba un rayo de sol oblicuo que lo hacía ver como el ser más hermoso de la creación. Me hizo compañía aquella noche, se marchó al día siguiente luego de mirarme por un instante. También, vino un grupo de adolescentes bastante raro, extremadamente andrógino, una humanidad redibujada. Pensé que harían cosas vandálicas conmigo, pero fueron respetuosos; me avergoncé por haberlos juzgado, es justo que yo esté de salida con mis prejuicios para que ellos puedan construir un mundo nuevo.

Nadie más vino, y, cuando vi millones de mariposas amarillas revoloteando dondequiera, decidí marcharme. El viento cerró la puerta tras de mí; al fondo, en la radio satelital instalada en el pasillo, siguió sonando esporádicamente la letanía entrecortada que nadie quiso atender:

—Aquí el presidente desde la Estación Espacial Simón Bolívar. ¡¡¿Alguien puede escucharme?!!

Los neonatos son nuestros tesoros. Son pocos, siendo nosotros muy viejos para protegerlos, una generación completamente perdida, fue lo que nos dejó la terquedad e incredulidad, no pensamos que nuestros hijos estaban realmente en peligro. Supusimos que, de nuevo, se trataba de otra estratagema para encontrar algún fantasma creado y alimentado por ellos; su hegemonía interplanetaria se mantiene a base de fantasmas. El placebo de la primera vez fue la carta de presentación de una "Justicia" a toda costa; ¿dónde estaban entonces aquellos defensores de la vida y las buenas costumbres éticas? Solo unos pocos se expresaron ante la futura posibilidad de una retaliación contra los médicos. Hoy, veo como mi amigo se sienta sobre la tumba de su hijo Habib Fida Ali, quien no soportó más el dolor de ver muerta a su hija Perween. Ahora, descansa a su lado.

A lo lejos, sonaba en la radio esta canción:

Tuskeegee #626
Somebody done got slick
when deadly germs are taking turns
seeing what makes us tick.

Tuskeegee #626
Scientists getting their kicks
when deadly disease can do what it please
results ain't hard to predict.

Tuskeegee #626
Pushed aside mighty quick
when brothers, you dig
are guinea pigs
for vicious experiments.

Sudado y agotado, dentro de su acogedor habitáculo de hormigón, Demetrio mira el líquido espeso y amarillento que ahora escurre de su mano; piensa en cuál será la función de esta sustancia, en este nuevo mundo de transición. Aprieta una mano, mientras con la otra abre la ventana para seguir con su rutina diaria, pero antes de anotar lo observado sucumbe ante el cansancio, pues, debido al autoaislamiento, su energía cada vez es menor.

Al despertar se dirige al baño, limpia su mano y el sudor de su cuerpo; toma su diario personal y lee las observaciones anotadas anteriormente.

25/11/2400. Ventana Norte, en dirección a los edificios y al antiguo parque mecánico:
De nuevo todos salen hacia su trabajo, de uno en uno. Sin embargo, he visto que esas dos casi siempre salen juntas, la prisa no las deja percatarse del cambio que se avecina con las malditas máquinas reforestadoras.

Al dejar su diario de lado, toma un vaso de agua, lo único que había ingerido en días; dando fe de esto su torso cadavérico y su tez pálida. Toma de nuevo su diario y se dirige a la ventana Este del departamento. El sonido de las máquinas trabajando a lo lejos le fastidia, observa con el ceño fruncido, cómo a medida que estas marchan, la ciudad va cambiando su tono gris por el verde y el azul "descontaminados". De pronto se ríe y anota en su diario: ¿Cuánto tiempo podré seguir aquí? ¿El verde también me consumirá?

Cuando el PTJ (Policía de Transición y Justicia) allana el departamento de Demetrio para interrogarlo por sus hábitos no convencionales, solo consiguen un cuerpo seco, una jeringa y una nota que dice:

"MI CUERPO NO SERVIRÁ PARA RECICLAR"

De un momento a otro no sentí más dolor, todo era tal cual Brandon me lo había participado. Mi cuerpo le fue entregado a mi familia y yo integrado a la red de Encarta; mi estancia en ese servidor fue breve, pues logré escapar porque deseaba ver a mi hija, Morph. Entré a la red consiguiendo la forma de instalarme en su iPhone 100 y desde allí pude verla llorar, reír, jugar.

Fue satisfactorio ver cómo crecía. Sin embargo, mi presencia era limitada; la encriptación de la mente humana es difícil y no sirve con todos los sistemas operativos. Compartimos muchas veces, al punto en que hablaba con total normalidad conmigo, como si estuviera vivo. Su madre y Brandon le decían que era imposible tener una conversación conmigo, pues yo estaba muerto. Luego de algún tiempo decidieron internarla en el psiquiátrico.

No soportando la ausencia de Morph recurrí a Brandon con un mensaje, en el cual le expresaba mis intenciones de volver al Proyecto Poltergeist, si la ayudaba a salir del sanatorio. Este accedió logrando convencer a mi esposa o "ex", de regresar la niña a casa. Pronto, mi hija volvió a su habitación; en mi último contacto con ella la noté diferente, los medicamentos le habían hecho daño. Se puso a hacer unos nudos que aprendió conmigo, me percaté de sus intenciones e intenté hacer que saltaran las alarmas... pero era tarde, ya sus lindos pies flotaban sobre el piso, se veía angelical, etérea...

39 días después de comenzar la cuarentena, Dorangel recibe los planos 3D que tanto necesitaba para imprimir y ensamblar su nuevo amplificador de realidad virtual (ARV Glu-E). Luego comienza con la calibración neuronal, pues el ARV Glu-E promete una mejora kinestésica del 100%, en la realidad virtual. Dorangel decide saltarse algunos protocolos, avanzando así a las opciones de:

ENSAYO O INICIO

Decantándose por esta última, poseído por un instinto visceral, introduce la escena que compró en la Deep Web, iniciando así la simulación.

Ante él, aparece el objeto de sus deseos, carne blanca, bien proporcionada, moviéndose espasmódicamente. Sin poder soportar más la necesidad de saciar su apetito, tan propia del encierro, comienza el festín mordiendo las pequeñas mejillas de su presa. Una bocanada de sangre empapa su lengua produciéndole una sensación que no experimentaba hacía más de un mes. No reparó en el llanto ni en el seguimiento, de los ojos aterrados de su víctima, que atestiguaban su deleite. Sin embargo, sintió un dolor profundamente estimulante, miró sus manos, las cuales por error había mordido. Sin aterrarse, dirige su vista hacia un espejo, observándose llega a la conclusión de que su cuerpo es inclusive más provocativo que el que yace muerto frente a él, excitado dirige ahora su ataque hacia sí mismo, obteniendo un placer casi inconmensurable. Un punto rojo de alarma aparece, pero la excitación le resta importancia, solo obtiene placer tras cada bocado. De pronto se siente caer y cuando abre los ojos ve el ARV Glu-E a un lado, la sangre, que emana del muñón donde minutos antes estaba su mano, tiñe todo el piso. Ante esta imagen, Dorangel opta por lo que le resulta más placentero, seguir el festín hasta el final.

ESCRIBIDORES-IMAGINADORES

Alejandra Decurgez (Buenos Aires, Argentina, 1977)

Es Licenciada en Psicología por la Universidad del Salvador, y trabaja como docente y terapeuta clínica. También ha estudiado Guión Cinematográfico en el Sindicato de la Industria Cinematográfica Argentina. Su guión *The Dive* recibió mención de honor en el Fantasmagorical Film Festival de Kentucky en 2015, llegó a segunda ronda en el Austin Film Festival y fue finalista en el Miami International Science Fiction Film Festival. En 2016, su guión *The Mantis* fue finalista en los mismos festivales.

Autora de las novelas *Mis muertos amarillos* (Peces de Ciudad, 2018), *Colores Verdaderos* (Niña Pez, 2019) y *Limbo* (Ayarmanot, 2020). Ha participado en las antologías: *Alucinadas II* (Sportula, 2016, en papel; Palabaristas, 2016, en digital), *Lista negra* (Pelos de Punta, 2016), *WhiteStar* (Palabaristas, 2016), *Breves de amor* (Sopa de Letras, 2018). Ha publicado en las revistas: *Próxima, Axxón, The Wax, miNatura* y *SuperSonic*.

Eliana Soza Martínez (Potosí, Bolivia, 1979)

Primer libro de cuentos *Seres sin Sombra* (2018). Junto a Ramiro Jordán libro de microficción y poesía *Encuentros/Desencuentros* (2019).
Antologías: *Antología Iberoamericana de Microcuento* (Comp. Homero Carvalho, 2017). *Armario de letras* (Caza de Versos, 2018). *Antología de cuentos de terror Macabro Festín* (Soy livre, 2018). *Letras y Misterios: Nuevas Crónicas Potosinas* (Ed. Juan José Toro Montoya, 2018) Publicado por el Gobierno Autónomo Municipal de Potosí. *Hokusai* (2019), *Antología de microrrelatos*, Revista Brevilla, Chile. *Cuentos Fuera de Serie* (Comps. Adolfo Cáceres Romero y Homero Carvalho Oliva, 2019); *Escritoras bolivianas contemporáneas*, Caballero, Decker y Batista compiladoras (Editorial Kipus, 2019). *Antología de cuentos del III Encuentro de Microficción*, compilado por Homero Carvalho Oliva, (Comunicarte, 2019). *Bestiario* (Sherezade, 2019). *Nocturnalia, antología de cuentos iberoamericanos*, compilada por Walter Saravia, (Amazon, 2019). *Herejes. Antología de cuentos navideños de terror* (Historias Pulp, 2019). *El día que regresamos. Reportes futuros después de la pandemia* (Pandemonium, 2020). *Brevirus* (Brevilla, 2020). *Rockabilly* (La Tinta del Silencio, 2020).

Leonardo Espinoza Benavides (San Fernando, Chile, 1991)
Médico cirujano, escritor y editor de ciencia ficción. Autor del libro de relatos interconectados *Más espacio del que soñamos* (Puerto de Escape, 2018) y de la novela pulp *Adiós, Loxonauta* (Sietch Ediciones, 2020). Editor general y colaborador de la antología chilena en tiempos de pandemia *COVID-19-CFCh*. Fue miembro de la Washington Science Fiction Association (WSFA) y pertenece hoy en día al directorio de la Asociación de Literatura de Ciencia Ficción y Fantástica Chilena (ALCIFF). Ha publicado ficción y no ficción desde el año 2008, participando en múltiples antologías internacionales y revistas hispanoamericanas dedicadas a la ciencia ficción y la literatura fantástica. Actualmente reside en Santiago de Chile, junto a su esposa Daniele y su perrito Hulky.

Maielis González Fernández (La Habana, Cuba, 1989)
Es graduada de Letras y fue profesora de literatura en la Universidad de La Habana entre los años 2012 y 2016. Egresada del Centro de Formación Literaria Onelio Jorge Cardoso (2014), institución que le otorgó la beca para escritores Caballo de Coral. Ganadora del segundo premio en el concurso de cuentos de ciencia ficción Juventud Técnica (2014), y del Premio Eduardo Kovalivker (2015). Ha publicado los libros *Los días de la histeria* (Colección Sur, 2015), *Sobre los nerds y otras criaturas mitológicas* (Guantanamera, 2016) y *Espejuelos para ver por dentro* (Cerbero, 2019). Además de haber aparecido en revistas y antologías en Cuba (*Ariete*, 2018), Argentina (*Revista Próxima*, 2017) y España (*Alucinadas II*, 2016). Sus artículos y ensayos sobre ciencia ficción y literatura fantástica se han publicado en varias revistas y antologías en Estados Unidos, Suecia, Argentina, España y Cuba. En 2019 tradujo, junto a Arrate Hidalgo, la novela de Nalo Hopkinson *Hija de Legbara* publicada por la editorial Apache.

Erick J. Mota (La Habana, Cuba, 1975)

Es licenciado en Física Pura por la Universidad de La Habana y cuenta en su haber con un curso de técnicas narrativas del Centro de Formación Literaria Onelio Jorge Cardoso. Escritor de ciencia Ficción y aficionado a la astronomía. Creador y editor principal del e-zine de ciencia ficción y fantasía *Disparo en Red* que se distribuyó por correo electrónico en Cuba entre 2004 y 2008. Con motivo de la publicación de su primer libro *Bajo Presión* (Gente Nueva, 2007), gana el certamen literario de Ciencia Ficción para jóvenes La Edad de Oro. Muchas de sus historias aparecen recogidas en diversas antologías y publicaciones. En 2010 publica en Casa Editora Abril un recopilatorio de cuentos, Algunos recuerdos que valen la pena. La Habana Underguater, colección de relatos que sale a la luz ese mismo año en la editorial Atom Press, para posteriormente publicarse como novela con el mismo título. Ha sido reconocido con el premio TauZero de Novela Corta de Fantasía y Ciencia Ficción (Chile, 2008) y Calendario de Ciencia Ficción (Cuba, 2009). Su relato "Memorias de un país zombi" acaba de aparecer en España: *Terra Nova, la Antología de Ciencia Ficción Contemporánea*, de la editorial Sportula.

Arisandy Rubio García (México)

Es licenciada en Psicología Social por la Universidad Autónoma Metropolitana. Su trabajo literario se orienta principalmente a la narrativa y actualmente figura en dos antologías de la editorial La Sangre de las Musas, una de Editorial Alebrijez y una de Endora Ediciones. Así mismo, cuenta con participación en las antologías digitales *Letras libres* de la Red de Escritores y Escénicas Potosí, y *Cuentos en cuarentena* de Editorial Amatlioque. Además, figura en diversas revistas y fanzines, tanto físicos como digitales, tal es el caso de: *Avión de Papel A.C., Caína Fanzine, Panopticón, Revista Letras y Demonios, Revista Fantastique, Minificción*, Editorial Aeternum, Editorial Letras Rebeldes, etc. Algunas de sus obras se pueden encontrar en: www.facebook.com/ARGarciaCuentos.

Mary Cruz Paniagua Suero (República Dominicana)

Artista independiente que trabaja en cine y teatro. Licenciada en Publicidad Mención Creatividad y Gerencia. Actriz y titiritera, egresada de la Escuela Nacional de Arte Dramático (ENAD), Santo Domingo. Directora de arte, egresada de la Escuela Nacional de Cine (ENACC), Bogotá. Co-propietaria de la productora El Fular de Thelma y Louise. Desde finales del año 2011, escribe para la *Revista miNatura*, especializada en el cuento breve de género fantástico, ciencia ficción y terror. Sus textos han sido publicados en la compilación *Mujer en pocas palabras*, de la escritora Ibeth Guzmán.

Álvaro Morales (Montevideo, Uruguay, 1978)

Licenciado en Psicología y psicoterapeuta. Ha publicado en las siguientes revistas: *Axxón, El Narratorio, Relatos Increíbles, Sinfín, Máquina Combinatoria, Cosmocápsula*. También en algunas antologías: *Ruido Blanco* números 3, 4, y 6, *Escritores acrónimos III, El hilo de la memoria, Kodama Cartonera, Calabacines en el ático, Gonzáles Rojas Pizarro*. Ha publicado algunos artículos académicos en blogs especializados como *Articulando* y *Psyciencia*.

Ave (Caracas, Venezuela, 1972)

Escritora, poeta y artista visual. Miembro fundadora de la Fundación Jóvenes Artistas Urbanos (FundaJAU), agrupación artística que materializa proyectos culturales en los andes venezolanos desde finales de los años noventa hasta la actualidad. Desde el 2017 forma parte del proyecto editorial *La Jauría Intergaláctica*, el cual está dedicado al género de la Ciencia ficción. Sus primeros cuentos de este género aparecen publicados en *El engrama, Antología de ciencia ficción tachirense* (Fundajau, 2018). Autora del poemario *Cuerpo yo alma tu* (Fundajau, 2007). Tambien ha publicado varios artículos de investigación en *Bordes. Revista de Estudios Culturales*, Universidad de Los Andes y Fundación Bordes.

Cristian Soto (San Cristóbal, Venezuela, 1988)

Licenciado en Castellano y Literatura egresado de la Universidad de Los Andes, Magíster Scientiae en Literatura Latinoamericana y del Caribe por la misma universidad. Psicólogo egresado de la Universidad Bicentenaria de Aragua. Docente de la Universidad Nacional Experimental del Táchira en el área de Lengua y Comunicación. Obtuvo la Mención de Honor del Circuito Cultural de Literatura (2012), Mención de Honor de la revista *Latina Intercultura*; Categoría: Relato Negro (2013). Publicó una selección de cuentos en *El engrama, Antología de ciencia ficción tachirense* (FundaJAU, 2018).

Obitual Pérez (San Cristóbal, Venezuela, 1972)

Miembro fundador de la Fundación Jóvenes Artistas Urbanos (FundaJAU), agrupación cultural venezolana formada a finales de los años noventa, aún activa. Participa del proyecto editorial de Ciencia ficción La Jauría Intergaláctica, y sus primeros cuentos de este género aparecen publicados en *El engrama, Antología de ciencia ficción tachirense* (Fundajau, 2018). Uno de sus relatos fue publicado en la revista digital *miNatura* #165 (España, 2018). Publicó de manera independiente una space opera infantil titulada *El niño astronauta* (Amazon, 2019). También publicó una antología de microcuentos dedicada al subgénero del *greenpunk* titulada *Crónicas verdes* (FundaJAU, 2019). Fue merecedor del primer accésit del I Premio Pragma de relato de ciencia ficción de la Fundación Asimov (España, 2020).

Wild Parra (San Cristóbal, Venezuela, 1991)

Licenciado en Educación mención Biología y Química por la Universidad de los Andes. Colaborador , desde 2013, de *Bordes. Revista de Estudios Culturales*, Universidad de Los Andes y Fundación Bordes. Escritor y editor de FundaJAU (Fundación Jóvenes Artistas Urbanos). Coordina, desde 2017, el proyecto editorial La Jauría Intergaláctica, dedicado al género de la ciencia ficción. Sus primeros cuentos de este género aparecen publicados en *El engrama. Antología de ciencia ficción tachirense* (Fundajau, 2018).

Omau (San Cristóbal, Venezuela, 1972)

Ilustrador y realizador de cómics. Estudió diseño gráfico en el Centro de Diseño Taller 5 (Bogotá, Colombia). Miembro de la Fundación Jóvenes Artistas Urbanos (FundaJAU), desde 1997. Durante varios años fue profesor de Diseño Gráfico en institutos universitarios tecnológicos de la ciudad de San Cristóbal, estado Táchira. Fue merecedor del 1° lugar en el Concurso Nacional de Caricatura de la Fundación Editorial El Perro y la Rana (2015). FundaJAU ha publicado varios números de sus historietas, como Noún y Contemplor, entre otras. Es el diagramador e ilustrador del proyecto editorial de Ciencia ficción La Jauría Intergaláctica.

José Leonardo Guaglianone (Caracas, Venezuela, 1983)

Formado en la Escuela de Artes de la UCV, se ha desempeñado itinerante e informalmente en labores como asistente de producción, caletero, asistente editorial, mensajero, escenógrafo, limpiador de playa, jalador de monte y corrector de texto. Ha ejercido como asistente curatorial de arte contemporáneo para la Fundación CELARG (2006-2009); como periodista cultural para el medio alternativo digital *Corneta. Semanario Cultural de Caracas* (2009-2011). Participó en el colectivo de investigación-acción y promoción en sociología de las juventudes y culturas urbanas Red de la Calle (2014-2015); como gestor de redes sociales y asistente del proyecto nacional Núcleos de Producción Cultural (2016-2017). Se ha desempeñado como editor de textos y libros en artes o ciencias sociales, tanto de manera independiente, como para la Asociación Civil Grupo Literario Nosotros (2006-2016) y para la Fundación Editorial El perro y la rana, del Ministerio del Poder Popular para la Cultura (2018-actualidad). Es parte del equipo de investigación y promoción del Centro de Estudios Caracas para el proyecto Vida y Cultura en la Caracas Insurgente, especializado en el tema de los muralismos y artes urbanas (2019-actualidad). A lo largo de su trayectoria profesional ha publicado algunos artículos, reseñas críticas, periodísticas y monografías académicas o divulgativas, tanto en medios impresos como digitales.

ÍNDICE

Ediciones FundaJAU
San Cristóbal, Estado Táchira
República Bolivariana de Venezuela
MMXX

CPSIA information can be obtained
at www.ICGtesting.com
Printed in the USA
LVHW021747061221
705421LV00015B/2545